PRAISE FOR LYNN COADY AND *THE ANTAGONIST*

". . . wildly enthralling, compelling . . . a bravura novel, tightly controlled . . . a readable, quixotic coming-of-age story, a comedy of very bad manners, and a thoughtful inquiry into the very nature of self. It's the sort of novel — and Coady the sort of writer — deserving of every accolade coming to it."   — *National Post*

"There has always been a lively, down-to-earth vigour to Coady's prose and to her protagonists . . . Credit Coady for making an empathetic character out of a 'big-mouthed bruiser' who throws his weight around and has a penchant for gross-out stunts. A deft blend of farce, tragedy, and wry social comment, *The Antagonist* is no mean feat."   — *Toronto Star*

". . . by turns angry, funny, tender, and sad . . . *The Antagonist* is a full-bodied work of fiction . . . Coady's previous books have received much praise and it's easy to see why, given all the gifts of storytelling on display here . . . a fine novel."   — *Globe and Mail*

"Hilarious . . . irresistible."   — *Edmonton Journal*

"*The Antagonist* is a crafty, technically-accomplished series of meditations on subjects ranging from manhood and self-knowledge to tricky father-son relationships. Brimming with hotheaded outbursts and recollections of jackass male behaviour, Coady's novel assures readers of steady bouts of laughter between substantial food for thought . . . memorably real and remarkably nuanced."   — *Vancouver Sun*

The Antagonist

Lynn Coady

ANANSI

Hardover edition first published in 2011 by House of Anansi Press Inc.

This edition published in 2012 by
House of Anansi Press Inc.
110 Spadina Avenue, Suite 801
Toronto, ON, M5V 2K4
Tel. 416-363-4343 Fax 416-363-1017
www.houseofanansi.com

Distributed in Canada by
HarperCollins Canada Ltd.
1995 Markham Road
Scarborough, ON, M1B 5M8
Toll free tel. 1-800-387-0117

All of the events and characters in this book are fictitious, and any
resemblance to actual persons, living or dead, is purely coincidental.

House of Anansi Press is committed to protecting our natural environment.
As part of our efforts, the interior of this book is printed on paper that contains
100% post-consumer recycled fibres, is acid-free, and is processed chlorine-free.

17 16 15 14 13   3 4 5 6 7

LIBRARY AND ARCHIVES CANADA CATALOGUING IN PUBLICATION

Coady, Lynn,
The antagonist / Lynn Coady.

ISBN 978-1-77089-104-3

I. Title.

PS8555.O23A58 2011   C813'.54   C2010-902173-0

Cover design: Bill Douglas
Text design and typesetting: Alysia Shewchuk

We acknowledge for their financial support of our publishing program
the Canada Council for the Arts, the Ontario Arts Council,
and the Government of Canada through the Canada Book Fund.

Printed and bound in Canada

MIX
Paper from
responsible sources
FSC® C004071

There will be time to murder and create.

— T.S. Eliot

Part One

1 |

THERE YOU ARE in the picture looking chubby and pompous, and it makes me remember how you told me that time you were afraid of fat people. That is, afraid of being fat, and hating those who were, so fear and hating, like of a contagion, the same way homophobes — guys who are actually maybe gay or have the potential for gayness within them — are thought to be afraid of homos. So want to annihilate them, make them not exist. You said you were embarrassed by it, though, your hatred of fat people, your fear. You knew it was shallow. You knew it was wrong. You thought it was a prejudice that was beneath the enlightened likes of you. And now, with all this time gone by, here you are in the picture. Looking chubby and pompous.

When you told me that, I remember being a little awed because we were kids, we were two young guys, and we hung out every weekend and we got drunk and declared, or might have declared, *I love you man!* at some point or another, but you — You — as much as you talked you never really said much of anything, you gave none of it away, whereas I was always yanking off hanks of self-flesh and shoving them bloodily at everyone around me, it felt like, half the time — *no please, take it, take it, really.* And people would accept them, those red bleeding chunks — because what choice did they have, I was a hulking drunken wreck who might fall on top of them at any moment — averting their eyes, embarrassed for both of us, as was only right.

Not you, though. I heard an expression the other day in reference to this other tight-lipped son of a bitch, actually it was the prime minister — *He keeps his own counsel.* And I thought that's perfect, that's perfect, that's Adam. The operative phrase being *his own,* the operative concept being *self.*

Point being, you kept your own counsel most of the time. You never turned to me in the midst of one of our drunk-stoned hazes to implore: Help me, man! I'm all fucked up! The way guys sometimes do. Not you, not like I was always doing, or felt like I was. You never said boo. I thought that was very cool about you for a while. I thought your head was just too full — heaving with profundity.

It is stupid the way young men admire one another, the cluelessness of it, the non-reasons.

And then, lo! He turns to me, does sphinx-boy, in the middle of a typical beered-up weekend rock and roll show on campus. Our mutual friend Tina is ripping up the dance floor in front of us. Tina has put on some pounds, the way girls do in just a handful of months, the same way they immediately take it off the moment it becomes apparent to them that guys aren't sniffing and circling the way they used to. Lately we've taken to calling Tina *Tiny* behind her back. A few months ago we would have been watching Tina dance with quiet horny awe but now she just looks fat and silly and we're embarrassed for her and disliking ourselves for thinking it because she's a cool girl, we like her, and why shouldn't she fucking dance if she wants to? And covering it up with asshole jokes.

And he turns to me, does sphinx-boy, face naked and craving in a way I've never seen. I lean in. My friend needs me!

"I think I'm prejudiced against fat people."

I have never heard such shame, such self-loathing in Adam's voice.

"That's okay, man," I reassure my friend. "Everyone hates fat people, they're fucking fat."

"No. I need to get over it."

I swing an arm around your shoulders and crush you against me, happy for the opportunity to be kind and big-brotherly.

"Look at her go," I say, gesturing to Tina out there undulating, eyes closed, jaw so slack her tongue is almost hanging out, dancing a sweat-slick frenzy. I found out later Tina was at that point well aware of her new nickname and had started taking speed to offset things.

"She's working it out there! She'll be back to baseline hotness in no time." I was right about that too. But that wasn't what you were worried about.

"I mean," you say, once I have released you, because I can tell it is awkward for you to continue your confession crushed against my manly chest. "It's me."

Of course it was you, Adam.

"I'm afraid that I'll get fat. I'm deathly afraid of it. Getting fat."

And look at you now, say it together everybody: chubby; pompous.

What a shitty way for me to begin! After you have been so nice. After all these years. I didn't even think you would write me back. And if you did write back, I never imagined you would say: Sure! Send me your story. I would be delighted to take a look, that's what you said. *Take a look*, that's very non-committal of course, but then, that's the Adam I remember.

Well guess what. I was being noncommittal myself. I was being noncommittal in that I was lying. That whole last email I sent was a lie.

First of all, I said *I haven't read your book yet but am very excited to do so*. But I have read it, Adam. I've read it a few times now.

Second of all, I was being friendly and nice in my email, but that was in fact not a true representation of how I am actually feeling toward you. I was baiting the hook. I wasn't sure you'd be particularly pleased to hear from me, if you would even bother to write back. So I thought I should be nice. I thought I should be all the things I knew — assuming you were still the old Adam — you would respond to: complimentary, admiring, affectionate.

Third, I said I had a story of my own. I said it was short. The first statement was the truth, but the second was a lie. I said I was trying to write and I would appreciate your help. That's not true either — I'm writing just fine at this very moment, I don't need your goddamn help. I said it wouldn't take too much of your time — not true.

You said, and I'm cutting and pasting here:

Sure! I'd be delighted to take a look.

So guess what? I am taking you at your word.

———

Okay, I thought I'd better go get another beer to help grease the wheels and now I'm back. So here we go.

I was born in a small town, like John Cougar Mellencamp and Bruce Springsteen. Remember how we all sat around arguing that time about whether or not Springsteen was a Jew? And Wade was so appalled — he couldn't get his head around the idea for some reason. And I got all in his face, having fun, like I was totally outraged: What are you, KKK or something? Jews can't sing? Jews can't be born in the U.S.A.? And he goes, No, Rank, no it just — it doesn't line up. In my head. It was like that time you told him Freddie Mercury was gay and the two of you argued all night until finally Kyle yelled, Dude! The name of the band is *Queen*. And the next day all Wade's Queen on vinyl mysteriously disappeared. Anyway, you said it didn't matter what Springsteen was, what mattered was we shouldn't say "a Jew." You said we should say "Jewish."

For years I went around studiously avoiding the term "Jew" because I didn't want to offend anyone — people like you, that is. And then one summer a guy I was working construction with used it in reference to his brother-in-law. And

I go, Look, man, I don't know if you're supposed to say that these days. And he straightens up and stares at me and goes, What's wrong with Jew? And I say, Like it isn't offensive? And he goes, I'm a Jew, dickweed. Am I offending you?

So thanks for that, Adam.

And — yes! What the hell! I am going all the way back and starting from day one, with my birth. I can do whatever I want, because it's my life and it's my story and it exists and has existed in a very specific way, despite what you have done. It is a thing that hangs in the air around me at all times, like if I didn't wash for a couple of months, which has sometimes been approximately the case — a personal stench made up from the chemical composition of my sweat, from everything I ate, from everywhere I went, everything I sniffed on the ground in front of me, all the crap I ever laid down and rolled around in.

You know all this, or I thought you did. I gave it to you, these intermittent chunks, I pulled off bloody hank of flesh after bloody hank and just handed them over and you were so coy, you averted your eyes and pretended to be embarrassed like the rest of them when really you were squirreling the hanks away and secretly stitching them together and building Frankenstein's monster.

———

Starting again. Beer the third.

I was born in a small town. That is not such a big feat in this country. You were born in a small town, John Cougar was, Springsteen the Jew, everybody was born in a small town. Whoop-de-shit. Let's not name a specific territory. We both know they are all the fucking same.

There was a dad, there was a mom. You know this too, approximately. The dad was a prick, the mom was a goddess. Gord and Sylvie.

Already this feels like a cliché, which is the fault of none other than Adam. It wouldn't feel that way if you didn't exist. It wouldn't be part of someone else's fairy tale, it would just be my own nameless stench, hanging over me. The biggest pisser? The fact that the cliché of me was all you really took, you boiled an entire life, an entire human being, Adam, down into his most basic, boneheaded elements. Good mom plus bad dad hinting at the predictable Oedipal (oh give me a fucking break) background of — voilà — Danger Man! One seriously messed up dude. Not very creative of you is what I'm saying.

Okay so anyway, she died, as you know, and left me with the prick. I know back in school I was always saying how my dad was a prick but I never got specific. What I didn't say was that he was a prick because he had Small Man Syndrome. I heard that term just a few years ago and immediately thought: Gord. Dad was about 5'5½" and found this intolerable his entire adult life. When I shot up at fourteen, he was delighted — it was as if he had added my height to his own.

Here's another cliché: every guy whose dad was a prick talks about that moment where he realizes he can take his old man — how empowering it is. But I always knew. I feel like I could've taken him at six if I wanted. I was a thug from the moment I popped from the womb, or so rumour has it. Ten pounds, bruiser hands and feet.

"How *old* is this kid?" my father is said to have hollered when the nuns brought me out from the cold storage room or the basement or wherever they stashed unwanted Catholic babies up for adoption — *ta da!* But Gord was suspicious. He thought they were trying to pass a toddler off on him.

Sylvie, however, immediately held out her arms to me, bracing herself, bending a little at the knees.

"The little bastard's old enough to *drive*," my dad insisted, watching as Sylvie heaved me against her shoulder into a burping position, which I made prompt good use of. Meanwhile a frost had crystallized the room. The nuns did not appreciate the B-word. Their slack faces tightened like sphincters. But what the tight-faced nuns failed to understand was that it had nothing to do with my illegitimate origins. Dad called people "bastard" as a matter of course. Anyone, really — men, women, children. Teachers, bankers, priests. Inanimate objects, even — a sweater with one arm turned inside out, a slippery fork. The nuns were just lucky he didn't call me a cocksucker, seeing as how he used the terms interchangeably, depending on mood.

Sylvie always told the bastard part of the story reluctantly, but not Gord. He loved to recount the glory of that moment. Not the story of my arrival, but the story of the day he used the B-word in front of nuns.

He bragged about it. That, and the size of me, which — once he had satisfied himself I was an actual infant instead of a masquerading toddler — he took credit for. He felt it reflected well, somehow, on him.

That's why the knowledge that I could take the prick never held any particular joy or pleasure for me. I didn't want to take Gord, it would've tickled him to no end, he would have loved it. *Look at that wouldya, broke both my arms and legs, that's my boy did that — bastard barely even broke a sweat!* I never wanted to take him. I just wanted to get away from him.

———

I had to stop for a while. I got a bit worked up after writing that and went off to drink and watch a little TV and now I am drunk. I just realized I can write you however I want — drunk or sober — and there is nothing you can do about it. Isn't this great. The freedom of the page. I think I remember you saying something about that. Sounds like something you would say. However I am making a lot of typing mistakes and this is incoherent but I will fix everything tomorrow so you can still read it lucky Adam. Freedom of the page. I think what I take issue with is this "freedom" concept of which you speak. Who gave it to you, that's my question. You just assume it. It's not legally enshrined as far as I know. Freedom of speech is a thing, but what you've done is a lot more complicated than simply giving utterance, isn't it. You have taken something, Adam. Let's be specific. You have taken something that was mine and made it yours. Without even asking. Like if you had said to me, You know what I think about you, Rank? I think you are a dangerously unbalanced thug with an innate criminality nestled somewhere in your genetic soup (quoting you now — surely you recognize this "luminous wordplay") which I assume has resulted from the early death of your sainted mother and subsequent oppression and, I'm guessing, abuse at the hands of your cartoon-villain father. If you said something like that — to my face, you know, like one man would to another — then I could say to you, Oh, hmm, I see. Well thank you for that Adam but that's a whole buttload of assumptions you just made and holy shit have you ever put on weight since last we met.

And that would be *fair*. I think that's what I'm getting at.

Oh Christ I read all this over and I see I haven't even got past the fact that I was born. I keep getting distracted. I'm going to send what I have so far because I can see it's going to take longer than I thought to get this down. Maybe I'll break the emails up from here on in.

Meanwhile my shoulders are all fucking bunched up from yesterday so I think I'll just go to the gym and start fresh tomorrow — start from the beginning, don't rant, save the insults, don't get sidetracked, just fucking hack away at the branches and weeds until I get to the clearing you've already hacked out for yourself — where you've built a little cottage and cultivated a little garden, where you thought you might lounge and relax and dream your lying bullshit dreams forever, where you are now standing, perhaps cowering, chubby and pompous, waiting for the bleeding, vengeful, earthquaking arrival of Reality, in the hulking persona of its raging representative, Rank.

Consider this the first chapter.

2 |

DO WHAT YOU WANT. Keep as much of a "paper trail" as you want, I haven't made any threats. What happened to freedom of the page? And I didn't use the word "bloody" five times, I only used it two times. You are counting "bloodily" and "bleeding," which are two completely different words. I can't believe I have to explain the fundamentals of the English language to a celebrated wordsmith like yourself. What I sent was a literary document, just like the one you published. How many times did you use the word "blood" and "bloody" in your book? A lot more than me I bet.

I contacted you on Facebook, I asked if I could email you my story, and you said:

Sure! I'd be delighted to take a look.

I'm keeping a paper trail on this end too you know.

Maybe now you're getting an idea how it feels to read something about yourself that you've had no hand in and have no control over. Like those cola commercials, when they were using footage of dead celebrities, do you remember that? Fred Astaire, smiling his slow, smirky smile at a refreshing can of cola in lieu of Ginger. And some people said it was ghoulish, it was like grave-robbing to sell pop.

So how does it feel to have your grave robbed?

To continue.

I was born, small town, prick, goddess.

I was just about to start writing about Sylvie. I thought I should commemorate her before anyone else, first and foremost, because she plays such a small role, ultimately, in the grand scheme of things, having died right out of the gate. But then, all of a sudden, I remembered who I was talking to and now I'm feeling protective of her.

She was still more or less freshly dead when I met you in first year — which made me the mess that I was, the emotional disaster zone you were eventually able to take such incredible advantage of. Let's just take a little break at this point and acknowledge a single fact: my mother had died, and you put it in your book. It wasn't a big deal, in your book — nothing that should have been a big deal was made into a big deal. It didn't have any consequence, my mother's death — I mean, *your character's* mother's death. Didn't kick off a police investigation or a funeral full of teeth-gnashing, clothes-rending mourners. It did nothing, it was a just a thing that had happened to this guy — *his mom died, by the way.* Background information. It's mentioned once and never again.

Imagine what you would have done with her if I'd given

you more to work with. Even now I don't trust you. So fuck you, Sylvie stays with me. You can have the prick — who I can't help but notice got even less play in your novel than my mother. Like zero. I find that puzzling considering how much I used to complain about him to you guys. Dead Sylvie was allowed in, but poor alive-and-kicking Gord barely made the cut. Which is hilarious compared to the reality because — you know. What I wouldn't have given and so forth.

All you guys from the house, you and Kyle and Wade, you wondered what the hell I was doing there half the time — why I bothered to hang out with people like you. I was feared and massive and you guys were — in the parlance of guys like me, guys who played sports — kind of gay. Right? I don't think you'll dispute that. I mean generally speaking. You sat around getting high and listening to Van Morrison when nobody in the world was listening to Van Morrison anymore. Wade even had a poster of Van Morrison. It was so embarrassing. And anyway I show up at that party they had for homecoming week in first year and I start making out with the poster of Van Morrison, like I've pinned poor Van against the wall and am sexually assaulting him, and you guys are like Oh my god that's the guy from the freshman mixer who chugged all the purple Jesus right out of the barrel and then vomited into the barrel and then started chugging that, who in Christ's name let him in? But you're delighted to have me, I can tell, because I am — and you sure as hell can't deny this now, Adam — a Character.

So that's why you hung out with me. I livened things up. I brought colour and physicality into your world. I shoved you into walls, got you in headlocks, squashed you up against unwilling women at various functions and held you there until both parties gave in.

But why did I hang out with *you* pussies? That was always the question no one on either side of the equation could capably answer. Why did I quit hockey in second year, losing my scholarship, so I could lounge stoned with you guys slouched in Kyle's idiotic beanbag chair wasting an entire afternoon flinging Wade's vinyl Grateful Dead across the room and into the sink?

Because Rank's fucking crazy, people used to say.

And that was correct. That's how I would've explained it too. But I'm a grown man now with the wisdom of many accumulated years and now I see that I was crazy in a very specific way. It was a layered kind of madness; it had texture. One, I was crazy with grief. So crazed I didn't even know it. I thought I was fine. I figured this was simply how life went for a motherless young man just kicking off his twenties. I thought, as I chugged my purple vomit to the cheers of countless admirers, things were chugging along quite nicely. Mom was dead, sure. But look how popular I was! And at least I was away from Dad.

And that's the thing — that's where I was mistaken. There's where all the underlying craziness, the bad kind of craziness, the kind that sneaks up on you — that snuck up on all of us — was lurking. In the knowledge I was kidding myself.

What happened happened, Adam, because I existed in a constant, desperate panic of aversion.

I hung out with you pussies because you were as unlike my father as any men I'd ever met.

05/25/09, 4:01 p.m.

I was born the illegitimate offspring of fornicators, passed like a puck to the nuns (which is what was done with us B-words in that particular time and place) and slapshot straight into the upstanding, two-parent home of Gord and Sylvie. Goal! Now I was somebody's son.

Fast-forward through my childhood, because my childhood is mostly her. Sylvie playing peekaboo (*I seeeeee you*). Sylvie telling me never to hide on her. Crying. Telling me it wasn't funny, it was no joke. I'd been under the porch step, directly beneath her feet as she called and called. At first it was funny, and then it wasn't. I heard her start to cry, and then I was too scared to move, too ashamed. Making your mother cry was the worst thing you could do.

Don't ever ever do that, she said. I want you right where I can see you.

It's funny how it's the memories of shame that hang on longest.

For example, I think about my life leading up to the moment you and I stopped being associated with each other — and it was an actual moment, wasn't it? You remember. A decisive, incontrovertible moment like the moment a blade comes down. Instead of one massive obstruction, you end up with two useless halves. But at least things aren't so complicated anymore.

Let me start that again. I think about my life leading up to the moment you and I stopped being associated with each other, and if I were to write the key incidents down on a piece of paper I'd end up with a kind of grocery list of shame. In fact I've done this, and in fact that is precisely what I ended up with. Bullet points. Shame-pellets.

I was ashamed that I worked at my father's Icy Dream as a teenager — not slinging soft-serve, but the other kind of work I did for him. Then I was ashamed when I tried out for hockey in order to get out of working at Icy Dream (as long as I was busy crushing my fellow man — be it on the ice or in the ID parking lot — my father was happy).

Then I was ashamed I played so well, which is something I can't really explain — the joy I got out of it when all I'd really been expecting, to be honest, was a means of shirking ice cream duty. And I was ashamed of my hockey scholarship, which no one — neither me nor Gord — saw coming. I was ashamed of the tweedy university it took me to. I was ashamed of going to university. I was ashamed that all of the guys on the team were like me and all of you guys from the house were nothing like me. That is, I was nothing like you. I was ashamed I quit hockey after only a year. I was ashamed to find myself hanging out with you pussies, with whom — to my continued shame — I had nothing in common. I was ashamed as my good standing with the university ticked away grade by dwindling grade, and that I no longer had any money to pay for tuition or housing. I was ashamed when I stopped going to classes and started bouncing at Goldfinger's.

At which point, it was like I had come full circle.

And then, as I think you know, the bullets blur together in a single, spreading oil slick of shame that coated me like some flapping, flailing seabird. Or maybe I am too big to compare myself to a seabird. More like some bellowing walrus flopping around on the oil-slick rocks, splattering his fellow marine life in filth.

And I understand wanting to get away from me at that point, I really do. Wanting not to be contaminated — pulled under in my wake, or rolled on top of in my panic.

But I've moved on, Adam. It's been a lot of years since then. I've put it behind me, as people do.

Except, not you. And you can only imagine my surprise. Adam: the first one to go, the first to get out of the way before shit could meet fan. Backing up, arms in the air. The guy who let me believe for the rest of my life I had been too much for him. That I was not worth the aggro; that he wanted no part of the bad-news contagion that constituted my life.

That it should turn out you wanted everything to do with it. That you should want it, in fact, for yourself.

3 |

MY ADVICE TO YOU ADAM is to sit back and enjoy the story. Okay? Stop whining, stop threatening (it's pathetic and besides I don't know how you expect to serve me "notice" whatever that means if you don't know where I am) and for Christ's sake stop interrupting. You're like one of those assholes at the movies who can't shut up, who keeps asking questions or complaining in a loud voice about how lame the dialogue is. There was a time when you used to let me talk and talk. For hours. Eyebrows going up, eyebrows going down. Thank god for your eyebrow movement — it used to be the only way I could tell you were still listening, that you hadn't abandoned your physical body at some point and were occupied bouncing from one astral plane to the next. I invested a hell of a lot in those twitches and furrows. And if anyone was looking for any more than a few twitches and furrows after they'd yanked off a hank of flesh and handed it over, they were in for disappointment, right?

Of course I know now why that was, what it was that made you such a wonderfully attentive listener.

Well now I'm giving it to you — all the stuff you felt you had to wheedle out of me on the sly. Look, it's all yours, unspooling like fishing line. So relax and just try to appreciate how magnanimous I'm being.

Where was I. We're skipping childhood because that's where Sylvie lives.

So, the Icy Dream. Gord blames Icy Dream Inc. for everything that's gone wrong in his life since the day he opened shop. He likes to imbue his failures with a cosmic significance, because this makes him a kind of Jeremiah in his own mind. For example he wasn't just some underemployed loser, back before he became my home town's emperor of ice cream, bouncing randomly around from job to job like a pinball — he's *God's* pinball, in *God's* own pinball machine, meaning the good Lord has always got a watchful, pie-plate eye on Gord.

Another example of my father's monomania: he always tells the story of how, once he got the loans together to buy some kind of franchise, he had "the choice" between an Icy Dream and a Java Joe's. Like it could only possibly be one or the other — the wrong choice and the right. As if some kind of celestial fast-food overseer descended from the heavens with a ID cone in one hand and a crumpled JJ's cup in the other — obliterating all possibility of, say, a Pizza Hut, a Mickey Dee's — displayed them both to Gord and thundered: *Pick!*

This would've been something like 1981. And the way Gord tells it, he scratched his head and said to himself: *Coffee?* Who wants to sit around drinking coffee all day? Who wants to *go out* for a coffee? ID was a magic land of ice cream confection — the kind of thing children clamoured for. The kind of all-forgiving place to which you got in the car and drove after a fight with the family, say. Everyone cools off and then you reappear bearing some kind of sweet, frosty olive branch and you're hero of the day. This had been a favoured tactic of Gord's long before he bought the franchise — maybe that's part of what inspired him to go with the Dream. He couldn't see coming home with a tray of large coffees to make up for his transgressions, no matter how many creamers and sugar packets he emptied into them. I remember Arctic Bars, Oh Henrys, two-litre bottles of root beer (A&W, the good stuff, not the no-name kind from Dominion) accompanied by a tub of vanilla ice cream to make floats. Sylvie always got a box of either Cracker Jacks or wine gums — she had strange tastes.

Point being, the way Gord saw it there was no insult, no trespass, no random act of prickery that sugar couldn't sweeten.

But coffee? Coffee was for harried office workers, management types. Ice cream was joyous, coffee was grim. Ice cream was celebratory, coffee was no-nonsense. Ice cream was of the people, for the people and coffee was strictly for grownups — medicinal, even — a kind of businessman's brain-lubricant.

Coffee's not what we're *about* in this here town, insisted Gord.

The town hasn't exactly boomed since then — they always said it would and it never did. Last I heard, however, Gord's Icy Dream is still in operation, still doling drippy soft-serve and flaccid burgers poking like tongues from out between two spongy, seed-flecked buns. Under new management since Gord retired. But of course you and I both know what *did* end up booming in the past twenty years. Coffee. JJ's. My dad's lone ID is currently surrounded by no less than six JJ's coffee outlets — there's the one on the highway leading north, and the one on the southbound route. There's the one in the mall near the industrial park, and the one in the strip mall downtown. There's the counter attached to the gas station and finally, there's the freestanding JJ's directly across the street from the ID. All of them thriving. No one in this town of 7,500 hardworking souls need go without JJ's mudwater for even five minutes, and clearly no one does.

"I never claimed to be a prophet," shrugs Gord when the topic of the Great ID Wrong Decision of 1981 comes up.

The weird thing is the *pleasure* he still takes in that epic failure of foresight. To him it proves his independence — his maverick spirit. Gord was never one to follow the herd, even if the herd was making truckloads of money.

"Coffee is for assholes," Gord will explain. His Last Word where Java Joe's is concerned.

It was a class thing, frankly. He associated coffee, in those days, with Management, and Dad has never done well with men of managerial timber. He planted Sylvie and himself into that particular small-town soil on the coast where he was born because of rumours of the any-day-now industrial boom. Soon, jobs would be given out hand over fist, the story went; Gord just had to get in line. So Gord got in line. And what did he do, once he was at the front of the line? Once he found himself sitting in the manager's office awaiting the just-a-formality, five-minute labourer's-job interview?

Gord called the manager an asshole, is what he did. The manager of SeaFare Packers, the only industry, thus far, in town. The reason why is lost to the ages, but Gord assures us his judgement was true and just and to have held his tongue would have constituted a serious moral lapse.

Thus began his career as an independent businessman, while the town, nurtured by SeaFare, built itself up around him. Gord established himself as a parasite of sorts. "I was a barnacle on the ass of SeaFare," he likes to say these days, always able to take pride somehow.

But he'd be damned if he was going to spend the best years of his life brewing coffee for those assholes.

Here's the irony — to this day I never go to JJ's. Not because of some kind of misguided loyalty to Gord, but the opposite. Surely you've been, Adam? Even a latte-sucker like yourself couldn't have avoided the occasional last-ditch caffeination stop at Joe's, right? So you'll know a patron doesn't exactly come across managerial timber stacked there in the booths.

You find parkas. Checked shirts and baggy pants — wife-bought. Fake leather shoes. Rubber boots. Work boots. Toques, ball caps. Bloated wallets in permanently deformed back pockets. Squints. Grizzle.

What you find hunched and huddled in the identical orange booths of Java Joe's are endless variations — young, old; fat, thin — of my father Gord.

05/25/09, 8:43 p.m.

I'll tell you what sucks about being almost forty, if you're me. Lots of men are angry at their fathers, yes, well into their forties and beyond, but at the same time, a lot of men aren't — or if they are, they manage to keep it in check. Lots of men go to see their fathers on the weekend, or call their fathers on the phone every once in a while, or take them to a hockey game, or out to Ponderosa for a steak. And the two of them are able to somehow be men together. They've arrived at that place through some mysterious process of maturation and tacit agreement.

I can't do that. Like there was this one time I brought a girlfriend home to meet Gord. Not that I wanted her to meet Gord, but I was trying very hard with this girl and I wanted her to see the coast where I grew up. Neither of us had a lot of money at the time, however, and Gord was still living in my childhood home, a two-storey farmhouse just far enough out-side of town to be inconvenient, which he'd bought to house Sylvie and their anticipated throngs of children. He'd kept it after her death and my departure and lived in it by himself, as if expecting one or both of us to return at any time.

I told myself there was no reason this visit shouldn't work out. I remember I was still trying to be normal at that point — trying to force a sense of decency onto my life. I didn't want to be the type of guy who was estranged from his father. I was trying not to be a lot of types of guy back then.

Kirsten was a girl from my church and the church had me convinced that if you said to yourself — I mean to God — Okay, God, I'm giving up my life to you now, it's all yours — and then just started acting like the kind of guy you wanted to be, the rest of your life would reorganize itself around that resolution. I was a wholesome, decent young man, I'd decided, freshly washed in the blood of the lamb. Therefore I had a wholesome, decent relationship with my father, who, when next we met, would somehow detect the godly aura rippling around my cleansed being and be instantly humbled and inspired to godliness and decency himself.

I can't blame the church for this delusion. It was my delusion, the church just lent it institutional support. On some level I knew that's what this particular church was all about — nurturing mass and individual delusions — and that's probably the whole reason I joined. But no doubt you'll recall how even in the old days I would radically clean up my act every once in a while, leaving all you guys at the house gob-smacked at my sudden puritanism. I wouldn't drink, I would go to classes, I'd make sure I was at the library on the days I knew Wade would be coming back from Goldfinger's with his stash. Sometimes I could go two, three weeks like that. But not much more. After that I'd get angry about something and need to arrest my thought process somehow. It's a pattern I've maintained my whole life.

So there I was — wholesome, decent, delusional — mentally pulling open the screen door of my childhood home for the first time in maybe ten years and thinking — I actually told myself this — It'll be great! My girlfriend and I will drive down the coast. We will stay with my father, and Kirsten will meet my father, and the two of them will get along. Gord always had a bit of a courtly side with the ladies. He'll take one look at her, I thought, and he'll be all "me dear" this and "me love" that — playing up the salty old Gael stuff because if goddess Sylvie found it irresistible surely all central Canadian women must — and it won't be grotesque or off-putting at all. Perhaps he'll take down my baby book for the two of them to titter over, seated side by side on the couch. *Looka the size a the little bastard! I said to them nuns, I said* . . . Perhaps we will barbecue in the evenings, drink beer, boil a lobster, reminisce about the days of Sylvie. It won't be painful. It will be healing, if anything (I was very interested in the idea of "healing" at this time). And perhaps, when the time is right, my girlfriend and I will even talk to my father about Christ.

Or perhaps Gord will talk endlessly about all the bastards and assholes who have betrayed and conspired against him, always casting an accusatory eye at yours truly, and perhaps yours truly will grit his teeth until he has to make a dentist's appointment and be fitted with a mouth guard to wear at night, and his stomach acid will churn until he can digest nothing but mushroom soup from a can and he will want, very badly, to get drunk and give nary a thought, for a couple of days, to how our Lord and Saviour, in all his compassionate wisdom, would've handled a trial-in-the-desert like Gord.

And perhaps all that new-found, Christ-inspired patience came crashing at last to the ground when Gord made the mistake of referring to his son as a hockey hero, or, more specifically, a *failed* hockey-hero, in the girlfriend's presence.

As in: "This fella here coulda been another Al MacInnis. Coulda gone all the way to the NHL if only he'd listened to his old man."

To which I pleaded: "Gord, don't be a goof."

"But no," continued Gord. "Listens to everyone but. Telling him he was no good. Story of his life."

Which of course would be a nugget of information to pique any girlfriend's interest.

"Really Rank? People said you were no good?"

"No, he's full of crap," I replied. With maybe a bit too much volume. "No one ever said I was no good. But nobody ever said I should go into the NHL either, except for you, Gord. Gord likes to imagine the whole world is busy judging my every move, going *boo* or *yay*."

"You're the one who thinks that," Gord countered, happy now to be arguing after all the uncharacteristic nice-making in honour of the girlfriend's visit. "Your exact problem's always been that you believe it. You believe the judgement, when you should be looking at the facts. Even when the judgement is clearly a load of BS."

This was about the time Kirsten started to realize that the father-son banter had shifted away from the great game of hockey into mysterious, dangerous new terrain. The big hint, she told me later, was the way I'd started moving my jaw minutely back and forth, producing a faint, unconscious twitch beneath my temples. Kirsten always called this my "warning signal." She said it reminded her of when a cat starts swooping its tail.

Which meant it was time to change the subject. "What say we put the steaks on, Gord. Or you know what?" I reached — maybe grabbed is a better word — for Kirsten's hand. "How about a prayer?"

This won me a sneering once-over from the old man. He wasn't exactly buying the new me. "Where I come from, you say grace before dinner, not ten times a day before you sit down and before you light the stove and before you wipe your ass — pardon me, dear."

"Oh that's nice, Gord, thanks."

"All I know is this: when the whole goddamn town — sorry, dear — turns against a boy for doing what's right, for doing what the cops are too goddamn — pardon my French, dear — chickenshit to do themselves . . ."

The ancient lawn chair beneath me gave a rusty squeal as I got to my feet, yanking on Kirsten's arm to make her do the same. This after months of painstaking effort trying to prove myself a gentle man — the blissed-out, easygoing kind of guy who walked in the light of Christ's love and all that.

I knew it wasn't going to work, is what I'm saying, and it didn't. My shiny new halo flickered and fizzled out like past-date Christmas lights. It was no match for Gord. We'd been in his company for scarcely an hour and the whole time it had felt like sitting inside a cloud of mosquitoes — every word he spoke a needly humming in my ear. It made me want to swat.

I announced that I wanted to take Kirsten down to Jessop's for a beer — her mouth just kind of dropped open at the word "beer," I remember, as if her jaw had abruptly unhinged. And I did take her to Jessop's, but first I took her to a motel on the highway and booked us a room, where we proceeded to argue into the night.

Kirsten didn't get it. She thought I was crazy and insisted I had to at least call Gord and tell him we wouldn't be staying the night as planned. She said she couldn't believe how rude I was being toward my poor old father. "What?" She kept saying. "So he's a little crotchety — so what?"

I yelled at her that he wasn't "crotchety," he was a fucking prick. It was the first time anyone had done any yelling in this relationship, let alone any wielding of the F-word. I could feel all my work with this girl — all my good behaviour and act-cleaning-up — start to flake away like dandruff.

"Sorry, sorry," I said fast. (The problem with being a man of my size is that I can't get away with displays of aggression in mixed company. I can't shout around women no matter how angry or frustrated I get because it scares the living shit out of them. They start cowering, and then I feel like a monster. I remember one time riding the bus I was sitting beside a baby and I sneezed — I just *sneezed* — and the kid nearly turned itself inside out with screaming. It's not a nice way to feel.)

So I got my act together and said some other things about Gord, trying to explain myself. I strove to paint Gord as a kind of evil genius. Every word he uttered, every gesture, I explained, was a jab at me — a perfectly timed, precisely aimed barb.

Admittedly, I was just desperate to get my girlfriend onside. I knew how ridiculous this portrait was even as I was painting it. Gord shrimpy in his polyester workpants, floating in one of my discarded hockey jerseys as he waved us a confused goodbye. Anyone who watches him in operation can see my dad is not exactly a man of strategic foresight. Gord is a nerve ending, an involuntary muscle — he fires according to certain stimuli.

"*Rank*," I remember Kirsten saying — this astonished girl who had accepted Jesus as her personal saviour when she was all of eleven years old and never looked back with even a hint of nostalgia on her pagan childhood. "He's an *old man*," she said. "He's a frail, little old man."

And then she held her arms out toward me, not in invitation, but as if to say *Behold*. She shook her head at me. As if to say *Good lord, you could snuff him like a birthday candle.*

And Gord is now twelve years smaller and more frail than he even was then.

And, look at this: I still can't stop talking about him.

05/25/09, 10:56 p.m.

All right. Jesus. Here we go.

I was born, and next thing I know I'm a teenager and my father runs the Icy Dream.

But you realize if I tell this story, it's just going to be more Gord.

I find, writing this, I keep getting caught up. Sometimes this is fun and at other times it isn't and other times it's not exactly one or the other. I just get caught up and forget who I'm talking to. Not *who* exactly, but what version of you, Adam. It keeps shifting around. I forget about the thief and liar on the back of the book, the guy who needs regular reminders of how portly he has become given that he was once so afraid of it because what kind of friend would I be if I didn't make him aware of the gradual bloating process to which he, middle-aged fatso, has succumbed?

I forget about him and I instead remember you. And I think by *you* what I'm really getting at is a person who doesn't exist. There's the angle-y Adam with glasses in my memory who I was at first a bit put off by because he never said much and had that quiet observer thing going on of which any sane person, I think now, would be suspicious. You reminded me of a certain type of spectator from my hockey games. Guys who'd sit directly behind the net and be so immersed in the action that even when the puck came straight at them and bounced against the Plexiglas in front of their faces, they wouldn't blink. They'd even lean forward sometimes, as if to meet it. So they were completely absorbed in the action, these guys, but at the same time completely apart. And they knew it, they never forgot for a second. They never doubted they were safe.

And instinctively, I didn't like that about you at first. It goes to show a guy like me should always trust his instincts.

Later — and this gets to the heart of the You I'm speaking of, the You who doesn't actually exist — I took the fact of how you sat and stared, how your eyebrows went up and then went down, how you spoke one or two sentences in response to my five hundred — and even those only after a long, agonizing, eyebrow-jimmying silence — I took all this to mean you must be some kind of oracle, a man of profound sympathy and insight. Someone, in short, who understood the way things were, who got it. Who maybe even got me.

One time, I remember, you put your hand on my forehead. You probably don't remember this. We were very drunk, or I was anyway, and dawn was going to break at any minute, and I was talking — I'd been talking for hours and it was like labour or something, like giving birth, I was working myself up and now I could feel it coming, I could feel it coming, I was going to tell it, and I broke out in a sweat and started talking faster, willing it to come but terrified and the next thing I knew I was telling it, telling you, and the fluorescent light from the kitchen was glinting off your glasses in a way that drove me crazy, so that I actually got up and moved at one point, closer to you, mid-sentence, just to change the angle so I could see what was happening behind your eyes.

But that was when you held out your hand, as if to stop me from seeing, or as if I had moved toward you precisely to receive a kind of benediction. You leaned forward and held up your palm like a traffic cop or Diana Ross mid-routine and you placed it against my forehead and your hand felt fantastically cool, which made me realize how heated I'd become with all this talking and confessing.

And everything stopped. I don't know how else to describe it. I wasn't talking anymore because words seemed not to exist. And that was wonderful — it was a wonderful feeling, the sudden nonexistence of words — like a cool shower after a long gruelling hockey practice.

And morning light started fingering its way through the gaps in Kyle's shit-green velvet curtains. Curtains he'd hung precisely to keep the morning light from doing this very thing and auguring its way into our hungover dreams, but curtains that consistently failed to hold up against the tenacious morning rays.

And long fingers of light, I remember, gradually stretched themselves across the room, illuminating the beer bottles. I'm sure you don't remember. Probably it only lasted for a second, your hand against my head. It would be years before I hooked up with my church but I think I had a moment of precognition then. Faith-healers, charismatics, weeping, shrieking supplicants, the laying on of hands and then — all that pain followed by all that peace.

But you know what Adam? Fuck this. That's what I have decided, just now. Fuck you, traitorous fat man, and you, skinny cryptic four-eyes, and most of all You — lying disappointment you have been, it turns out, all along.

4 |

06/01/09, 1:12 a.m.

SURPRISE! RANK HERE.

Adam, this has begun — there's no way around it. That's
what I've been realizing this past week. I gave up writing to
you and I felt this incredible relief — no doubt you did too. In
fact that was the only thing that tainted my relief — knowing
you were probably relieved as well. But fuck it, it was over!
It had been started, but now it was stopped, and so was over.
Cooler heads prevailed and all that. I'd just go back to doing
what I've been doing all along — working and coaching and
going to the gym — and you would go back to whatever it
is you do — vampiring the good and the real out of people's
lives — and we'd forget about each other as we'd already
done and should've kept right on doing.

So let's take another run at this, shall we? I've been reading over what I sent you so far trying to figure out why in
God's name I can't just settle into a nice, neat, chronological

version of the story of my life. I keep going off on these point-less tangents. It seemed like such a simple idea at first — all I had to do was sit down and write it out. But it's actually a lot harder than you would think.

Now that I've read everything over, however, the problem has become clear. It appears I'd rather talk about pretty much anything other than working for Gord at the Icy Dream. But if I don't the rest of the story can't happen. Which is precisely the hurdle, come to think of it.

The interesting thing about this whole process is that I find myself realizing what I think about everything at the exact moment I'm typing it out. Then I sit back and read it over and go: *Huh.*

Is that how it works for you? This never really occurred to me before. I have to admit I kind of imagined you sitting around rubbing your hands together and cackling to yourself as you plotted out your miserable theft, not just typing away and suddenly looking down and going, Oh hey, check that out. I just completely screwed over a guy I used to be buddies with.

And I've also just realized that even though my outrage resulting from the above has led me to launch myself at you across the ether hollering *Hey nice story you thieving bastard but guess what, I have the real story right here — so get comfortable, chump!* That is, even though I was completely gung-ho when I initiated this little back and forth between us, there is a big part of me that keeps trying to bow out.

But I am going to do this, Adam. Neither of us is getting out of it. Every time I think fuck this and fuck you — and I think it with approximately every other sentence — I imagine your relief at never having to open another email from me and it propels me right back here in front of my ancient computer, constantly hitting the wrong keys and having to go back and start again in all my enthusiastic umbrage.

Gord used to go over the counter. That was the crux of the matter. I had two jobs at Icy Dream — well, three, if you counted working the till and manoeuvring the soft-serve into two perfect undulating bulges balanced in the cone — three bulges if the customer ordered a large. That was something I eventually got very good at, executing perfectly undulating soft-serve — I felt like a sculptor at times. So I did that, I even took a bit of pride in it, but I was mostly at Icy Dream, according to Gord, to "bust punks' skulls." So I busted punks' skulls, but I also had a third job, a private job that I had not been assigned but ended up inevitably assigning to myself.

And that was to keep Gord from going over the counter.

The problem, which my father could not have foreseen when the Celestial Fast-Food Overseer descended from the heavens and demanded he choose between ID and JJ's, was the existence of punks. Punks abounded in our town, as they do all towns, big and small, and were the bane of Gord's existence as a small-business owner.

Everywhere kids went in our town they promptly got thrown out of, was the thing. Nobody wanted teenagers anywhere out in public. I knew because I was one. I was the worst kind of teenager — superficially speaking, that is — the kind that grownups like the look of least. Big and thuggy. I could take them. I could take anyone, obviously. And if you put me with another two or three guys, no matter what the size of the others might be, we were terrifying. We were punks.

I remember getting thrown out of the mall once — for doing precisely nothing. We'd been sitting on one of the benches outside the Pizza Hut waiting for it to be time to go to a dance when a cop sauntered up carrying a grease-pocked bag of garlic fingers and told us to get lost. Our very existence was offensive to the other mall patrons, he explained. They couldn't abide the sight of us, a clutch of jean-jacketed menace huddled on the bench.

The cop didn't call our parents or curse us out and it was, as far as this kind of thing went, a pretty innocuous incident, which is why I didn't think it was something I should keep from Gord. But it turned out it was. When I mentioned it the next day at dinner he took a fit. I didn't raise you to be a goddamn punk, he screamed, handing me a bowl of mashed turnips. So why are you going around hanging out in the mall like a goddamn punk?

I wasn't doing it like a goddamn punk, I protested. We were just sitting there.

Sitting there like a goddamn punk! Give me the salt! Like you got nothing better to do!

I *don't* have anything better to do.

Then you get your ass home if you don't have anything better to do! Help your mother! Do your homework! Straighten up your goddamn room! Where the fuck is the butter?

And so forth. There was no arguing with Gord on the punk front, not since he opened Icy Dream. Punks streamed in at all hours, hot and cold running punks, and Gord discovered his group nemesis. They scared off the kind of customers Gord wanted — moms with kids, for example, not to mention the considerable number of people who shuffled in solo just to buy a single cone or hot fudge sundae, some small confection to brighten up their lonely, ho-hum lives. These customers were depressing, yes, but at least they didn't make trouble. There is not much sadder than a fat guy in his fifties sitting alone in the back of an Icy Dream plastic-spooning soft-serve into his mouth, but there is one thing sadder, and that's watching the same guy flinch every time the jolly group of teenage dicks in the next booth erupt into gales of comradely yet somehow malicious laughter.

The punks would invariably order small orange pops and skulk in the corner booths spinning coins and shooting the shit under their breath until the gales of brain-dead testosterone-stupid laughter erupted, a sound that was like the pig-squeal of microphone feedback to my father's ears. For a while he tried the "Eat something or get out" tactic, at which point the punks would invariably pool their change and place a single order of small fries to see them through the next hour of customer alienation.

Get the hell over there, Gord would hiss at me then, and tell those punks to pound salt. Or else you'll bust their skulls, tell them.

They have drinks, I'd say.

They don't have drinks! They got a cup full of gob after chewing on their goddamn straws the last hour. Put your hat back on.

Usually when I had to confront the punks I would remove my paper hat because it made me feel like a tit.

I look like a tit in the hat, Gord. They won't take me seriously.

You don't look like a tit in the hat! It's your uniform. A

uniform gives a man an air of authority.

An Icy Dream uniform does *not* give a man an air of authority.

You take pride in that uniform. You have nothing to be ashamed of. That uniform puts food on the —

Oh Jesus, I'm going. I'm going, Gord.

Stop calling me that! If you're too cool to say Dad you can damn well call me Mr. Rankin.

Calling him Gord was still a new habit at that point. I'd acquired it not long after I turned fifteen. It hadn't been intentional, the first time I'd done it — I can't even remember what the circumstance was — but once it was out and in the air between us I could tell I had kind of broken Gord's heart. After that I couldn't seem to stop.

Hi guys, I would greet the punks.

And what would happen next depended entirely on the punks in question. Sometimes the punks were my friends. They would smile up at me with their greasy, fry-fed faces, make an ungenerous remark or two about my hat and I would respond with a cheerful threat to shove my hat up their asses. After some back and forth along these lines I would tell them they should come back between around five and seven next time because that's when Gord went home for supper and then we could all hang out and I would give them free Cokes if they were nice to me.

Meanwhile, I'd say by way of wrapping things up, my dad requests you remove your dirty punk asses from his family establishment.

But Rank, Scott was thinking he might like a fudgy bar. He hasn't quite decided yet.

We don't want your business, boys. You bring the tone down. Bad optics, scuzz like you chowing down on our fudgies.

Why don't you chow down on one of *my* fudgies sometime, Rank?

Ha ha ha. Oh my god. Nice one. Get out.

And the guys would snort and smirk just so not to lose face entirely, then shuffle their way out the door taking care to look extra dangerous and sullen for the benefit of Gord, scowling away by the fryer.

Those were the good days.

On the bad days, guys like Mick Croft showed up.

Mick Croft was one of the town punks who actually *was* a punk — not just a gangly, belligerent, functionally retarded teenage boy like the rest of us. He dealt drugs — of course — and brandished knives — of course — and had been expelled for kicking the gym teacher, a man with the unfortunate name of Mr. Fancy, in the ass when Fancy was bending over to gather the volleyballs into a canvas sack. Fancy had just called Croft a loser in front of the whole class. Take a good look, guys, he'd said, at what not to be if you want to achieve anything in this life other than a welfare cheque. And then Fancy made the unbelievable move of turning around to get the volleyballs and showing Croft his sinewy glutes. It was like, Croft is rumoured to have protested, the man was offering it up.

That was the effect Croft had on adults — he enraged them, moved them to say the kind of things you should never say to a sixteen-year-old kid, no matter how much he pisses you off. Men in particular he provoked to tantrums. Croft had flunked enough grades to be in a couple of classes with me and I remember the entire room sucking in its breath when a red-faced Geography teacher took hold of either side of Croft's desk — with him in it — and yanked it with an effortlessness born of pure animal rage to the front of the classroom. When everyone was going around asking what had prompted Fancy to denounce Croft like that in the gym it turned out to be because Croft had forgotten his shorts at home. Which sounds like nothing, but we all understood how little the shorts would have had to do with it. What it had to do with was Croft's attitude. Croft had a smirk that made you want to take hold of either side of his mouth and pull his face apart. It wasn't a smirk like that of other punks. It was a smart smirk, and was usually accompanied by a smart remark. And when I say smart, I mean *smart*. Croft wasn't your typical idiot punk like say his compadre Collie Chaisson who did time in the Youth Centre for putting his fist through a convenience store window and leaving a multitude of perfect, dried-blood fingerprints polka-dotting the cash register.

So it was no surprise that Croft would be the first to send my father lunging over the counter at Icy Dream, hands clenched to throttle and punch — simultaneously if at all possible. I will never forget that first time, grabbing Gord around the waist like a child and hoisting him backward as every muscle in his tiny body strained in the opposite direction. He actually had a boot on the counter at one point, but instead of using the leverage to launch himself at Croft, he was thwarted by me hauling him back at just the right moment and using the momentum against him. Croft was wide-eyed, having shot a good three feet back from the counter, skeezy smile quickly affixed to mask his shock. In his mind he was already sitting in some sweaty basement telling the story to Chaisson and his other dirtbag friends. Gordon Rankin man! Little fucker comes at me right over the fuckin counter man! Lost it. You goddamn punk! You little asshole! Like he can't even talk he's so pissed. Like in-co-*her*-ent with rage. So I'm ready to go right? Grown man coming straight at me, fuckit, he's the one who'll be charged, not me. I'm just a widdle kid. Lucky for him the gland-case comes to the rescue.

No one had ever called me a gland-case before I met Croft. I remember being a little shocked by it — the audacity. It wasn't the kind of town where guys got mocked for being big. You got mocked for wearing colourful shirts, or using words with more than two syllables, but not for being big. Big was considered an achievement. Total strangers all but stopped me on the street and congratulated me on it. Croft was the first person to make me feel like a freak.

I remember walking by him at a dance. Croft started bouncing up and down and making earthquake noises. I glanced around and grinned to show I got the joke, but also to let him know I had heard the joke and to determine if it was the kind of joke that required me to walk over there and set a few things straight. Croft grinned back at me. Huge and chimp-like. At which point I stopped smiling, allowed myself to slow down a little, upon which Croft held his hands up in the air, all innocence and goodwill.

I kept walking. *Fucking gland-case*, I eventually heard, enunciated loudly and with care from somewhere behind me. When I turned around, Croft and his cronies had dissolved into the crowd.

Here's a snippet of how the conversation went between Croft and Gord moments before my father's attempt to take flight.

Gord: What can I get you today, son?

Croft: Coke.

Gord: I beg your pardon, now, I didn't quite catch that.

Croft: Coke.

Gord: You'd like a Coke, would you?

I should explain that Gord is already doing a slow burn at this point. I can all but hear the rant bubbling away in the foreground of his brain: *goddamn little Christer no respect doesn't even know how to ask for something it's the parents off doing god knows what don't even instill common courtesy let alone basic please and thank you think the world owes them every goddamn thing they get.* So it's only at this point that Croft, who has been paying no attention whatsoever up until now, actually turns his nasty focus on my father. So I see this. I am standing at the grill supposedly waiting for it to be time to turn the patties over but at this point I have pretty much forgotten about the patties because I witness the way Croft's bright little eyes are taking full measure of Gord and the tendrils of smoke slowly wafting from my father's ears.

No, I think. Not the smirk.

Croft allows the smirk to just kind of ooze across his face like syrup over pancakes.

Croft (enunciating loudly, precisely the way he did when he called me a gland-case at the dance): Yeah, bud. I said a Coke. *Coca. Cola.* I wanna teach the world to sing.

(Chortles from the skeezer crew lined up behind him.)

Gord (with a hideous patience that tells me he is revelling in the accumulation of adrenalin that's taking place as his ire is stirred. Now the two of them are practically dancing together): It's not that I can't hear you, son. I may have a few years on you, but I don't have any trouble with my hearing.

(Oh Christ, I think, he's called him "son" again.)

Croft: Sorry, bud. Guess it must be the Alzheimer's setting in or something.

(More skeezer tittering. Even though it isn't quite time, I rapidly flip all the patties on my grill to get this particular obligation out of the way.)

Gord: My problem, *son*, is with you. And the fact that you little assholes keep coming in here . . .

Croft (flipping his hands into the air at the word "assholes"): I just want a Coke! I'm just thirsty!

Gord: . . . and you sit in the back corner both scaring people away and reeking of maryjane . . .

Croft: I don't even know Mary Jane! I never touched her!

(skeezers holding their sides at this point)

Gord: . . . and then you have the goddamn nerve to come up here and grunt at me in my own restaurant. "Coke" (Neanderthal grunt-speak here). "Coke, *bud*. Gimme Coke."

Croft: Look, *bud* . . .

That's what did it. The slavering insolence of that third and final "bud." I dropped my flipper and hurled myself forward, reaching Gord just before his extended hands could secure themselves around Croft's neck.

There was a lot of yelling. The word "punks" occasionally leapt like a salmon from an otherwise undifferentiated stream of obscenities where my father was concerned, whereas on Croft's side of the counter, as he and his crew sauntered (but sauntered somewhat hurriedly, I'd like to point out) toward the door, I heard — along with their own laughing, obscene stream — the words "Crazy" and ". . . should call the fuckin cops!"

Once Croft et al. had taken off, I yelled — still clinging to Gord — something around the restaurant about complimentary single cones for everybody, but everybody was too busy gathering up their bug-eyed children and herding them toward the exits to notice. The only people left to take advantage of the offer were a few workers from SeaFare grabbing burgers after their shift, and they seemed to regard the incident as a kind of floor show. They laughed and applauded and generally made me regret the free ice cream I ended up doling out to them.

"Nice reflexes there, Rankin."

"You shoulda let him go off on that little tool."

"Why you giving my food away to those assholes?" Gord wanted to know once I had rejoined him behind the counter. He had yelled at me for burning my patties but otherwise seemed cheerful and refreshed after his lunge at Croft, like he'd just woken up from a nap.

"Because you attacked one of the customers," I explained. "Those assholes are only ones who didn't run screaming out the door."

"'Customer' my ass, goddamn little punk! *Sorry, bud. Coke, bud.* They oughta give me a medal."

So about twenty-five minutes later, a pair of Mounties came strolling through the doors.

"Here they come," I said. "They got your medal, Gord."

06/01/09, 11:32 p.m.

And now I find myself starting to panic a little, for a couple of reasons.

Because I just told you another whole slew of stuff about Gord and reading it over I can see that I still haven't got to the heart of the thing. I can feel you still aren't getting it — my father is coming across to you the same way he came across to my Jesus-freak girlfriend all those years ago — as a foul-mouthed but mostly harmless "character." The same kind of creature I must have been to you and Wade and Kyle when we all started hanging out — a shape in the distance; a figure on a screen, behind Plexiglas. You lean forward, no matter how dangerous the guy's antics might become — no matter how much he shrieks and sweats and bares his teeth — knowing he can never touch you, ultimately. You can watch him and see him and go home and think about him, even be disturbed by him a little. But it's not like he can ever step off the screen, or out from behind the glass, and blunder his way into your life.

That, as they say, is entertainment.

It's weird because I've held this stuff in my head for so long, been so consumed and convinced by it, but when I pour it out onto the page, into you, it emerges as this completely different thing, like juice turned to cider, or cider to vinegar — I'm not sure which is the better example in this case, but my point is: it's the same thing but it's *changed*. It's not worthless — you wouldn't necessarily throw it away as a result — but it's *changed*, and now you have to figure out what you're going to do with it, because this is not the end result you had in mind.

The other thing is, after feeling the whole time I've been writing you like I'd rather shove both hands beneath a lawn mower than write about the Icy Dream, about five seconds into it I realized I was enjoying myself.

And finally, I know I vowed to keep you away from Sylvie, but I'm starting to figure out that if I keep digging into this, it's inevitable that my shovel has to scrape against my mother's coffin at some point.

So what do I do then?

Do I do what you did? Do I yank Fred Astaire from his mausoleum, force his cold, dead fingers around a can of cola, put on some music and waltz him round the graveyard, calling, *Come one, come all?*

06/02/09, 12:01 a.m.

How about you just trust me when I tell you she was perfect? Can't we just take that on faith and move on? How would you feel if your mother died? Well, that's how I felt, even three years after we buried her, when I was nineteen and you and I became acquainted with each other. Maybe you even know what I'm talking about — for all I know, your mother has passed on too by now. So think about how that felt and get back to me. Was it bad? Okay, well it was bad for me too. It's never good, obviously. But it was worse for me — I don't care what happened on your end of things — it was worse for me and we both know why.

It's important we get this right, Adam, the story of Gord and Sylvie. It's important because you presumed to write

a book that featured you-know-who. Let's just go with the
name I came up with earlier, let's call him Danger Man: a terrible guy who performs a terrible act. An act with a flat-out
crappy outcome, an act that is shocking and horrible — but
also, here's the kicker — inevitable. Why inevitable? Well, it's
built into the character's DNA, you see. They don't call him
Danger Man for nothing. According to his creator, the guy
has an "innate criminality" swimming around in there. A
born thug, born bad, born to lose. It's fated: the guy's a biker
tattoo waiting to happen.

That was me, Adam — in your book and nineteen years
ago. You're not going to deny that it was me, right? I notice,
for all your whining, you still haven't denied it.

And here's the gravy: Danger Man? *Oh yeah. His mom died,
by the way.*

It's not enough, is what I'm saying. *Insult to injury* is what
I'm saying, Adam.

Anyway, on to Gord. Poor old Gord who didn't even merit as
brief a cameo as Sylvie-the-corpse in your magnum opus.

Picture redneck wed to goddess. Finally Dad finds himself
in charge of something, in a domestically ordained managerial position all his own, and he makes his authority felt. No,
Adam, he doesn't hit. Gord is not a hitter of ladies, he is at
heart a courtly little bugger, as I've already said. But he sneers.
Croft had the smirk, Gord had the sneer, every bit as infuriat-
ing to the observer. He berates. He insults.

If I give you specific details then I have to give you Sylvie,
which I am still not willing to do. But I'll give you this much.

Picture a sort of spark. A flicker of light — there's a flaw in the film. The glare of the projector comes blazing in. It's startling, but after a while you get used to it, the way you can get used to a fuzzy TV channel if there's nothing else to watch. Picture a sort of stationary glimmering — a small, steady radiance of sweetness and light. Oh, Gordie, the glimmer murmured to me one day after I'd finished kicking a hole in her bottom cupboard. Such cheap materials, in the house that Gord built.

Gord himself had just finished calling the glimmer "goddamn useless" before sashaying off in the truck to Home Hardware to buy a couple of lamps for the living room which, he'd suddenly decided, was poorly lit and which Sylvie, if she'd been any kind of worthwhile human being, would have fixed before poor, busy, put-upon small-businessman Gord had to have his consciousness affronted by the experience of an inadequately lit room.

"Useless idiot," added Gord as he pulled on his boots. He wasn't screaming anymore, but often with Gord, as in this instance, the post-screaming moments could be the worst. Just as Sylvie was likely starting to let herself feel relief that the screaming had finally come to an end, that she no longer had to hunker in the trenches as verbal machine-gun fire tore up the air around her, and just as she poked her head above ground hoping for the all-clear, Gord would lop it off with some quiet remark along the lines of *useless idiot*. And then go cheerfully on his way.

"Fucking . . . assho— . . . fuck!" I was saying as I removed my foot from the cupboard once he was gone.

Oh Gordie, the glimmer murmured then, wanting to make me feel better. Because that was what the glimmer was put on earth to do. Even in the daily exhaustion of dodging Gord's machine-gun fire, she never gave any indication that anyone might deserve or require comfort other than her baby boy.

It's okay, the glimmer assured me. He really never talks to me like that . . . Dear, you made such a *hole*.

"He *always* talks to you like that!" I sputtered — talking to the hole and not the glimmer. I often couldn't look directly at the glimmer, she shone so pure and bright.

No, no, the glimmer assured me in her voice that was like no other mother's. Other mothers, it always seemed to me, either barked or shrieked. Their voices were either shrill and silly — a strained, desperate pitch deliberately tuned to convey: "I'm just a nice lady! Don't concern yourself with me!" Or else sharp and harsh, a sort of debased version of the previous that announced: "I am so sick of trying to pull off this nice lady shit, now pick up your socks."

Not the glimmer. Her voice was always low and soothing, like the coo and flutter of overhead doves.

No, no, she cooed and fluttered at me, wafting over to close the cupboard door as if that would hide the hole. He doesn't. He really doesn't.

"When?" I yelled. This was the worst part — now I was yelling at the glimmer. I was yelling at her for having been yelled at. "*When* doesn't he talk to you like that? He *always* talks to you like that!"

No, no, the glimmer cooed. He's nice to me, Gordie. It's just sometimes he wants to show off — you have to understand that.

"Sometimes he wants to show off," I repeated with complete incomprehension.

He's just trying to impress you, said the glimmer. You're his boy.

"Impress me," I repeated.

Otherwise he's fine, said the glimmer. Don't worry.

Otherwise Gord was fine. He sneered and berated and called my mother "goddamn useless," but only when I was around. Otherwise he was fine.

That's when the dread began to settle around me like ash.

That was my first major hint from the universe.

5 |

HERE'S ADAM. Look, everybody!

Lope-de-dope, gangly through the quad, awkward artsy four-eyes. His body doesn't fit him somehow. He stoops, but in the strangest way. In a backwards kind of way. His hips jut a little forward, his hands dangle a little behind. A type of guy that other types of guys, hockey-team kinds of guys for example, want badly to scrape across the pavement. It is an instinctive, gorilla sort of thing, a phenomenon Dian Fossey might have witnessed. Culling the herd. Stamping out the genetic weaklings.

Once, in first year, Adam said, in the middle of a party, the word "methinks." He was talking to girls, clearly a pretty new experience for a guy like him, one of the girls had opined something about something else, and Adam was actually going to quote Shakespeare at her — the line from Hamlet about the lady protesting too much — but his new friend quickly wrapped a forearm about Adam's windpipe to spirit him away before too much social carnage could be inflicted. So the quote came out kind of: "Oh *ho* (the oh *ho* being what put the friend on alert). Methinks the *gwaaaa*."

"What the hell is wrong with you?"

Adam singularly unappreciative as he rubbed his overlong neck: "What?"

"Don't say 'methinks.' Don't ever say 'methinks.'"

"It was a quote from . . ."

"For fuck's sake I know it's a quote. Don't quote!"

Adam just hadn't found his niche. There were girls you quoted at, and girls you didn't. And once he learned to distinguish the girls ripe for the quoting, he knew enough not to quote Shakespeare, and not to stand there with a look of anticipation on his face as if to say: Oh boy! Time to quote! No, he figured out his routine pretty quick. You lounge, you smoke. Perhaps you twirl the ice cubes in your glass of mid-range scotch that by second year you've decided makes a more distinctive impression than a beer bottle dangling from an index finger. You never look at them directly, the girls who like to be quoted at, because that makes it seem as if you're deliberately quoting as opposed to just thinking out loud, following the profound and languorous train of your own thoughts. Rattling off a little Beckett here, a little Kafka there. What's that? Neruda! Adam did extremely well with Neruda, it was all you heard out of him for a while. The thing about the blood of the children in the streets. Betraying something of a social conscience. He doesn't just live in his head, this guy, not Adam. He'd be at the barricades soon as the first shot rang out.

None of which made the guys who wanted to scrape him against the pavement any less eager to scrape him against the pavement, you understand. If anything it stoked the evolutionary-determinist fires: Cull herd! Squash faggot! Fortunately, Adam, as previously mentioned, had a friend. The same friend who was considerate enough to crush his windpipe at such a key moment in his social development. A big, strong, popular friend, genetically blessed if cursed with a tragic past and a disastrous readiness to trust his fellow man.

Adam was afraid of fat people. He was afraid of a lot of things. Rare meat, for example, made him gag and run away, wrists a-flapping, like a high-strung little girl. His friends found this out during an outdoor barbecue one early spring day in first year. It was too soon to be barbecuing, there was still snow on the ground, but everyone at Kyle and Wade's house decided it was time for winter to be over so they put on shorts and flip-flops, spun a few of Wade's Beach Boy records and bought some steaks for grilling.

They grabbed either side of the horrific couch — a Sally Ann special, natch, as this is a period in a young man's life, although the young man never knows it at the time, that is riddled with clichés. You drink to excess. You carry the horrific couch out into the yard, sit it in the snow. You are so crazy! Little do you know you are caught up in some kind of Star Trek time warp, where in a million universes exactly like this one, throughout every possible history of every such universe, a billion college dorks exactly like you are doing exactly the same thing and declaring to their exact same selves: We are so crazy! Who'd have thought to bring a couch outside in early spring?

(I think sometimes I felt it, Adam, and that's why I behaved the way I did. I felt the weight of those million universes, those billion clichés. Wade: pothead music freak. Kyle: pothead Future Leader, offhand alpha male, even with me around. You: geek; me: jock. All we wanna do is drink and get high and listen to guitar rock and talk about some interesting shit we might have read or heard, god forbid, in class, and have sex with girls, all the time, in all sorts of horrifying ways. And we talk about those ways. And we listen to Van Morrison. And suddenly I can't stand it, I am suffocating under the weight of the billion college dorks who came before me — who exist on every side, in all the invisible universes — and I eat the by-now grievously abused poster of Van Morrison off the wall. I don't even take it down first, decently ripping it into bite-sized morsels with my hands. I just lean into the wall and tear off chunks with my teeth and tongue and lips; chew and swallow — ahm, num, num like the Cookie Monster. Ahm, num, num as Wade gazes from behind his peevish cloud and mutters: *Hey*, man.)

Adam was afraid of rare meat. His big, popular, handsome friend unearthed this bit of information during the springtime barbecue. The big popular handsome friend had guzzled a jug of alcool like it was Mountain Dew and he was feeling the massive weight of the innumerable universes of college dorks who had guzzled innumerable jugs of alcool before him, so he blundered over to the barbecue, grabbing the still-semi-frozen steak off the rack (none of them knew how to cook in those days, no one thought to defrost it) and started tearing into the semi-frozen, mostly raw cowflesh with his teeth. He just stood there growling with the steak in his hands as his good friends — his band of brothers — gaped. He looked like some kind of upright animal, a monster, the Wolfman maybe, tearing off chunks of flesh like they were chunks of a Van Morrison poster and going *ahm, num, num,* blood trickling down his charismatic chin.

And that's when Adam lurched to his feet about to run, but threw up instead.

Ha, ha, ha! declared the friend before throwing up himself.

06/06/09, 1:14 p.m.

Good times, Adam. Like Paris in the twenties. Do you remember Kyle saying that — that was his line: *It's like Paris in the twenties in this place!* Whenever our interactions with one another grew particularly squalid. Like the time in second year we both ended up having sex with that one girl because she was so drunk she came back from the bathroom and forgot which one of us she'd been with previously, so went to you after having been with me, and then when I showed up wondering what the hell was going on everybody just kind of shrugged it off like — *Oh . . . Sorry.* And then I passed out on the floor beside you guys and I can only assume you just kept at it, because neither of you seemed particularly happy to be interrupted. Or the time Kyle slapped a girl he had in his bedroom (I still believe he did this, Adam) and we all heard it and stared at one another for a minute and then went back to our beers and conversation. Or the time Wade came back from Goldfinger's clutching his stash and terrified for his life.

Or that time I made someone die. Again. Remember that?
Well let me remind you. It was like Paris in the twenties.

06/06/09, 2:59 p.m.

Do I feel real to you? Do you feel that I actually exist, pound-
ing keys two-fingered here at my kitchen table, or is it more
like receiving email from a figment of your imagination? Is it
like I'm a ghost coming back to haunt you? It sounds stupid,
but that's what it was like for me, reading your book. We get
freaked out by ghosts because they aren't supposed to exist,
right? They're not real, in the same way the past isn't real,
not really — and what are ghosts except the past floating
around, occasionally taking shape and going booga-booga
in your face? Strictly speaking, what's past doesn't exist anymore. And it shouldn't. And you don't want it to. And there it
is, swirling up around the light fixture, trembling your tabletop, banging on the other side of the wall. Notice me — take
me into account. I'm not supposed to be here; here I am. That
is, here we are. Together again.

That was an experiment, when I was writing about you earlier, the way you came across back in school. How'd it feel
reading that? I was trying to do what I felt you did to me and
Sylvie — take you over. You'll notice I didn't make stuff up
exactly, but at the same time I wasn't really being fair, was
I? I was brutally honest, as they say, which is never quite
indicative of truth per se. I was making a smarmy story out
of the person you innocuously were, out of the hackneyed

college-guy life you were innocuously living. You couldn't help it — you were nineteen, twenty. You were an idiot. We were all idiots. But not all of us end up being immortalized at our personal peak of idiocy do we? Or, say, at very nearly the worst moments of our lives. Not many of us are lucky enough to encounter a hungry young wannabe in the midst of our suffering, a would-be storyteller nearly lobotomized by the dullness of his own existence, famished for some kind of genuine emotional content.

And then I come along. And I am nothing *but* emotional content.

Anyway, the experiment failed. I got caught up again and lost sight of who I was writing about exactly. I started having a kind of weird, dreamy fun and next thing I knew I was writing not about you, exactly, but about us. All of us, back then.

Or, fun is not the right word. Let's just say I get caught up and leave it at that.

06/06/09, 11:48 p.m.

Hey shitheels. What's the deal? I thought we had a back and forth going on and now you leave me hanging in the breeze. WTF, as the kids say. I'm baring my soul for you here, yanking off one strip of flesh after another and feeding it into cyberspace. This is supposed to be a dialogue, not To Be or Not To Be, if you know what I mean, not a one-man show. A meeting of minds so to speak. Methinks the a-hole needs to drop a line, is what I'm saying. I mean I know I told you to shut up but I didn't actually mean shut up. I meant it would be kind of nice if you could not talk to me like I am some kind of psycho stalker freak for a minute or so. You certainly had a great deal to say earlier, about the serving notice and the paper trails and whathaveyou. How can you create a paper trail if you don't ever write me back?

In conclusion, get with the program.

Your pal,

GR

06/07/09, 8:38 a.m.

OK so I had some beers last night and got bored and was checking my email for word back from you, which I have started doing a tad too compulsively lately, and I guess I was feeling sort of fed up with the radio silence. Sorry about that. I hereby vow not to waste your time with random drunken harangues anymore. We're not pen pals; I get that. I didn't exactly kick this whole thing off in the spirit of friendship and, let's face it, you didn't pause to solicit my opinion at any point when you were busy chronicling The Life and Times of Danger Man. So just ignore that last email and we'll continue.

Back to Gord. Needless to say, the Mounties didn't give him a medal the night he flew at Croft. But they didn't exactly give him a dressing-down either. Who could fault Gord, after all, an upstanding member of the small-business community, for wanting to kill Mick Croft? *Everybody* wanted to kill Croft — kids, teachers, small-businessmen and Mounties alike. This was nothing new.

At the same time, though, Croft was a kind of subliminal hero in our town. He was such a little bastard, and somehow he got away with it. On the surface, of course, everyone predicted dire things for Croft — he was the kind of guy a decent, God-fearing little town like ours was desperate to dismiss. Croft was insolent, criminal and rebellious. Surely he would come to no good. But in our secret outlaw dreams, I think, we rooted for him.

Croft was eighteen when he was expelled for kicking Mr. Fancy in the ass but only in Grade 10 because he'd been held back a couple years. So instead of sliding into some menial production-line gig at SeaFare like any self-respecting dropout, he moved into a two-bedroom apartment above the woeful Chinese restaurant on Howe Street and set up his drug-dispensary in earnest.

How do I know? Because I went there every couple of months. Croft was the man to see, like it or not. He was to my hometown what Wade was to the student body back in our beloved college days.

I was fifteen but about twice the size of Croft, and for all intents and purposes a man. It's weird to think back to it now. I was always big, as I think I might've mentioned, but at fourteen I kind of exploded into manhood. I shot up an extra foot, putting me at 6'4", I sprouted hair overnight like a werewolf — except the hair didn't disappear after the full moon, but sallied forth from the ground zero of my crotch to obliterate my entire torso. My voice — already deep — plummeted into Darth Vader Luke-I-am-your-father territory and I had to shave practically twice a day to keep from looking like a prospector. You'd think that would be weird, and it was weird, but

I'll tell you what was weirder: other people — the way *they* changed, behaviourally, in response to what had happened to me physically. Almost overnight I went from being alternately marvelled at and teased for being the big lumpy kid I was, to being deferred to and even respected as a grown man.

Imagine one day the neighbourhood mothers are gleefully feeding you hot dogs to see how many you can down in one sitting, tousling your hair, exclaiming over your "big, hungry boy!" status as they pour you another glass of milk, and the next day those same ladies, who thought nothing of shouting at you to take your shoes off at the back door and wipe your pee off the seat next time, are blinking up at you respectfully and asking if you think they should replace their furnace now or give it another winter. Lady, I'm fourteen! Gimme another hot dog. But no more hot dog marathons for this strapping young man, suddenly they're setting the table and frying me steaks and having to stop themselves from pouring us both a couple of fingers of scotch and plunking their mom-arses down onto my lap, practically.

I'm exaggerating to make my point, but you get it, right? And the problem with being a boy in a man's body is that, basically, in this world, it isn't a problem. It's commonplace. There are lots of boys in men's bodies walking around — I work with a few of them. Some of them are my age, trembling on the precipice of the big four-oh, and some are even older. What I'm saying is, a lot of boys don't bother growing into men, because they don't have to — their bodies have already done it and it turns out that's all anybody requires.

Which is to say, Adam, that when you are fourteen and you walk around looking like you are twenty-two, you rapidly figure out a few things about the human condition. First, being a grown man gives you this instant, irrational power. It doesn't matter if you haven't graduated from junior high yet, it doesn't matter if you spend most your evenings picking your nose in front of *Family Ties*, and it doesn't matter if you have done precisely nothing in your life worthy of your fellow man's respect. Doesn't matter — you have it. Everyone figures you can fix their cars, that you know what kind of aluminum siding they should buy, that you can file a tax return. And they turn to you, this is what's astounding — they turn to you, these ladies with the bashed-up furnaces — in all your assumed expertise and aptitude.

Meanwhile you just want to eat hot dogs and pick your nose. And you *do*. You *do* eat hot dogs and pick your nose. And nobody *notices*. It doesn't seem to sully your newfound respectability one bit.

So imagine you're not just a grown man at fourteen but (and sorry for how this sounds) imagine you're a *spectacularly* grown man. That you tower above other men. That your voice is deep and authoritative — your pronouncements, therefore, not to be denied. That your forearms and chest and genitals are practically carpeted. If being a grown man endows you with instantaneous authority, what do you suppose a body like mine was telling people?

It told people, I think: *Make way.*

It told people: *Trust me.*

Some people it told: *I am your hero!*

It told women: *I'll take care of it.*

Men it asked: *How could I have anything but contempt for you?*

It said: *Prove it. Prove to me how big you are.*

06/07/09, 1:27 p.m.

So I was fifteen and Croft was eighteen, and I was the obvious choice among all my friends to head to Croft's upstairs apartment on Howe every few months or so and purchase a few fragrant rabbit-turds of hash and multiple baggies of what my father so quaintly called "the maryjane." There was never any discussion of this among me or my friends; it was simply understood that Croft was a dangerous skeeze, known to deal with bikers and carry knives, and therefore it fell to Gordon Rankin Jr., fifteen-year-old colossus, to do business with him. Everyone assumed I was invulnerable and would have no problem with this, and in fact I didn't. I wasn't scared of Croft. I wasn't scared of anybody. Because when people make the kind of assumptions about you that I describe above, Adam — that you are basically a 214-pound superman — it is kind of hard not to assume it right along with them.

I went to see Croft not long after Gord took that run at him. I don't think it occurred to me that the incident at Icy Dream would interfere with our business interactions, so when I climbed the steps to Croft's apartment, the woozy stench of cheap meat and sesame oil from the Chinese restaurant filling the stairwell, I'd pretty much forgotten the whole affair. Like I said, I was fifteen years old. Not all my higher brain functions had gelled at that point. I was fantastically oblivious to danger at that age — or even the idea of consequence itself. It never occurred to me, for example, that there was any reason I should bring a buddy with me to Croft's — none of my friends had any interest in attending these transactions, and they all had complete confidence in my ability to handle myself. Therefore, needless to say, so did I.

Imagine how any given small-town petty-criminal teenage headbanger circa 1985 would decorate an apartment and — bang — there's your mental image of Croft's drug shack. A lot of red light bulbs, a lot of smoke, a lot of heavy metal odds and sods (skull candles, flying-V ashtrays — you get the picture). The guitar in the corner, the amps, the preposterous stereo system, so tweaked and extravagant it might as well have been sculpted from solid testosterone. The grimiest of couches placed behind a wooden slab of a coffee table that in its squat massiveness had a kind of sacrificial-altar thing going on. Croft probably chose it for that very quality, now that I think of it (and by "chose," of course, I mean hauled it out of the dump or his grandmother's basement or somewhere). Because the coffee table definitely performed a ceremonial function during these meetings. This was where Croft cut, measured, tested and finally bequeathed his product.

Croft's bright little eyes lit up when he opened the door. "Dude!" he greeted. This I should mention was long before people in my part of the world started saying "dude" all the time, but ever since that California stoner movie with Sean Penn, Croft had adopted the expression as his own as if in tribute. That, and "bud." He also went around exclaiming "You *dick!*" more than was strictly necessary.

And if you're expecting an atmosphere of criminal intrigue to take over at this point, Adam — sorry. I was one kid buying dope from another, just as millions of kids do every day. I sat down on the couch across from Croft (and the cow-flop of hash that was splayed on the table between us), placed my order, and waited for Croft to saw me off a few chunks like I was waiting for a slice of ham at Easter dinner. We'd been through this a bunch of times. He didn't give me a sinister look when he pulled his knife out of his back pocket, his eyes didn't glint as he extracted the blade, he was barely paying attention to what he was doing, and so was I. I just sat there feeling vaguely depressed by my surroundings. Croft's skeezer entourage lounged around sucking beers and bobbing their heads to Lynyrd Skynyrd. Collie Chaisson had his eyes closed and was playing air guitar. My own eyes were tearing up from the smoke. I remember thinking to myself, as Croft invited me to help myself to a beer from a cooler sitting near my feet, that I should feel jealous of him living this outlaw, parent-free life, and I wondered why I didn't. I downed the beer and didn't pursue the question, but the answer is pretty obvious to me now: I was only fifteen. I had no desire, conscious or unconscious, to live like Croft. I craved, like any kid secretly does, rules, decency, wholesome surroundings. I didn't want this, or anything like it, not yet. I still wanted my mother.

"So dude," said Croft, rolling a chunk of hash into a ball between his fingers. "Your dad, man. Fuck."

I placed the emptied beer bottle between my legs. So we were going to have the conversation after all. "I know," I said. "Sorry, man."

"Lost it, bro."

"I know," I said again. For lack of anything else to do, any other kind of this-conversation-is-over gesture to make, I picked up the empty beer again and made a point of pretending to drain it.

At this point Collie Chaisson's freckled eyelids flew open and he stopped playing air-guitar mid-riff. "Holy fuck man fucking *guy!*" he exclaimed. "Like, *flying* across the counter man!"

I slouched deeper into the chair and let my arms dangle over the armrests, deciding to just go limp and permit the stupid inevitability of Chaisson's play-by-play wash over me.

Croft was smiling down at his drugs, shaking his head in a seen-it-all kind of way. "Angry little man," he remarked.

I sighed. "Yeah. Short fuse."

But Chaisson wasn't finished. "So he, like, he *comes* at the Mickster, right?"

Chaisson was actually preparing to tell the story from start to finish. Not only that, he was acting it out, leaning forward in the chair with his arms extended straight out in front of him, fingers spasmodically clenching, exactly the way Gord's had been. Even Chaisson's face was twisted into a unpleasantly accurate imitation of Gord's furious little knot of blood lust.

"And he's like 'You *blankety* little *blank-blank!*'"

Blankety? I stared at Chaisson.

"Dude," interrupted Croft, and I was glad he did because we both knew if Chaisson kept going I would eventually be obliged to respond. Much as I wanted to distance myself from Gord, I couldn't let this skid sit there guffawing all night about how ridiculous my tiny, angry father had made himself.

"We were all there, Col," continued Croft, still not looking up from his work. "No need for the floor show."

Chaisson immediately sunk back into his chair, glancing over at me and frowning just a little when he realized how hard I had been staring at him this whole time.

Then, a massive piece of furniture at far end of the room began to tremble and grunt — it was actually a guy, a guy in sunglasses who I'd originally assumed to be passed out when I first arrived. Now he was hefting himself out of a chair that had previously seemed a natural extension of his body, so snugly did it fit his lower half. I sat up and watched as he trundled over, still grunting, to join Croft on the couch. He was almost equally tall as wide, with a balding pate and grotesque little ponytail nestled in the folds of flesh insulating the back of his neck.

"Jesus, Croft," he grunted as he approached. "I can't watch this anymore."

Croft smiled up at him. "What?"

"What," repeated neck-fat. "What. It's like you're sitting there crocheting fuckin doilies is what." He took the knife from Croft's impassive hand and briskly finished the job like an executive chef chopping onions. A second later, he'd wrapped the chunks of hash and shoved them, along with the requisite baggies of pot, across the table at me.

"Good?" he said to me.

"Um," I said.

"Hey man," said Croft. "I'm just trying to do a good job by this guy. This guy's a good guy."

"How nice," remarked neck-fat, peering at me through his sunglasses. I didn't know how he could see a thing in Croft's red-lit living room. "So is the customer happy?"

"I think so," I said, rapidly counting the baggies. "Uh, yeah. Yeah, this is good." Thank you neck-fat, I thought to myself. This is exactly what was needed — someone to step forward, punch through Croft's leisurely, lord-of-the-manor pace and move this business along. I stood up from my chair in order to yank my wallet from my back pocket.

"Forty," rumbled neck-fat.

"Wait a sec, Jeeves," said Croft. "I thought we'd give my buddy Rankin a little discount."

"Why that's adorable," said Jeeves, gazing up at me — and could his name really be Jeeves? "And why would we want to do that?"

"Little dust-up at his dad's restaurant the other day. Just wanted to say no hard feelings."

I was still standing there with my wallet in my hand, practically hopping up and down with the need to get this over with and go meet my buddies behind the mall. The parking lot behind the mall seemed the most wholesome place in the world all of a sudden.

Abruptly, the mountain man heaved himself to his feet and extended his hand to me.

"Call me Jeeves," he said.

"OK," I said. The top of Jeeves' red-shining head came level with my nose, which meant he was a pretty big guy. And, as I contemplated his stringy skull, I realized that he had about twenty years on the rest of us.

And he still hadn't let go of my hand.

"Oh," I said. "Rank. Gordon Rankin. Call me Rank."

"Rank," repeated Jeeves. "Like pee-yew, right?" He smiled and wafted his other hand in front of his nose.

"I never thought of that," I said, thrown, because I really never had. I realized for the first time that I had basically been insisting people call me Stinky since I was twelve years old.

"You're a big fucking guy, Rank," remarked Jeeves. He pumped my hand and finally let it drop.

"Yes," I agreed. "I am a big fucking guy." I had trained myself at this point not to automatically respond "Thanks," when someone made this remark.

"Well why don't we say thirty-five, big guy?"

"Thirty-five, sure," I said, digging through my wallet and glancing over at Croft. Because why was I doing business with this Jeeves guy all of a sudden? Croft gave me one of his sweet smiles, the same kind, I recalled, that had sent the Geography teacher into such paroxysms. The thing about Croft was, he had something of an angelic face. When he smiled his bright blue eyes tended to dance — he could light up a room. That face, I think, was what really sent people like Fancy and the Geography teacher over the top. Being a badass little shit is one thing. But being a badass little shit who follows up his snotty remark with a smile that melts your heart is too much to ask of anyone's patience.

06/07/09, 7:05 p.m.

Adam, I notice you still haven't emailed me back. I know I told you to sit back and enjoy the story, so maybe you are just being obedient and, if so, I appreciate that. And sorry again, really, for my drunken e-nagging earlier. I just want to let you know it's okay if you feel the need to remark upon any of this. It kind of helps me to keep going if I know someone is digesting the story and responding to it. I guess it's nice to have an audience, to know I'm not just whistling into the void. When I asked you that question before, about whether or not I felt real to you, if it felt like you were getting email from a figment of your imagination, it wasn't rhetorical. I was genuinely wanting an answer. It kind of bugged me when you didn't answer.

I know I came off a little psycho previously but I was just pissed off because you were being so defensive with that "serving notice" shit. Why is it you can't seem to get around the whole "innate criminality" thing when it comes to me? You turned me into a criminal in your book and you are treating me like a criminal even now. Just because of a few emails. But they're *my* emails, right, therefore they must have an innate criminality nestled somewhere in their genetic soup.

I told that story about Jeeves because I knew it would ring a bell with you. Aha, you'd think, that's why none of it was new to him. That's why he settled into that world so comfortably, treated those people like he'd known them all along. Wrong, Adam. That was the first and last time I ever met Jeeves. Pretty innocuous, right? Just a bunch of dirtbags sitting in a crappy apartment drinking beer, dealing hash and pot. Sound familiar at all? Replace the dirtbags with a clutch of fine young college men and what do you have? No guns, no prostitutes, no intravenous drugs. I bet you had all these big expectations — Rank running with bikers, some kind of enforcer, beating the crap out of rival gang members, all at the tender age of fifteen. Innate criminality and all that. You'd lap it up. *Ahm, num, num.* You'd be on to your next book in a flash.

But Jeeves didn't have anything to do with what happened next — or very little anyway. Like I said, I never saw him again. Jeeves wasn't the problem. The problem, as always, was Gord.

6 |

I JUST REMEMBERED I didn't tell you what the Mounties actually said when they showed up at ID a few hours after Gord flew at Croft. And I should, because it kind of began there.

They arrived just as Gord and I were closing up, so Gord invited them in and we all sat across from one another in a booth like four kids on a double date.

There was this one cop called Hamm. The best way I can describe him is rectangular — the guy was all corners. Even his moustache was a rectangle. If it had been any smaller, he'd have looked like Hitler.

Hamm's partner was one of those cops whose job it was to be unobtrusive. To just sit there recording everything, saving it for later, and fade into the background meanwhile. Therefore, I can't tell you much about him, but the way I just described him reminds me of a certain someone. So let's call him Constable Adams, in homage.

Gord had learned somewhere, at some point, that Constable Hamm's first name was Bill and kept referring to him by it. By his full name, that is — Bill Hamm. I had no idea why. Gord was the kind of guy who did this sort of thing sometimes — resorted to random rhetorical flourishes.

"I'll tellya something right now, Bill Hamm," he began before we had even quite settled into the booth. "If I'd managed to get my hands around that little Christer's neck you'd be drawing a chalk outline over by the counter, there, rather than having this nice little talk with me."

I threw my head back and stared at the ceiling. We were going to jail.

But Hamm chuckled. "Now, Gordon," he said. "You can't —"

"You explain to me what I done wrong, Bill Hamm. Explain it to me right now."

"You can't attack —"

"Why is it a load of drug-dealing little shits are permitted to come into my place, sit back there using bad language and stinking of dope, and I'm not allowed to do a goddamn thing about it?"

"Gordon, you have every right to —"

"Then! The minute I try to defend myself. The minute I assert my rights, you assholes — pardon my French, Bill Hamm — you fellas, you show up here —"

"*Gordon*," said Hamm. "Let's step back. Let's not get angry. We're just here to find out what happened. We got a report of a disturbance. We just want your side of the story."

"When you should be out there arresting every last one of those little bastards! Not here harassing me and my boy."

Hamm and I sighed simultaneously.

"You should be *thanking* this boy," added Gord, taking the opportunity to thwack me in the sternum with the back of his hand. "This son of a bitch right here, Bill Hamm."

"And why is that?" said Hamm, eyeing me, abruptly deciding to let Gord take the conversational lead.

"He's the only thing kept me from ripping the little bastard's head off. He's the law and order around here."

I met Hamm's gaze and tried to get some ESP going between us. Don't worry, I transmitted. Sanity exists here at Icy Dream. No teenage heads will be torn asunder.

But Hamm didn't look reassured. In fact the amused indulgence that had been dancing in his eyes while dealing with Gord dropped out of them completely when they met up with mine.

"You know, Gordon," he said, sitting back. "That's not actually what I hear."

Gord was as surprised by this as I was. That anyone could hear anything but good about his boy.

"What's that supposed to mean? What do you mean that's not what you hear?"

"What I hear is that the boy starts fights in the parking lot is what I hear."

Gord and I looked at each other, both astounded and both of us realizing simultaneously, I think, that, strictly speaking — keeping within the letter of the law — it was true.

Gord's reply, therefore, was entirely predictable.

"Horseshit! That's goddamn horseshit is what *that* is, Bill Hamm!"

After all, I was there to bust punks' skulls. Gord had made that clear from the moment I started working with him. And it's not that I literally busted anyone's skull exactly, it's just that I threatened to do this to some random punk pretty much every weekend and — yes — I even got into a tussle or two. The thing is, there were a lot of little shits of the Mick Croft mould who knew Gord couldn't stand the sight of them and who would therefore get liquored up and wander in around closing time precisely for the sport of it.

They had been banned from the restaurant, which of course my father had every right to do. So Gord could have easily called the cops to get them kicked out of there. But Gord didn't want to do that. He liked to handle these things, he said, "himself." Meaning getting me to handle them.

So my job was to take off my hat (my own stipulation), stalk over to wherever the punks happened to be seated, and growl at them to vacate the premises immediately. If they didn't, I was within my rights (according to Gord) to wrestle them out the door — but I rarely had to do this. What happened more often than not was that the punks would tell me: Fine. We'll just be in the parking lot then.

The parking lot, I'd say, is our property, and we want you off it.

You got it, man, they'd say. And go wait for me in the parking lot. They'd smile and wave at me through the window if I didn't go out right away. Or sometimes they would be in the Legion parking lot, immediately next door. The two parking lots were separated only by a sign and a concrete rail — it was easy to get them confused.

That, apparently, was what constituted me "starting fights."

But Gord was all over the situation before I could even draw a breath in my own defence. He leaned forward as far

as he could in the booth so that the table between us and the
cops cut into his scrawny chest.

"You listen here, Bill Hamm. Let me tell you about this
boy. This boy is at the top of his class at school [this was not
strictly the case]. This boy is here, working at his dad's business four nights a week. I don't let him work any more than
that because he has to do his school work. We're saving to
send him to a good college when he graduates [if this was
true, it was the first I'd heard of it]. This boy can do anything
he wants with his time, but what does he want to do? He
wants to help his old man."

Constable Hamm was holding up his hands and opening
and closing his mouth, desperate to get a word in, because it
was clear Gord was only getting warmed up.

"And I'll tell you. When I see drug-addled little shits like
Mick Croft staggering around town, Bill Hamm, it makes
me sick. But you know what else it does? It makes me *weep*.
I weep for those boys, Bill Hamm. Because what do they
have going for them? Do they have two stable parents who
look after them? Do they have a family business to help run
that keeps em off the streets at night? Do they have anywhere near the gifts or advantages of this little bastard right
here? [Another thwack in the sternum.] No! They don't!
And so I weep! I weep for them! But I'll tell you something
else! This boy works his ass off four nights a week to help
me run a clean, decent business. When those lousy punks
wander in here cursing and pouring booze into their Cokes
and lighting up joints in the back of my restaurant, you're
goddamn right he's gonna kick their asses. He's gonna kick
their asses right out of here! He's gonna kick their asses

all over the goddamn parking lot if he has to. And do you know why?"

"Gordon," said Bill Hamm.

"Do you know why? Because his father told him to, that's why."

With that, Gord slapped his palms down onto the table between us and sat there panting with righteousness. Constable Adams, I noticed, was scribbling furiously into his book.

"Gordon," said Bill Hamm again, once he could be certain he wouldn't be interrupted. "I only want to say this to you once. You call us. You don't sic the boy on them. I know what you're doing — you think you've got a secret weapon here. He's under eighteen and a minor so the rules don't apply. You think you've got a one-man vigilante force."

I glanced over at Gord, surprised that the cop would give him so much credit. It was far too calculated. Gord had no master plan: he just wanted punks' skulls busted and was thrilled to have someone around who could capably get the job done. It never occurred to me that he might be taking the legality of the situation into account when he sent me out into the parking lot. And by the way, had the cops entirely missed the fact that it was Gord who had nearly throttled Croft this evening, and me who held him back? I felt myself getting angry at approximately everyone present.

"Excuse me," I interrupted. "I was trying to stop it. I didn't want anyone to get hurt. I was trying to calm Gord, um, Dad, down."

"That's right!" exclaimed Gord. "Like I said, I was ready to castrate the little bastard. If this boy hadn't held me back . . ."

"I don't particularly believe that," remarked Constable Hamm, stunning us both into silence. He sniffed, then, causing his rectangular moustache to bounce around a little. "What I believe, Gordon, is that you let these kids provoke you. You enjoy it. If you didn't enjoy it, you wouldn't be sending the tank here after them every weekend — and believe me, we hear about it when you do. The boys over at the Legion think it's better than TV. If you didn't enjoy it, you'd be calling us, and we'd take care of it."

A thoughtful stillness, entirely uncharacteristic, came over my father.

"And what would you do?" he sneered after a moment — the famous Rankin Sr. sneer. "You said yourself, these are kids. You people can't do a goddamn thing but shoo them off home."

"We come over, we tell them to leave, they leave," replied Hamm. "It's boring, for us and for them. After a while, they find something else to do, and you don't have to worry about them anymore. But you don't want that. You want your showdown in the parking lot. You want your dogfight."

Dogfight. I thought about the handful of standoffs in the parking lot, Gord's face on the other side of the restaurant window. Safe behind glass, miming punches, cheering me on.

At that moment, my father seemed to lose interest in the conversation. "Ah — bullshit," he muttered.

"Anyway," said Hamm, standing up. Adams followed him out of the booth as if they were conjoined. A second later Gord and I stood too. "That's all we wanted to say tonight, Gordon. We wanted to let you know that we're keeping an eye, and we're happy to drop in anytime you need us. You just give us a call next time."

"Wonderful," said Gord, shaking Hamm's extended hand so fast it was like he was wiping his hand on a dishtowel. "My

Christ — haven't we all just accomplished so much." And
with that, he turned away and disappeared into the kitchen,
leaving me to show the policemen out.

That's when Constable Bill Hamm turned to me and said
something I never forgot. It was only the second time he'd
looked at me, and for the second time in our conversation, the
fake-friendly light he'd held in his eye while talking to Gord
flickered into nothing.

"I know you," he said then. "Understand that, Mr. Rankin.
I see exactly where you're headed, son."

I stared back at him for a moment, making no sound
because inside my head I was sputtering at the injustice of
these words. "What?" I managed to sputter out loud, at last,
to the cop. I wasn't asking him to repeat himself, I didn't say
it like "Pardon?" I spread my hands as if to gesture to everything — the entire world surrounding me. It was my "I just
want another hot dog" gesture. *I'm only a kid*, is what I was
trying to transmit to Constable Hamm. It's not my fault you
have to tilt your chin upward to fix me with that null-eyed
stare of yours. I've only been on this earth for fifteen years.
Please don't say this kind of thing to me.

"*What*," repeated Constable Hamm. "You know what. We
both know what."

He turned his back — no handshake, nothing.

And that was my second big hint.

It wasn't fair, but it was — it turned out — true. That's what
made Bill Hamm a kind of oracle. He wasn't talking about
right or wrong, good or evil, justice or injustice. He was a
man plugged into the cosmos, a moustachioed fortune teller,

just talking about the way life was — the way it was going to be. He was talking about fate. Fate's representative stood in the Icy Dream that day like it was the temple at Delphi — and duly he pronounced.

Not bad for a university dropout, eh? I remember almost nothing from my undergraduate career, but I do remember the stuff you and I talked about, the classes we took together. You were studying English — very unoriginal, Adam — and you'll recall that I was doing a basic humanities mishmash in the hope of discovering an aptitude for something other than skating at high speed directly into other versions of myself. Is it any surprise the stuff from Classical Lit would stick with me all this time? If you're going to believe in one or more gods, I remember thinking, the gang from Mount Olympus made a lot more sense than the guy I'd been hearing about most of my life up until that point. Who are you going to believe runs the show if you are a citizen of Planet Earth with any kind of awareness as to what's going on around you? Are you going to buy into the story about this great guy, who is actually somehow three guys, one-third human, and he loves everybody equally, and all he wants is for everyone to behave themselves? (But, oh yeah, sometimes tsunamis at Christmastime. Sometimes bombs on civilian populations. Sometimes mothers dying horribly.) Or do you believe in this self-absorbed pack of loons who couldn't give a shit what happens on earth but just for fun decide to come down every once in a while to screw with us?

At nineteen years of age, three years following the extinguishment of Sylvia LeBlanc Rankin, glimmer of pure light, I remember feeling like I'd found a new religion. This was something I could believe in. It didn't require me to feel bad, to do penance, to confess or be contrite. It required nothing. This cosmology fully expected and understood my exasperation with what the universe had inflicted on me thus far — and didn't care. The gods were dicks — end of story. They had all the power, and guys like Homer and Hesiod and Ovid were damned if they were going to let them off the hook for their dickish behaviour. Not like us Judeo-Christians. Not like we do with our own white-bearded fucker-in-the-sky. (And if that sounds harsh remember I do have some experience with this. I served on Our Lord's custodial staff as an enthusiastic whitewasher of His mysterious ways for longer than I care to admit. In the hope that He'd return the favour.)

So that was good, that helped me for a while. *Oh*, I thought, *Oh! You don't* care. *That's right*, the cosmos patiently affirmed. *You're not punishing me*, I gradually figured out; *you don't hate me. Hate you? Har, har*, chortled the universe. *Dude! You see a parade of ants trucking along and you cut off the route with a bunch of rocks or something just to watch them run in circles. As flies to wanton boys and all that.*

It was weirdly reassuring. I was an ant — I was a fly. Sylvie was just another bug to them. So was Gord. So had been Ghandi, Saddam Hussein and Princess Di. All of us specks. Nothing personal. That felt good. I could deal with that.

Except of course you will recall what happened next — in what direction this new religion ended up taking me.

7 |

06/11/09, 5:44 p.m.

DID I EVER tell you Gord's famous pick-up line, from the first time he introduced himself to Sylvie? Sad. Two hicks working for isolation pay deep in the blackfly-riddled thickets of Northern Ontario.

"Well mother of Christ, they got Frenchies all the way up here now, do they?"

Another excerpt from their storybook romance that Sylvie never cared to talk about. It wasn't the insult to her language and people, mind you, but the cavalier name-in-vain-taking of Our Holy Mother. Sylvie was about a hundred times more Catholic than Gord. It was all about Notre Dame in Sylvie's neck of the wood, so my old man's offhand blasphemy — as natural to Gord as scratching his nuts — came very close to losing him the ball game.

Not close enough, unfortunately for every last one of us. If the gods were keeping a pie-plate eye that day, they decided to let the ants go marching blindly forward.

Sylvie was wearing hip waders for the occasion, standing with a fishing pole up to her knees in the Firesteel River as my dad came sloshing over, heedless of soaking his pants, more than a little sloshed himself.

"They biting?" he hollered, slipping on a rock as he approached and having to steady himself against her.

Sylvie frowned as she teetered, bracing her stomach muscles. Not yet annoyed, as she tells it, only perplexed. She didn't understand how any self-respecting young man from a no-doubt rural, fishing-and-hunting background similar to her own could come sloshing through the river toward her, hollering greetings, and then exhibit, peacocklike, the sheer, splendored idiocy to ask, "Are they biting?"

"No," replied Sylvie. "Dey aren't biting."

Gord, as unperceptive as he'd already proven himself to be, didn't miss a beat when he caught wind of the accent.

"Well mother of Christ," he remarked. "They got French-ies all the way up here now, do they?"

How is it my life unfurls from a seed as insignificant and stupid as this, Adam? And what kills me is, it isn't even my seed. I was adopted, for the love of god. It's not my life; they weren't my parents. Somewhere, perhaps at precisely the same moment, two giants came together. You know how that happens — the tall girl no one will ask to dance. Until a man even taller comes along, surveys the room with scorn, like *Check it out, short-ass losers*. And together, they take the floor. She inclines her endless neck up at him, at last, in gratitude.

Or, I don't know. All I know are here are these two tiny little people standing in a river in Northern Ontario as the gods keep watch, or don't. A drunken east coast stereotype insults a fine-boned French girl of slender means. Problem is, they have both nothing and everything in common. They are hicks. They are broke. They are working at the building site of a hydro electrical generating station for isolation pay at White Dog Falls because the world has nothing else to offer them as yet. It is 1965 and kids their age are rioting in the cities, upending the socio-sexual landscape, but my soon-to-be parents are farm people, terrified of cities, of drugs, of the irreligious, of those who walk around wearing entirely different coloured skin from them. The world is changing, rapidly, dizzyingly, and change is something they've both been raised to fear. They have this in common: they want no part of it.

And that's the only explanation I come up with when the question comes to mind, as it so frequently has throughout my life. You know the question: Why did she marry the prick? We all know why she stayed with him: Notre Dame. The abiding influence of Mother Church and her sacred bellyful of domineering fathers. Our Lady of the Sit There and Take It. But why marry Gord in the first place? The world had nothing else to offer, maybe — nothing so comfy and familiar as some freckled knee-jerk French-hater telling her she's useless.

Sylvie had this terrible story she used to tell about her time up North. That is, *she* didn't think it was so terrible — to her it was just a footnote to one of the handful of heroic-outdoorswoman narratives that she cultivated pre-Gord. She was proud of those days, because she was one of the only women working up at the hydro electrical sites when they were being built — these places were nothing but backhoes and Quonset huts, not to mention about fifty men for every woman. She would talk about day-long trips by freighter canoe to Moose Factory, about choking back the contents of her stomach during convulsive, vertiginous flights along the Abitibi River in two-seater planes. Sylvie seemed to be wearing hip waders in most of these stories, if not an ammunition vest and deer scent. It's hard to picture it now, and was hard to picture it then, listening to her talk about those times while watching her fuss with her favourite elephant teapot or tape a colourful swath of fabric over the hole I had kicked in the cupboard in the house that Gord built.

But in those days, Sylvie was a badass. She shot ducks out of the sky. She wrestled pike from the rivers. She castrated bucks. And then she met Gord.

This story she told was about a goose hunting trip to James Bay that she took with none other than her new, red-headed boyfriend — this Rankin fella — and another girl she worked with at the site's "office" (i.e., a trailer plunked down in a field of mud) just so no one back at camp would get the wrong idea.

And I'll tell you now that thinking about this story always sends a little shudder through my intestines. Because on this particular occasion, I think, the gods really were watching. This was the moment in Gord and Sylvie's lives — in my life, by extension — when the gods shifted forward in their divine Barcaloungers, scrambled to turn the volume up on their jewel-encrusted remotes.

That is, the trip to James Bay was cursed. Or divinely ordained, depending on how you look at it. It was still early days with Gord, and he was doing his best to macho it up

for the ladies, giving Sylvie, who needed no help whatsoever, pointers on her shooting technique, offering Myrna his
sweater when the evening got chilly — a move he regret-
ted because Myrna, who was a big girl, wore the sweater all
weekend and ended up stretching out the chest, rendering it
unwearable to anyone not sporting a pair of 38Ds. He even
tried to banter with the two Indian guides, who refused to
be bantered with and at the end of the day always set up their
tent and fire several deliberate feet away from the rest of them.

Still, things were fine until the middle of one night when
the Indian guides broke their silence to plunge into everybody's tents and shout at them to pack everything up immediately because the tide was rushing in.

I don't quite understand the geophysical logistics of this,
but the way Sylvie tells it, they got stuck. Their boat was
on one side of the water, and they were on the other, and
the tide somehow stayed put another two whole days. They
couldn't get out. They ran out of smokes. They had nothing
to do. Their food was gone and so they tried boiling one of
the geese they had slaughtered over the weekend. The smell
was obscene and Sylvie couldn't eat it. Monday went by, then
Tuesday. They were, of course, due back at the site. They
began to starve.

Quite the test of manhood for our buddy Gord. And
how'd he fare? Sylvie never said, really. They were basically
stuck on a spit of land with nothing to do but try to figure
out how to make boiled snow goose palatable. Gord didn't
have a lot to work with, no matter what reserves of masculine ingenuity he might have been carrying around with him.
You'd think the Indians would've had a few tricks up their

sleeves, but no. So much for the one-with-nature stereotype —
they hadn't even known the tide was coming in. They just sat
around their fire, occasionally taking pot shots at any random
flock of geese that happened to be passing overhead. At this
point, those honking, sky-encompassing flocks — the sheer
numbers of them sailing overhead in almost intelligible pat-
terns — added insult to injury. Nobody wanted to see another
goose again.

One thing about the Indians, though, was that they didn't
seem too ruffled by the predicament. They were content to sit
and wait for nature to take its course.

"They were patient," remembered Sylvie. "So we decided
to just be patient too."

Being patient doesn't sound like a particularly Gordian
strategy to me, but then again, this was a time before Gord
was really Gord and Sylvie was really Sylvie, as far as I'm
concerned. What I mean is, over the years I've become more
and more convinced that the James Bay Goose Hunt Calam-
ity of '66 represents a kind of hinge in my parents' lives. It's
one of those before-and-after moments. The gods saw it.
That's why they stuck the two of them out there on that spit
for a while — to let things really soak in. To make sure the
changes *took*.

I don't know how it worked for Gord exactly. Who knows,
maybe he wasn't a prick before then. Maybe the insult of it all
— the unsociable Indians, the boiled goose, the wrecked, tit-
imprinted sweater, is what pushed him over the edge; maybe
before that he'd just been another lovable leprechaun of a
working man. Like I said, I don't know. It's not a story Gord
ever told. It was a story Sylvie told.

So I know how it worked for Sylvie — and I know exactly when it happened for her.

Sylvie used to begin the story on the Saturday just before they got stuck. She had wandered off on her own across a marsh (in her hip waders, natch) because she had grown tired of Gord talking all the time and telling her what to do and then always taking the shot before she could. ("I just get so *excited*," he'd apologize afterward.) So she wandered off on her own, not too far, she promised the guides, and sat for a while in a clearing on the other side of the marsh, kept just cool enough — even in her heavy waders and long underwear — by the relentless, whipping wind, and just warm enough thanks to the blazing October sunshine settling across her skin like a cat across a lap.

Wilderness. Sylvie in the wild, hat pulled down, wind in her ears. I like to picture her like that. She stayed there for the next hour, she told me, because it was so peaceful. She got one goose — it practically landed at her feet — and then another, which plopped into the middle of the marsh. Well it was time to get going anyway. She felt the freezing water strain against the rubber of her waders, hugging her legs like pleading children, as she sloshed forward to get the second goose.

But just a few steps in, something bucked at her side, almost throwing her off balance and into the drink. It was goose number one, still kicking at life.

Criss! she yelped, grabbing at it.

But goose number one had no interest in being groped. Goose number one had come to, discovered itself to be gut-shot, dangling from some Frenchwoman's scrawny shoulder, and was entirely taken aback. It made its feelings known to my mother.

She sloshed her way back to solid ground holding the thrashing goose out in front of her, barely able to keep it still.

For all her experience in the bush, this had never happened before. Usually when Sylvie made a creature dead, it could be counted upon to stay that way. Not this guy, though. Reason being, Adam: this was a gift from the above-mentioned gods — a honking, feathery thunderbolt, if you will. Celestial provocation.

"I was gonna have to break his neck," Sylvie related to me whenever she got to this point in the story. "I thought to myself, *Câline de bine, I'm gonna have to break his neck.*"

There was always something poignant about my mother's bestowal of gender upon the goose (in which case I guess I should say gander). You might think this was her French-speaker's habit of sexing every noun — but Sylvie had spoken English right alongside of French her whole life and never had that habit. I believe it was just my mother's way of getting across the intimacy of that moment. The fact that she had found herself confronted with a being, an individual — how else to put it: a *dude.* A dude whose outraged, flappy-winged life she needed to extinguish then and there. There was no way she could make it back across the marsh with a thrashing goose in tow.

So she began to throttle the goose.

Creak! Went the divine Barcaloungers, shifting forward in unison.

I remember her first telling me this story when I was ten or so, and I remember feeling at this point in the narrative exactly what I'm feeling now, as I tell it to you. A dread. A kind of teetering feeling, like a car halfway over a cliff.

"But I couldn't choke him."

What do you mean you couldn't choke him? You felt bad? You showed it mercy?

"No I mean he just . . . wouldn't choke."

It wouldn't die! Sylvie throttled and throttled the snowy bastard, and still it kicked, still it thrashed. Let it be known: this was one hell of a goose. I mean have you ever seen the necks on those things? They may as well have been designed with ready-made finger-welts, they're so chokeable.

So Sylvie knelt down on the ground, the better to throttle her goose. She squeezed and shook and strangled, for god knows how long.

"And he just wouldn't choke!" ends this part of the story.

Now there are a few things I don't understand here. Premier among them, of course, being why wouldn't the dude choke? Even putting that aside: I mean, my god, Sylvie could've simply twisted the thing's head around a few times like a bottle cap, couldn't she? I'm sorry if that sounds horrible, but this is life and death. She does not want the goose to be alive at this moment, she wants it to be dead, and when you want something to be dead, I would think, you have to be prepared to get a little extreme. Playtime, as they say, is over.

So what did Sylvie do next?

"I thought: I better kneel on him."

Mom! You *knelt* on the goose?

"I tried to, like, kneel his breath out of him."

Adam, do you see how this is horrible? Sylvie in the wilderness, the wind off the bay, the silence in the wind, the struggling goose, the living goose, shot out of the sky, my mother and the thrashing goose, throttling the goose, strangling the goose, the wind in her ears, in its feathers, kneeling, at last, the better to throttle, the continued thrashing of goose, the endless moment of no-death, no end in sight, the angelic wings, spreading and contracting, spreading and contracting.

The goose does not want to go down.

So Sylvie *knelt* on it.

Sylvie (I thought at ten, and ever since), *don't do it. Don't kneel on the dude.*

She knelt on it a nice long time. Who knows how long. Until the goose was finally good and dead.

Then she picked it up, flung it back over her shoulder, and waded to the other side of the marsh, where my father stood waiting.

8 |

06/27/09, 2:04 p.m.

SORRY IT HAS been so long. Or maybe you don't care — I can't help but notice Chub Central continues to maintain its radio silence. The old ignore-him-and-he'll-go-away tactic I suppose? Well guess what, Adam, I've done more than my share of market research on that one, and I'm here to tell you: he doesn't. He won't.

You're not going to believe this but I called Gord the other day. I was feeling a little stalled since last we spoke. That goose always takes it out of me. I had to hit the couch for a while. I lay there for a good couple of days asking myself if it was really such a great idea to set aside my summer vacation for this. If this is really what I want to spend the next two months gnawing away at. Usually, I'll take on some project or another. I'll work on the house or volunteer at the Y to do some coaching. Not hockey, if that's your assumption. The kids are all about soccer these days. Hockey's time, it seems to me, has come and gone. The players stopped seeming like demi-gods around the time they started seeming more like rich, whiny babies, and the playoffs have been depressing pretty much since Gretzky left for L.A., and most kids' parents can't afford all that gear anyway.

Fortunately and speaking of which, the Confederations Cup is on the sports channel, so it wasn't like I just spent two days staring at the ceiling. I first started watching soccer back when I started coaching — teaching myself about the game and figuring out how to give a shit about it — and now I look forward to the soccer finals more than I ever did Lord Stanley's bashfest. I happen to live in a neighbourhood with a pretty big Greek contingent and they always go bananas at this time of year. I can wander from one block party to the next, being handed napkinfuls of baklava and shots of ouzo with every step I take. When Greece won the Euro Cup a few years back, there was literally dancing in my street — the party went on for days. (Oh and I'm not going to get any more specific than that about where I live, by the way, because I could be anywhere, Adam. I'm a ghost, after all. Maybe I'm on the other side of the continent from you. On the other hand, maybe I could get up out of my chair right now, take a stroll a few blocks over, and knock on your door. Who knows, right? Not you.)

So anyway, right around the time Italy was going up against Brazil I started thinking about Gord and how disgusted he would be; how he always hated soccer because Europeans played it and Europeans are by definition homosexuals, even though the Russians have proven themselves able to play hockey every once in a while like respectable hetero males.

And then I found myself snickering up at the ceiling thinking how fun it would be to call Gord up and tell him that I was watching soccer on TV and describe to him how much I was enjoying it, especially that one player with the flowing chestnut hair and taut buttocks.

So one day, after a great many beer, I did.

When I drink a great many beer, you have to understand, I soften up a little about Gord. That is to say, I go from my sober default setting of wanting to never look at or speak to him again, to my great-many-beer status of wanting to call him up and provoke him.

"How's it going, fucknuts?"

"Well piss on a plate! Is that who I think it is?"

"It is who you think it be."

"Well isn't this a surprise. Stay right there now son and let me turn off the TV."

That's when I lost a bit of my great-many-beer glow, realizing at once how happy I'd made Gord with my phone call, realizing I was actually sitting there on the line waiting for him to come back and talk to me.

So I hung up.

But of course he called me immediately back.

"Guess we got cut off there."

"Guess so."

"These goddamn phones! They make you buy new packages every year that are supposed to save you so much trouble for more money and the service just gets worse and worse."

"They make you buy them, do they."

"Well they don't give you any goddamn choice. This young one called me up the other day, some kinda accent on her, I can understand maybe every third word, Oh we're offering this new service . . . "

"Just hang up on them, Gord."

"Well I would but I'm too polite. So I say maybe one of you assholes can tell me why every time I pick up the line now the goddamn thing goes boop boop boop like a busy signal?"

"It means you have a message, Gord. It's like an answering machine."

"What's like an answering machine?"

"Like — an answering machine that's inside your phone. They gave you voice-mail on your line — it's internal voice-mail."

"Well that's dandy but who said I wanted any goddamn voice-mail, internal or external? I get my mail in an envelope, and it goes in my mailbox, and that's all the internal mail I need. Then I take it out and, by Christ, it's *ex*ternal. Whoopee-ding, aren't I high-tech."

I could tell by the tone of his voice, by the sprightly lilt to his *goddamns,* that my father was thrilled to be speaking with me.

"Hey Gord, guess what? I'm watching the Confederations Cup on TV. Big soccer finals."

"Is that a fact? Watching a bunch of fruits run around in their shorts now, are you?"

"Sure am."

"Well to each his own. Live and let live I always say. Just as long as you keep those types away from me."

"It's not gonna be easy Gord. You're a good-looking man."

"Oh kiss my ass."

"Don't say that to *them.*"

Gord wheezed himself a scrawny chestful of laughter at that one. Ah, father-son queer bashing. How did I get into this?

"Hey Gord?" I called over his delighted gasps for breath. "Listen, I gotta go."

"No you don't, you just got on for Christ's sake," he said, hacking up the results of his laughter — into a Kleenex, I hoped. "You didn't call just to tell me you're sitting there watching fruits in shorts."

"Actually I did."

"Well I hope you have more than that to say for yourself these days."

And then I thought: Oh well. Gord's not good for much, but he does constitute a living archive of sorts — which, as I think I've already indicated, is why I've avoided him most of my adult life. But undertaking this little project with you, I suddenly realized, was going to require a complete readjustment of my lifelong MO.

So what the heck, I thought, time to open up the archive.

Was this a bad idea? Yes. Did I open, and swiftly down, another beer precisely to drown out the clamouring voices of my better, smarter angels, who were telling me this was a bad idea? Yes.

"Gord," I said. "Hey Gord. Do you remember when I almost killed Mick Croft?"

And Gord — you're not going to believe this — he was ready for it. It's like he had spent the past twenty-odd years like a runner, coiled on the starting block, poised for the pistol.

"That little fucker," Gord began. "I will tell you something right now, son of mine. That little fucker was looking to get his head kicked in pretty much the moment he poked it out of his mother's you-know-what. And now I'm going to tell you something else. You didn't almost kill him, that's bullshit. It was self-defence and everyone in this town knows it, and has known it, for the past twenty-three years."

My god. Gord had kept count.

"We did this town a favour, you and me. We were the fucking clean-up squad. Bill Hamm and his keystone cops up there at the detachment couldn't do anything about it, but oh my Christ, they sure as hell could come after me and mine once we finished doing their goddamn job for them, couldn't they?"

"Me, Gord," I said, spastically thrusting my hand into the beer cooler I'd stationed by the couch when the Cup began. But all I got this time was a fistful of ice. "You were in the restaurant. You were on the other side of the glass from where I was."

But Gord was off. Gord had been coiled and ready too long to slow down now.

"Almost killed the little bastard — if only! How many kids did *he* almost kill pushing his drugs? Not to mention that knife he was always carrying around for the love of god and everyone and their cousin's dog saw it. All those half-drunk tools over at the Legion. If that useless lawyer had any kind of clue what she was doing we wouldn't have . . ."

I was just digging around in the ice at that point, had been this whole time, my hand was going numb. And I knew I couldn't do this.

"*Me*, Gord," I said. "You're all: we we we."

"Wee wee wee all the way home," rejoined Gord. "Listen here, son. You did nothing wrong and I will go to my grave with those words on my lips, Gordie, that you can believe."

"It's everyone else's fault, right? The lawyer, the tools at the Legion . . ."

"It was his *own* goddamn fault! Are you gonna sit there and tell me different? Oh, he had a hard childhood, is that it? Oh boo-hoo, maybe his old man gave him a tap with the hairbrush every once in a while. Oh no, they fed him too much red meat. They didn't buy him fancy sneakers, wouldn't get a big screen TV for his bedroom. My god, when you think of it, they should have named a holiday after the little asshole."

"FUCK, GORD!" I roared into the phone.

"DON'T YOU CURSE AT ME!" he roared back. And here we were at last. "YOU'RE NOT TOO BIG FOR ME TO . . ."

"YES I AM TOO BIG! JESUS! STOP BEING SUCH AN IDIOT! I'M JUST TRYING TO HAVE A CONVERSATION WITH YOU!"

"Well who's stopping you?" Now he just sounded perplexed. Oh, I remembered this tactic from long ago and far away. Gord switches tracks — shifts with stomach-turning swiftness from wrath to bewilderment. *Who, me? Lovable old Dad, screaming, making threats? You're mistaken, sir.* And then you hear yourself panting and feel your face throb as you make rigid your neck tendons in preparation to holler some more at the poor, bewildered old man.

"I knew calling you would ruin my day," I told him after a while. "You're a lunatic, Dad."

"Well you know I always love to hear from you, Gordie."

And can you believe this, Adam? He was being utterly sincere. Utterly proving my point.

Brazil won, by the way.

9

07/01/09, 10:57 a.m.

WHAT YOU CAN'T account for, when you punch a person in the head, is how they are going to land. You can be as careful as you like. You can account for the fact that the man in front of you is a small man and you are a large man. You can pull your punches, always keeping in mind, however, that the small man is known to enjoy knives so it would be best for all concerned if you laid him out quickly and more or less completely. Also keeping an eye on the surrounding skeezer cohort, any one of whom may hurl themselves at you in wounded outrage the moment their beloved Mickster loses steam. So a single, decisive shot to the head is what's required here. We want the Mickster down and out. We don't want him reaching into his back pocket, signalling to one of his generals. We don't want to prolong this process long enough, say, for Collie Chaisson to dash over to use the payphone at the Legion, give Mick's friend Jeeves a call for example. We don't want reinforcements, please god. The wrath of bikers, raining down on Icy Dream.

So we get this over with. And we don't, we absolutely do not, give the little man bouncing around behind the glass his fun. We give him as little fun as possible — that is our eternal goal. Ditto the alky losers on the other side of the parking lot, hanging off one another in the doorway of the Legion, brandishing beers and smokes like cheerleaders' pompoms.

The story of how we got to this point is stupid and — this is funny to say considering the freight-load of consequence it produced — inconsequential. That is to say, it doesn't really matter how we got to this point. The point itself is what matters, the point of fist into face followed hard upon by head into pavement. The story leading up to that point is a story that could've lead up to nothing, or anything. It could've led up to me saying, "Croft, dude, buddy, seriously. Don't pass around a hash pipe in our parking lot." And Croft's blue eyes lighting up with friendship and understanding. "Dude! For you? Anything." And he and the boys restuff themselves into Croft's toylike Ford Escort and away they trundle off to the drug den on Howe Street there to smoke and drink, crank the amps and play "Smoke on the Water" 'til their fingers tear open. That could just as easily have happened. I was a preferred customer after all. But no. Why? Guess why. Right.

Gord.

Yes, it has to be admitted, Croft threw down the gauntlet. He was a provocative little shit as I think I've already established, and a hair-trigger reactionary like my father was as catnip to him. There's no question in my mind Croft wheeled his Escort into our parking lot that night looking for more

than soft-serve and a place to smoke hash. This was a recrea-
tion for Croft and company — a field trip. This was like going
to the park to play Frisbee.

It was a Friday night around eight o'clock when Chaisson wandered in. Not a bad opening gambit on Croft's part,
because Chaisson himself hadn't done anything to explicitly
offend my father except for chortle in Croft's wake from time
to time. He was Mick's keychain — pure nonentity when he
moved outside the outlaw circle. There was something dully
universal about Chaisson in his ball cap, soft teenage waist
spilling over his belt, face so obliterated by freckles you wondered how he could see through them all. He could've been
any local doofus from any small town anywhere, stopping
into the Icy Dream for a dollar sundae. Which is what he
ordered when I moved to the till to intercept him.

Gord was in back washing trays, but not so far back he
couldn't have taken Chaisson in with the slightest turn of his
head. I just had to hope that nonentity quality of Chaisson's
overwhelmed any association with Croft in my old man's
memory.

"Hey man," said Chaisson, scratching his gut in a great
show of nonchalance. Which caused me to glance immediately out the window and into the parking lot.

To see, of course, Croft leaning against his Escort, reaching over to hand a customer's pipe back to him.

"Hot fudge sundae?" said Chaisson.

I turned back to him. "That it?"

"Yeah."

"I'm gonna need you guys to take off out of the parking lot
as soon as you get your food," I told him.

Chaisson parted his freckled eyelids a little wider than usual and I got a glimpse of his weird burnt-orange irises, identical in colour to his hair. "Who?" he said, peering out the window. "I'm not even with those guys, man." He had nowhere near the finesse of Croft when it came to this kind of bullshitting — didn't come anywhere close to achieving the same sarcastic, fake-innocent flourish that Croft had long ago perfected. Chaisson just reached up under his T-shirt to scratch his belly more aggressively.

"Chaisson," I said, leaning forward and speaking low. "Fuck off, okay? We ask once and then we call the cops. New policy."

Before he could protest, I turned my back and went to make his sundae. The unfortunate thing about a fast-food franchise is that food prep happens in view of the counter. So you can't secretly gob on a random asshole's sundae, for example, just before adding the hot fudge, should the spirit move you to do so.

Croft would've known I was full of shit about the cops, but I was hoping Chaisson wouldn't. Croft had long ago intuited how much pleasure Gord derived from these encounters — that my father would never hand the fun off to the cops. That's what kept Croft coming back — he'd found a new playground, complete with willing playmate.

I stuck a spoon into the bulge of ice cream and shoved the sundae across the counter at Chaisson.

"Go."

"All right, man, Jesus," said Chaisson, dipping his head to tongue the tip of his sundae like it was a nipple. His lips came up chocolated. He pawed a booklet of napkins out of the dispenser as I looked on in disgust.

Maybe I shouldn't have made my disgust quite so manifest. Maybe that's all it would've taken to defuse things.

As it stood, Chaisson shot me a look of resentment — a look of hurt feelings, almost — as he slouched out the door and into the parking lot, where Croft made a great show of having not seen him in ages. He spread his arms wide, welcoming his long-lost friend into his smoky circle.

I looked at the clock. 8:12. Forty-eight minutes 'til closing time. The restaurant was dead as it usually was at this hour and Gord had already begun cleanup. I could hear him wrestling with the inventory somewhere deep in the kitchen's bowels. Good. I just had to make sure he stayed in back, away from the windows.

I was just about to turn and yell that I thought I'd get started mopping the floors out front when I noticed a blaze of ice-blue in my peripheral vision. I glanced out the window again and what do you know. Gord in his ID smock had appeared in the parking lot and was striding with great purpose toward Croft and his entourage.

He had taken the garbage out early, I suppose, and heard the voices, caught an acrid whiff of smoke. And what I should have done then was, I should have called Bill Hamm. He had left his card, and I had even made a point of scotch-taping it on the wall beside the phone. I should have proven Bill Hamm wrong, shown him what a good, law-abiding boy I was, proven once and for all exactly who the raving Rankin was in this establishment.

So why didn't I?

Because I was only fifteen fucking years old, Adam. I ran outside to help my father.

Things were already underway. The dicks out front at the Legion were silent and leaning toward us like pointer dogs on full-bodied alert. Chaisson was holding his sundae out before him, taking slow deliberate bites to demonstrate the unquestionability of his status as a food-buying patron of Icy Dream with therefore every right to be on the premises. Croft was smiling happily, leaning against the open door of his Escort and explaining to my father that he possessed every intention of going into the restaurant to place a food order, it was just that he had paused to speak with his good friend Collie Chaisson, who had recently emerged from doing same. Loitering, Sir? Wouldn't think of it.

"And what about that goddamn smoke I'm smelling? What about illegal substances being consumed on my property?" demanded Gord — Gord who was pretty much one giant, pulsating tendon at that point.

"It must've been those guys who just left, Sir," answered Croft, referring to the skids who had booked it at the sight of my father stalking toward them in his ice-blue smock and paper hat. Croft recently had switched to calling Gord "Sir," when it became apparent the insincere use of the word drove him even crazier than "bud."

"That's not even the point," I said as I jogged over to the group of them, taking my place in restraining-distance behind Gord. "The point is you're banned, man. You're not supposed to be here one way or another."

"Dude!" appealed Croft. "I'm not still banned am I? Come on, I love this place. Best fries in town."

"We're within our rights to call the cops," I said, before Gord could chime in. I wanted that information, that evocation, front and centre.

Croft spread his hands, smiling wider in mock disbelief. "For buying fries? You're gonna call the cops because I wanna buy some fries?"

"Get your ass back in the restaurant, son," said Gord to me, not taking his eyes off Croft. This directive, I knew, was pure showbiz. Gord had kicked off a routine, and I could only respond by rote.

"You go back in, Dad," I said, "and call Constable Hamm."

The first part of the sentence was dictated by our routine, the second of course was my own improvisation. He shot me an appreciative glance as if to say, *Nice touch!*

But he didn't deviate from the script. "Get your ass back in there," he repeated. "No one's watching the till."

"And someone's gotta make my fries," added Croft.

Cue Gord! Wrath mode! Uncontainable rage! He lunged, I restrained. It was downright boring at this point. Croft backed up, hands in the air, laughing, as I got my father's swinging limbs under control.

"I will take that fryer and I will shove your pimply punk face in it," Gord was saying, among other things. "Howya like your french fries then!"

"Inside," I was saying. "Inside, back inside Gord, come on."

But he just kept flailing and cursing and threatening, moving Croft and his cohort to new heights of merriment, and I knew he would keep it up until I returned to the script, until I delivered my big line. No improvisation would be broached at such a key moment.

"*Dad*," I said. "Go back inside." I felt Gord's muscles slacken in anticipation — he could feel it coming.

"I'll take care of this," I said. Loud enough to be heard over the laughter, the cursing.

Everything stopped — the obligatory momentous pause. What a bunch of drama queens they all were. Gord went still, the perpetual skeezer laugh track warbled into silence, Croft's wide, guffawing grin compressed itself into a soundless smile and he crossed his arms, waiting. Even though I was standing directly behind Gord, I could feel my father smiling back at Croft. Such fun the two of them were having. Gord shifted himself out of my grip, straightened his apron, adjusted his hat, and turned away without a word. Back into the restaurant where I knew he would station himself behind a window, nose practically against glass, and the phone would sit there on the wall behind the counter doing nothing.

Already the handful of drunks out front at the Legion had metastasized into an enthralled flock, beers moving toward mouths in slow motion.

At the last moment, I remembered to take off my hat.

"Let us go then, you and I," said Mick Croft, pretty face beaming.

07/01/09, 11:12 p.m.

And where the hell did he get that?

I can assure you I almost crapped pants when I came across it five years later. Flipping through one of those massive, massively expensive intro readers they made us buy in undergrad English. Needless to say, it's a line I'd never forgotten, being the last words I ever heard out of Mick Croft.

And there I am, Adam, there I am, jump ahead if you will to the time when we, when you and I, became acquainted with each other. I am alone and motherless and at university, I have drunk my own vomit in public, eaten posters off walls, inhaled raw frozen cow — what won't I consume? — and very recently walked out of the locker room in the middle of a playoff game at the insincere behest of my coach who told me if I didn't do what he wanted I could "walk away right now." (I still relish the bug-eyed, juicy-veined full-facial flush it provoked when I stood up without even taking off my skates and did exactly that.) So I didn't even have hockey — my one and only justification for being there — to ground me at that point. So there I am in the library, flipping through the anthology, having decided to "buckle down." I knew I had it in me — I'd always been able to lock myself in a room for a couple of days, study like a madman and jack up a dwindling grade at the eleventh hour. I just had to lay off the purple Jesus for five minutes and crack a book. By Christ, I decided, if I couldn't be a jock I would damn well prove myself a scholar — *Tee hee!* tinkled the celestial laughter.

And that's when they hit me with it — the punch line to the elaborate practical joke the gods had set into motion that evening in the parking lot of Icy Dream. Do you remember that board game from the seventies, Mouse Trap? I got it for my birthday one year and it never worked, but in the realm of the metaphorical it functions as a pretty apt parallel for the course of my life from that moment in the parking lot to that moment in the library, bookended as it was by those seven words. The game features a series of random plastic doodads — a bathtub and a boot and a bucket, for example — all set up to interact with one another in frankly stupid and unlikely ways (the boot kicks the bucket, out of which falls the ball, which rolls down a ramp), and at the end of this rickety and dubious process, down comes the mouse trap.

So there they were glaring up from the page, Croft's famous last words, emanating wave after wave of uncanny terror at me. Not to mention the creepshow pertinence of the lines that followed, as if someone — some malignant entity — had affixed a kind of psychic spigot directly into my past and let it drip, one word at a time, into the book. The patient etherized on the table, the night spread out against the sky, the tedious argument of insidious intent. The muttering retreats.

From your lips to God's ear, Mickster.

It was like — well. You know what it was like, Adam? It was like a certain goose had walked over my grave.

That was the same day, by the way. That was the day I shoved my books into my bag, headed over to the house, announced my dismissal from the hockey team, ransacked Wade's room for hash, dragged you out to the liquor store with me, came back with a great many beer and a few forties in tow, wondered where the hell Kyle had gotten to, drank and drank and drank, slowly began to peel from myself one bloody hank of flesh after another, carefully fed them to you like a mother bird feeding a chick, groaned like I was about to give birth to something, sweated and drank, watched your eyebrows rise and then descend, switched position, leaned forward, gave confession, found your hand against my head, went silent, lost words — rested.

"Let us go then, you and I," said Croft.

I punched him in the head, and he went down.

Part Two

10

07/04/09, 1:15 p.m.

IT DIDN'T HELP my case that once he regained consciousness all
Croft could do was sit around blubbering. It didn't help me to
have this sweet-faced boy quietly bawling his eyes out in front
of the judge throughout the entire proceedings. And I mean
the *entire* proceedings — non-stop. It was a brain-injury thing,
my lawyer assured me and Gord and Sylvie — Sylvie whose
own eyes filled immediately at the sight and sound of Croft.
But it wasn't that he was actually sad, the lawyer murmured
to us kindly — it was just that he was brain-damaged. That
was all, just a little brain damage. Either way, it didn't help
my case.

There was no jury because it was juvenile court and thank
god because there's the sweet-faced bawling boy fresh out of
a coma, and in this corner here's the hairy, hulking six-foot-
four monster accused of aggravated assault. Oh, and here's
the hulking monster's father, by the way, who can't keep his

mouth shut, who keeps jumping up and calling the Crown attorney "dickface," to the delight of the gathered townsfolk who are taking such keen advantage of the proceedings being (and whose bright idea was this?) open to the public. Rankin Sr., keeping things entertaining as always, having more than once referred to the lawyer defending said monster as a "this dumb bitch here," who had to be very nearly forcibly restrained from delivering similar epithets in the judge's direction. I kept wondering if there was any way I could casually lean over and put a headlock on my father without tarnishing my image even further in the eyes of the court.

Meanwhile, there is Sylvie and there is Croft; the two of them drenching their respective sides of the courtroom.

"You're just making it worse!" Gord would holler at her during recess. "Making us look guilty — oh, his poor mother, they're going. Stuck with a bad son like that. Like he done something wrong!"

Sylvie would just shake her head and blow her nose, so I spoke up.

"Gord? I'm going to kill you."

"Now now now now now," my lawyer, Trisha, would interrupt at around this point.

"Just let me handle this, son. You're under a lot of stress."

"No, I'm serious, I'll kill you Gord."

"OK!" said Trisha, clapping her hands together, smiling her face-eating Marie Osmond smile. "We stop this. We change the subject now."

"*She* stays out of the courtroom," proclaimed Gord, pointing at Sylvie. "She's ruining everything."

This coming from the man whose outbursts had nearly got

him kicked out of the courtroom twice already that morning.

"The crying mother does not stay out of the courtroom," explained Trish — Trisha had astounded me throughout this process in her dealings with Gord. The enormous, face-eating smile acted as a bulwark against every "dumb bitch" he could chuck her way. "The crying mother is the only sympathy vote we get, fellas."

I looked at Sylvie tiny in her chair, clicking her rosary beads between white fingers with shredded fingernails, and I thought someone should go over there and comfort her. Or else someone should've just scooped her up and carried her out of there — some flannel-wearing Canadianized Superman — dump her in the woods in Northern Ontario, give her a gun, something to shoot. Put her back in hip waders and let her evolve into the backwoods amazon she was always meant to be.

I never thought it should be me, however — clearly I was not the superhero for Sylvie. I'd turned out to be as big a downward drag as Gord — maybe bigger. For all his daily shouts and insults, Gord had never reduced her to puddles before — not even close. With Gord, she shook her head, rolled her eyes and assured me "He never really talks to me like that," usually after he'd just finished talking to her like that. But the puddles? The puddles were new. The puddles were for and by yours truly. You could say I was the author of the puddles.

So no. It never occurred to me to shift out of my rigid, fist-clenching gonna-kill-Gord carriage and put my arms around my mother. I was a contagion, after all. I was a destructive force. I was an injurer of men's brains.

I later learned that once Croft stopped crying, he developed epilepsy. Also, he had no idea who I was throughout the trial. He didn't remember anything from before his skull hit the pavement. I think the memories came back a little later, but at the trial, he was a blank slate, an innocent. And in this state of purity (the kind of literal born-again status that my church later had me convinced even a Great Contagion could achieve if I just bashed my head against the pavement of Christ's love long enough), Croft had gone from being a badass with an angelic quality to a sheer, full-potency angel — a weeping one at that.

It did not help my case.

But then, what could?

Somewhere in there, my sixteenth birthday happened.

07/05/09, 12:37 a.m.

The night was preparing, in that slow, summertime way, to spread itself against the sky — the sun smeared like a broken egg yolk along the horizon. And I knew the world had flipped itself over like an all-beef patty, done on one side, when I heard the sound Croft's head made when it struck the pavement. Okay, the sound was bad, but the truth is, I knew it was pretty much game over the minute I felt my fist invade his skull. In the name of getting-it-over-with/avoiding-knife-punctures, I had decided I would have to knock Croft out. This was something I had never attempted in all the nights of parking-lot punk-grappling previous to this. Usually, these sessions mostly involved peeling guys off me and shoving them into the sides of cars. I hadn't realized it up until the moment I hit Croft, but those fights hadn't been fights at all. They'd been play. We'd been like kids brandishing lightsabers at one another in the schoolyard. We'd been getting our exercise.

And I realized those fights were nothing so immediately, so assuredly, because of the experience of my fist smashing into someone's face — an experience I'd never had before. Because of the way it made me feel, instinctively, on some kind of primal, sub-literate level: *Poor Croft! Poor Croft's face!*

Because it crunched. I felt how it crunched in a couple of places.

I felt Croft's bones absorb the force and velocity I threw at him; I felt how easily they shuddered and gave way. I felt this in my own bones; in the bones of my fist. It was simply a vibration; it didn't cause me any pain at all.

That said, it was a vibration that transmitted precisely what I was doing to Croft's face at the moment I did it, meaning that even as I was doing it, I was regretting it.

I flashed on a memory of accidentally breaking an egg in one hand; standing there cradling the runny mess of it.

Which was around when Croft's blood announced itself in a deluge from his nose: *Surprise! Look how red I am! How much of me there is! Wow, I'm not slowing down, am I? Now it's a party!*

Some of it hit me as Croft was going down, very warm against my very cold skin — I'm surprised it didn't sizzle — hot and snotty.

Then came the sound — and the party was over before it could even get cooking.

It didn't echo. It was so loud — so loud, Adam — but it didn't echo. We were in a parking lot — everything echoed.

The shouts of Croft's pals, my cornball, pro-forma threats (*back off, man*), the excited cries of the Legionnaires next door, Croft's final taunt. These noises ricocheted against the cinder-block walls of the Icy Dream, flung themselves back at us like near-simultaneous mockery. But the crack of Croft's skull did not echo. It was this blank, bottomless sound, with no layers, no resonance. A sound unto itself.

But how could the sound (the man behind the glass wonders to himself as he sips at his hot chocolate, turns up the collar of his coat) possibly have been any worse than the crunching bones, the sudden blood-parade?

Adam, the sound was worse.

———

I heard that sound a second time not long after, in the middle of one of my hockey games. My coach and former social worker, Owen Findlay, had a strict no-fighting rule, which outraged a lot of parents, not to mention the opposing coaches, because he pulled guys off the ice the minute he spotted a tussle taking shape, which was no fun at all. If the ref didn't call it, he simply walked out onto the ice himself — fans howling for his killjoy blood — and put an end to things. He had also vowed to kick anyone who got into a fight off the team no matter how good they were or how much clout their parents might have on the town council or school board. I didn't realize at the time how unique Findlay was in this regard. It's probably safe to say you and I would never have met in the hallowed halls of academe if the gods had presented me with any coach in the world who was not Owen Findlay.

Still, shit happens on the ice. Helmets get knocked off, kids go flying, skulls crash against solidity. And I should add none of that used to really bother me, before Croft — before I set foot into the grownup world of consequences — the innocent "before" juxtaposed against the catastrophic "after." Before Croft, I might have even got a little irritated myself with Owen's hard line on fighting. If some guy whammed me into the boards so hard it stole my breath, what was the harm of shoving a not-so-friendly warning? Most guys expected and — I'd venture to say — enjoyed it when you did.

But barely a year into the catastrophic after, I made it happen again: that sound. It had been a nice, easy check, I thought, as far as these things go. Clean. I'd practically said "Excuse me" as I knocked the guy aside. Still, his face hit the lip of the boards, and down he went. That's when I heard it. The players surrounded him and the coaches surged forward and meanwhile I was moving in the opposite direction, away, off the ice, I didn't even stay to see if the kid, a pudge-faced winger named Chisholm, was okay. I turned away the moment the sound reached my ears, but that didn't keep me from witnessing the blood-parade again (*Hi Rank!*) this time pouring from Chisholm's mouth. It skipped across the ice, Chisholm's blood, happy to be set free, and I went straight to the locker room and pulled off nearly all my gear I was sweating so much. Then I just sat on the bench. Then I got up, headed to a stall, threw up, and sat down on the bench again. I drank some water. I sat there. After a while, Findlay came looking for me.

He knew my story. Findlay, as I've mentioned, was a social worker in the non-hockey part of his life. He was the guy who got me out of the Youth Centre early so my punishment wouldn't mess too much with the school year. At some point during the fog of my fifteenth and sixteenth years, Owen had taken over coaching the high school team, the one I'd tried out for pre-Croft as a means of getting out of spending all my free time working for Gord.

Before that, I'd only played shinny, for fun. I was one of the few guys in my town who wasn't gunning for the NHL from the moment I learned to skate — very likely a subconscious (or maybe not so subconscious) response to Gord's oft-voiced fantasies of becoming the next Walter Gretzky. High school hockey wasn't going to get me any closer to the Stanley Cup, but it was still hockey, therefore the one activity Gord would cheerfully let me off work to pursue.

But I was careful to never let my father see how much I loved it. Because if he knew I loved it, I knew he would wreck it. Because pretty much the moment I first set foot on the pond with a stick in my hands, I realized in a secret and essential way that hockey was actually *mine* — not Gord's, not my NHL-crazed buddies', not even the NHL's itself. It was mine. It was the only thing in my life that shut out the noise, all those desperate voices — the ones that sounded like Gord (anger, fear) and the ones that sounded like Sylvie (sorrow, fear). All it took to break through to a more serene plane of existence, it turned out, was some hard skating, a beautiful pass, the magical-seeming synchrony of human minds and bodies when a play goes just right. It had to do with that feeling of being caught up in something bigger, of *team* in the purest sense — when you're as individual as you've ever been while knowing you're completely unalone. Completely *with*. Thinking back on it now it seems to me that hockey was the church I found before I found my church; the institution that brought home to me — a hell of a lot more effectively than any droning priest ever could — the virtues of Communion and Grace.

So it was my escape, in short. But it couldn't be my escape if I let Gord turn it into another trap, which is why I showed zero interest in the leagues as a kid. Otherwise it would've been drills at 6 a.m at the pond on weekends. It would've been coaches filing restraining orders to staunch the flow of apoplectic phone calls, death-threats shrieked from across the street. It would've been pitying, disgusted looks from other parents.

High school hockey felt lower-stakes and therefore a safer bet. And once I was sprung from the Youth Centre, Owen placed me back on the team without even asking me, practically. He just told me what time to show up for practice, and because he was Owen, I did. At the time it made sense — as much as anything could make sense in that catastrophic after. Hockey had always been my escape, after all, and the idea of escape was sounding particularly good around that time.

But when Chisholm's cranium hit the ice I came up against one of the biggest downsides to living in the after — the realization that no matter how hard I played, how much I tried to lose myself, escape wasn't really on the menu anymore.

Now Owen stood in the doorway of the locker room, a bright blue Icy Dream toque perched on his head — a gift from Gord — watching me shake and sip water. "Chisholm's fine," he said after a moment. "He'll sit out the rest of the game. Not too happy about it."

"He could have a hairline fracture," I said. "He could go home and say good night to his mom and go to sleep and not wake up. Sometimes brain injuries — they have to settle in." I was babbling. I was basically regurgitating everything I'd learned in court about the danger and insidiousness of brain injuries courtesy of the Crown prosecutor during my trial. "He's just forgetful, or something, can't quite put words together and if it's not treated, all of a sudden he's in a coma or he has a fucking hemorrhage . . ."

"Rank, he's fine, he had his helmet on."

I stared up at Owen. "No he didn't — it came off. I heard the crack."

"It stayed on, Rank. You heard his helmet."

"Bullshit," I said, parsing my memory. My memory was insisting that the helmet had come off.

"He's fine, trust me. Are you coming back to play?"

"I don't know, Owen."

"I would like it if you came back to play."

"I threw up."

"Do you feel better?"

I thought about it. "No."

"You have to trust me that he's okay," said Findlay. "And you have to get up and come back to the game. Okay? And then you'll feel better."

It relieved me a little that he gave me a directive. That he told me what had to be done, and what would be the result. But I was still too scared to budge.

"You want me off this team," I told him.

"No I don't. Don't tell me what I want."

"This is what happens," I explained. "This is what I make happen."

It was the first time I'd said it out loud. Sylvie was a year into her grave, I was seventeen years old, and that was the first time I'd said it out loud.

07/06/09, 6:43 p.m.

Anyway. Findlay eventually got me off the bench. And I finished the game, and Chisholm really was fine. I kept on playing season after season, harder than ever, thinking that at some point if I could just get my blood whooshing loud enough in my ears, if I could just lose myself in the glory of a really great play, I could disappear into it like I used to — that little hatch in my mind would finally drop open again, flushing everything away but what was happening on the ice. But what do you know: just when I was ready to give up, an entirely different escape hatch revealed itself. My game got noticed. I was offered a scholarship, of all things, applied for a student loan on the strength of that, and next thing I know I'm on my way to university — where I met you.

Ready Adam? Because we're finally getting to the good part — the part you'll recognize. This is where I, the all-powerful author, get to explore my exciting new character. Let's really zoom in on him, what do you say? What kind of narrator would I be if I didn't ruthlessly delve into what makes good old Adam tick, warts and all — oh yes, warts and all! The insecurities, the conglomerate of loser qualities to which he is oblivious, the nerdy tics, the wincing attempts at self-aggrandizement. (And yes, I realize I've skipped over a significant detail, a key incident that occurred sometime between crushing Croft's skull and packing for university, but I believe I've already outlined that particular scenario to you in one boiling regurgitative flush and just maybe I'd prefer not to go into it again, okay?)

And so, to begin.

Actually before I begin I feel like I should mention I ran into Kyle not long ago. I wish it could have been Wade, if it had to be anyone — Wade, I imagine, even after all these years, would have blearily stuck out his hand and rambled about his new speakers or his new Guns N' Roses box set or his new insert-whogivesashit-here — but it was Kyle. And as you'll recall, there is nothing bleary about Kyle in the least.

"Oh my freaking god," said Kyle once we'd locked eyes the way teenagers once were rumoured to lock braces when making out. That is, we were stuck together, suddenly and inextricably. Kyle's head jerked forward on his neck like a bird's, his mouth fell open, and I knew there was no denying the mutual recognition. The next second he was loping over to me with that same easy, chest-forward stride he used on campus, the walk that made you think his grandfather must have founded the university or something.

Do you wonder where we were, Adam — Kyle and I, meeting up after all these years? I'll tell you. We were at a Winners in downtown Toronto.

I had deked in off the street to get dry and maybe buy an umbrella because I'd been walking around downtown and the sky had been hanging overhead in a cluster of great grey bellies before finally it belched once then opened up.

How long ago was this, wonders the man behind the Plexiglas. What time of year was it? What was Rank, townie shitkicker extraordinaire last time we checked, doing wandering downtown TO?

Who knows, Adam? Not you.

If Kyle was at all dubious about approaching the shitkicker apparition in question, he didn't let that dull his politician's twinkle. He transferred the two ties he'd been pawing from his right hand to his left and waded in to make my re-acquaintance. Firm handshake, followed by that direct yet easygoing half-smile that got him laid with such maddening efficiency back in school. Cool blue-eyed greeting.

"Rank," he said. "Man!"

"Hey. Kyle, right?"

I don't know why I threw that in, that question — *right?* Like there was any doubt either of us remembered one another. Kyle — hemp-wearing student union president, rugby captain, Guatemalan-sweatered, pothead friend to all — he let it pass, or course. Faked along with me.

"That's right, that's right. Kyle Jarvis." He even spoke his last name for me as if I needed a reminder. It was almost embarrassing how readily he accommodated my bullshit. "How you doing, man?"

"I'm good," I replied. And so on and et cetera. You know how these things go. Maybe I should write the rest of the conversation as translated subtext just to hurry things along.

Kyle: Jesus Christ I don't know what to say because last time I saw you you were running from the cops after what you did to that guy!

Rank: Yeah I know — crazy, right?

Kyle: And you disappeared and none of us ever thought we'd see you again!

Rank: Yup — same here.

Kyle: I am dying to ask you what the hell happened! But I can't because we're standing here in Winners and for all I know you've been in jail the last nineteen fucking years! It's very awkward, even for a suave son of a bitch like myself!

Rank: Yes, I can see that, Kyle, but rest assured you're doing very well. How about I change the subject? Tell me, what's your story these days? Venture capitalist? Hotshot parliamentarian? Jet-setting —

Kyle: I work at City Hall.

Rank: Well piss on a plate.

For those last two remarks, I have switched back into the non-subtextual — that's what was really spoken. Kyle looked only slightly thrown by my Gordism — I could tell by the excess teeth he showed me when he grinned.

"Well, hey, it's really great to see you. You look good, Rank. Fit." I saw him eye my pecs just the way he used to do when we were kids. You'll recall, Adam, how Kyle was never quite comfortable with the idea that any guy could have a natural advantage over him. He was that way about your superior GPA too, I seem to recall — all the things charm and orthodontics couldn't necessarily help a young man achieve. "Are you living in Toronto now?" he wanted to know.

I replied, perhaps truthfully, to Kyle's question then.

We were already beginning to extract ourselves at this point in the conversation. Kyle had intuited there would be no going for coffee and getting caught up, a suggestion I could practically see hopping around behind his nice white teeth. This incident at Winners, he eventually realized, was a cosmic oversight; no more than a blip in the time-space continuum — best to just let things blip back to normal. Kyle and I were never meant to intersect again — how could we be, after things had ended so perfectly and decisively all those years ago? Like a novel, come to think of it. It was just the gods, again, unable to leave well enough alone, celestial George Lucases writing bad sequels nobody wants to see.

Kyle started to turn away to pay for his ties ("Paul Frank," he confided, waggling them at me) — and I was content. The encounter was everything it should be — acutely awkward, but blessedly brief and inconsequential. We would go our separate ways and soon would shake each other off like rain.

Except Kyle remembered something. And when he remembered this thing, he turned around. And when he turned around, he met my eyes again. And in this meeting of eyes was the memory of the last look that occurred between us, that look of nineteen years ago. Which had marked the moment Kyle lost it all — the chest-thrust, the half-smile, the unflappable gaze. All the stuff he'd been busy practising and cultivating to get himself to precisely this point in his life. But back then, none of those traits had solidified yet. They wobbled like Jell-O in unguarded moments; they could still be displaced, wiped clean, by, say, a terrible act, a terrible thing. Kyle stood revealed as a kid in such a moment, a scared boy, and like a scared, helpless boy, would look around, for the first time in our acquaintanceship, for somebody else to take charge and tell us what to do. But if Kyle wasn't going to take up that mantle, certainly nobody else would — certainly not the stammering mess of Wade, certainly not the repulsed, already retreating Adam. All the guy could do, ultimately, was resettle his helpless blue eyes into those of the perpetrator, the author of this terrible act and thing, take a calculatedly large step away from the scene and say a useless thing like: "Whoa. Whoa Rank, Jesus, man."

Anyway, that wasn't what Kyle was remembering that rainy day in Winners. That's what I was remembering. Kyle was remembering something else.

"Hey!" he said, holding up the ties again as if to flag me down. "Remember Grix?"

I stopped mid-stride and pretended to think about it. "Glasses," I said.

"Yeah, yeah, with the glasses." Kyle was back on his game now, growing more comfortable as he moved toward the cash and the distance grew between us, calling to me over his shoulder like we were old friends, like we had just seen each other the day before and might see each other again the day after.

"There's a bookstore over by the food court," he told me, digging around for his credit card and ignoring the cashier the way guys like Kyle always do. "Go check it out. Grix has a book in there."

"No way," I said, genuinely surprised. Also this: pleased.

"Seriously, he was in the paper on the weekend. I Face-booked him to say congrats."

This new verb: to Facebook. *But you're like forty years old,* I wanted to say.

"Look him up," said Kyle. "Adam Grix."

"I know," I said, nodding. "I remember."

Kyle's ties had been rung through and bagged — he'd managed to exchange neither words nor eye contact with the cashier the whole time — and now he was on the opposite side

of the counter from me. This was our goodbye. He waved a
hand and smiled, and I raised a hand and smiled in return
without even thinking about it. It was as if in that moment of
being mutually happy for our friend we'd forgotten that none
of us were friends — that we hadn't been since 1990.

I let that feeling, that forgetting, carry me all the way to
the other end of the mall and into the bookstore.

11 |

07/21/09, 11:24 p.m.

Hi Adam,
You have received a friend request from Rankenstein.

12

07/26/09, 11:00 p.m.

I KNOW. SORRY. Not very nice of me to write such a big set-up to the exciting Adam portion of our story and then go and leave you hanging for three weeks. Did you think I'd said to hell with it again and didn't bother to tell you this time? Did you think it was the last you'd ever hear from me? Did you hope? Were you sorry?

I've been wondering, whenever I had time these past few weeks, what you might be thinking. If I would maybe get a line from you, finally, wanting to know what's been going on, why I just cut things off all of a sudden. Gord doesn't have a computer, needless to say, let alone internet, so whenever I got a chance this last little while I would deke over the library to check my messages. Nope — nothing. I even checked the spam folder: dick enlargers and Nigerian investment opportunities.

Aren't you even curious? I mean after all, we've made it

this far, you and I. Despite your early jitters and my monumental inability to get to the point.

I see that you have deleted your Facebook account. I don't blame you — Facebook freaks me out too. I only started my account to find you after that time I ran into Kyle, but it never occurred to me (and I suppose this makes me pretty stupid) that people would use it to find me too. It's sort of creepy how viral the thing is. The second I friended you, the entire class of '91 starts pouring in for a reunion party. There's Kyle: *Hey Mystery Man awesome running into you downtown. We should grab a drink sometime, what's your sched this week?* And then, just like in our college days, Wade comes tumbling after: *Rank! No way we all thought you were dead or something what's the story??*

That's when I panicked and actually emailed a couple of kids I work with to find out what you're supposed to do when all these unsolicited voices from the past start honking at you. The kids assured me I could just click *ignore* and all would be well, and if *ignore* didn't work then I could *block*, no worries, no more voices — no more ghosts. So I blocked (Wade: *Yo, slacker, friend up!*) and ignored (Kyle: *Rank in all seriousness I've thought about you a lot over the years . . .*). But then Tina came knocking. And Tina's friend the championship highland dancer, the one who used to get shitfaced and then cross two hockey sticks on Wade and Kyle's kitchen floor so she could perform a sword dance at four in the morning, and she'd make the bagpipe noises herself as she hopped up and down and it always had us in hysterics. Janine. Whose name, along with everything else, I'd forgotten until the moment she tried to friend me. And Scott, from the hockey team. And

Mitch, also from the hockey team, who tells me he now lives next door to Scott and their families take vacations together, which is weird because I distinctly remember them throwing punches at each other at the student pub during a Tragically Hip show. *Ignore, block, ignore, block.* But it's no good because with every friend request it's like I have to *go over* these people again — I have to confirm their continuing existence beyond their existence in my memory. With every block and ignore, it's like I'm doing the opposite — every time I click on a name it's an acknowledgement.

And then sometimes you just get these total doozies out of left field:

You have a friend request from Colin Chaisson.

It was like, as long as all these people existed only in my memory, it was just a short step to the belief that in fact I'd mistaken memory for imagination and, in fact, these people were actually figments — just like the events that they participated in — part of a long, dark dream that only you and I shared, Adam. (And it was hard enough when I discovered you shared it, when I found it immortalized in your book — immortalized, but in such a freakily offhand sort of way. Somehow enshrined and chucked aside all at once.) Now I had to contemplate that my private, guilty dream was out there, scattered across the internet in fragments, embedded in other people's memories like ancient chunks of pottery waiting for some archaeologist to come along and piece it together.

Then Kyle again: *Hey Rank. I really hope you don't think I'm being nosy — seriously that's not what this is about . . .*

But I didn't want to shut down my account as long as yours was up there. I had no good reason for this really. It was just a kind of superstition. So that's when I got the idea to deactivate my old account and change my identity.

And now I'm Rankenstein — no photo, no info. And nobody tries to friend me because nobody knows who I am.

But you're not even out there anymore, my only friend, my reason for being.

You're not anywhere — not even in the paper. I check the newspaper every weekend, and the web of course, but it looks like all your reviews and interviews have pretty much trickled off. How's that feel, by the bye? And how come you don't have a web page? Stephen King has a web page. Wouldn't it be good for business? What's it like to have disappeared so all-of-a-sudden? On this end, it's a feeling like you've been absorbed back into my imagination where you should've stayed in the first place — you've reverted to being a ghost.

Well, whatever. I believe in you Adam, even if you've disappeared. I know you exist, like the fairies in Peter Pan — if I shout and clap my hands you live; if I shrug and turn away you die. But I won't — I won't let myself forget. I still carry around your book, and it still has your picture on the back, and you, old friend, are still looking pretty porked-out. My emails haven't been bounced back, and so I figure you're still out there — *lurking,* as the kids like to say — so I am going to proceed as such. I'm going to clap my hands and shout, like I've been doing all along.

I do believe in you, you big fat fairy. I do. I do.

Now let's get you caught up.

I get this phone call the other day — the same day I wrote to you about Kyle. Young guy — young voice. "Oh, hello there

— Gordon Rankin?" Which nobody I know actually calls me. So I'm immediately thinking: telemarketer.

"Who's this?" I demand in my best belligerent-psycho grunt.

"Might I speak with Gordon Rankin?"

"Identify yourself!" I yell. Because I hate how these assholes will try to reel you in, get you off-guard, happy to be chatting to a friendly soul, meanwhile the second you've done something as innocuous as cop to your own identity they tick a box, press a key and forward your digits to a million assholes exactly like themselves, all in pursuit of your credit card number. I never make it easy, or pleasant, for them.

"Owen Findlay," said the voice, after clearing its throat, "gave me this number."

I sat down then. "Okay," I said after a moment.

"So, now . . . Would this be Gordon Rankin Junior?"

And that's when I noticed the accent. And that's when I sighed, realizing what kind of phone call this was going to be.

So Gord fell off the roof is what happened, and broke his collarbone and his right ankle. What was he doing on the roof? He was being an idiot, characteristically, replacing the shingles by his seventy-five-year-old self. Fortunately someone happened to be driving past and saw him plummet. He was lucky — it's not a busy road in particular. He might have lain there trapped on his back like a turtle, obscenities rising feebly from the overgrown lawn, for the next twenty-four hours if this had not been the case.

"I'm Father Waugh," said the guy on the phone.

"Father wha?" I said.

"Yes."

So, Jesus, the priest was calling. It was like getting a call from fifty years ago — from a time when the parish priests called their communities "flocks" and wandered around town bringing the Host to seniors, praying with the sick and making sure no one was dancing to rock and roll. It was so old school. Of course, I hadn't been back home for years, not since that time with the born-again girlfriend. But back home didn't change.

Except for the fact that the priests were younger than me now.

So, as young Father Waugh tells it, he was wandering around the hospital — as apparently priests still do — visiting seniors, sorting out who was going to need communion from who would need last rites, when this student nurse rushes past him purple-faced and a shout follows her down the hall along the lines of (and needless to say the priest relayed this line in euphemism): "I can handle my own goddamn wanger when I piss thank you lady!"

My dad.

Handling his wanger was one thing, sure, but what about everything else? Like feeding himself for example? Here was a laid-up senior citizen with no family on hand — Father Waugh took an interest, naturally. Social Services was called, of which none other than coach Owen Findlay is now grand poobah. Gordon Rankin, you say? Findlay got out from behind his desk and drove to the hospital himself.

And apparently they would never have been able to dig up my number if it hadn't been for Findlay. Gord refused to give it up. "Don't bother the boy," he insisted. But Findlay had my address from the occasional Christmas card — when I remembered to send them — and looked me up.

This is what passes for bureaucracy in my home town. The priest contacts the head of Social Services, who goes home and digs through his old Christmas cards.

"Listen, Father," I said to Waugh, feeling ridiculous — I don't think I've ever called another human being "Father" since my confirmation. "If Gord doesn't want me, you know . . . that's fine." I knew how lame it sounded, how bad-son, but in my defence I hadn't quite digested the severity of Gord's injuries at that point. I had forgotten how stubbornness and irrationality can mingle so potently in my father.

"Well, whether he wants you or not, Mr. Rankin, he's going to need some assistance above and beyond what the public health nurse can offer."

"Can you call me Rank?"

"I . . . you want me to call you *Rank?*"

"That's what people call me. Didn't Owen call me Rank, when you were talking to him?"

"I don't recall, no. He just called you 'the son.'"

For some reason, I started to feel upset.

"So what then," I said, "I have to come out there? Me and my dad don't get along, you know."

"I didn't get that impression at all, uh. Rank. Not at all. I'm surprised to hear you say that."

"You said it yourself, he doesn't want me to come."

"Well the impression I got was that he felt you're too important to bother with what-all that's happening down here. And perhaps he's not important enough."

I snorted, because I didn't know what to say at that point. I could hear something peevish and familiar in Waugh's voice, something I hadn't heard in a long time. Good old redneck reverse-snobbery. *My! Isn't the cityfella special?*

"It seems to me," continued Father Waugh, voice prissier by the moment, "Mr. Rankin holds you in very high esteem. You wouldn't believe how delighted he was to speak with Owen Findlay about you. Owen brought some pictures along of your hockey days and the dear old fella's eyes just lit up. He thinks you walk on water, is my impression. Like a god."

The priest threw this last line out just a bit dismissively as if to add: Poor deluded old fart. My back went up. The gods, I wanted to tell Father Waugh, are *known* for being shitheads, okay? So maybe the dear old fella's not as dumb as you think. Gods don't rush to the side of ailing mortals. They never help you in your time of need. They would double over in disbelieving glee at the idea of answering someone's prayers, after which they might deliver a nice thunderbolt or locust plague by way of extending the joke. And do you really think your guy is any better, Father? You think your guy isn't just Zeus with better PR?

Anyway, long story short, I'm on a plane to the coast. Or a train. Or maybe it's close enough I can just drive for a few hours.

Who knows, right? Not you Adam.

So it turns out Father Waugh is something like thirty-six, clearly gay, clearly in denial about it because he's never left this oh-so-Catholic coast except to go to seminary. The sight of him makes me feel sorry for both him and the Catholic Church combined. Because let's face it, Waugh is probably the only kind of priest the church can get these days after so many years of scandal and disillusionment: holy-terrorized hillbillies who grew up believing every word of the hairy-palm story, the it'll-rot-off-if-you-even-think-about-it stuff. So he's this roly-poly self-made eunuch with an accent thicker than my Gaelic-speaking grandmother's and a really rather grotesque way of talking about his elderly parishioners like they were his personal collection of teddy bears.

For example, Father Waugh on Gord: "God love him, but he's a lively little fella." This is not an endearment prompted by Gord's height. Everyone is a "little fella" in Father Waugh's Care Bear cosmology, and the women are "dear little dears."

Gord loves him, of course, because Father Waugh is of another century. He is exactly what Gord intuits a priest should be — a creature outside of masculinity, outside sexuality itself and therefore comfortably inhuman.

Sorry to go on about Father Waugh, I just had to vent because I've been seeing a lot of the pudgy bastard lately. He takes good care of his parishioners, I'll give him that. He's here checking up on Gord every other day, and because I am a good east coast boy, and Gord harangues me if I don't, I have to make the fucker *tea*. Every. Goddamn. Time.

—

This new laptop is destroying my wrists. I went to the Radio Shack at the strip mall downtown yesterday, which is exactly as I remember it except for being called The Source, and bought the crappiest laptop I could find. The keyboard is freaking infinitesimal. The other thing is, I find I have to write when Gord is sleeping because otherwise he is at me all day, even if I go into my room and close the door. He'll just sit in the front room nattering away with the TV cranked up, bashing on the wall with his crutch whenever something comes on that I simply *must see.*

"Look son, look! [Triple crutch-bash.] Get in here! She wants her tits chopped off! Fourteen years old and says she wants to be a boy! What's she gonna do for tackle, that's what I wanna know. Good luck on that front, girlie. Christ! Gordie! Look at the tattoos! [Double crutch-bash.] Kick her out of the house and let her try living on the streets looking like that, see how she does. Let her pay her own room and board for a while. Single mother, obviously, lookather, lets the foolish thing do whatever she wants. Sure, wear an earring in your eyebrow, who gives a shit, live and let live. Look at *this!* Jesus Christ, the mother's got tattoos herself! [Quadruple crutch-bash.] Get *in* here, for the love of god and *see* this!"

So what I'm saying is, I don't necessarily have the time and concentration I was once able to bring to this little project. Just to let you know in advance.

But guess what. I've looked over the last few emails and now I remember exactly where we left off.

Adam!

13

07/27/09, 10:31 p.m.

KYLE AND WADE are the most popular guys on campus, reason being that both last year and this they have rented (correction: their parents have rented) an entire house just for the two of them. It isn't a big house, or a particularly nice house, because who is going to rent that kind of house to a couple of twenty-year-old boys? So it is a student house, meaning a dive. But it has a huge yard, a cavernlike living room, and three bedrooms (they call the third the "crash pad" and make it available on a first-come-first-served basis to shitfaced compadres). They have of course named the house. The house has been dubbed, with equal parts reverence and irony, the Temple.

Kyle Jarvis is a magic man, gliding through the echelons of undergraduate society with ease and impunity. He plays rugby, so he might mingle with the jocks. He plays guitar and, god knows, loves himself some weed, so he's cool with the hippies. He pulls down grades — a boy of his background dare not falter in this regard — which gives him an in with the keeners. Finally, barely out of his teens, Kyle is already an accomplished cocksman. You'd want to kill the bastard if he wasn't such a decent guy.

Wade Kotch, on the other hand, Kyle's best friend since Grade 6, enjoys loud music and is mostly majoring in hash. The pair are basically a middle-class echo of Mick Croft and Collie Chaisson — like if some overseeing deity had attacked a portrait of the aforementioned hoodlums with a paint-scraper and chipped away the layers of criminality and skeeze. There goes the smartass smirk in favour of the winning half-smile. *Chip-chip* go the remnants of Chaisson's freckled spare tire to reveal the concave gut of Wade, swathed in one of those ugly-ass raw-cotton hoodies that was practically a Gen-X uniform in those days. *Chip chip chip* go the ball caps. *Chip* go the homemade knuckle tattoos — all the nastiness flaking away until at last they stand revealed, this wholesome new version of Croft and Chaisson: Jarvis and Kotch. Couple of really good guys.

Getting back to Kyle. The thing about Kyle's magic is, it makes him a uniter, an axle. He brings the disparate social echelons together in their mutual attraction to himself. He knows this; everybody knows this. So when these diverse campus factions — typically so opposed — are gathered together one raucous evening at the Temple ("gathered in Dionysian worship," Kyle likes to joke), the venue is understood to constitute a no man's land, a place of peace. No sectarian conflict will be tolerated.

So say some thug from the hockey team spots some skinny wiener in his kill-me uniform of a cardigan and glasses, decides

to dispense with introductions and instead to pick the wiener up, hoist the now squirming wiener over his head, and
march over to a nearby open window to the ecstatic cheers of
his hockey compadres. Kyle, in such a circumstance, could be
relied upon to bound across the room, station himself between
the thug and open window, sternly point at the thug with the
spout of his beer bottle, and say, like dog trainer to a misbehav-
ing mutt: No. No, Rank. Not here. Not in this house, man. No.

Chastened, knowing he has violated the code of the Temple, the thug reluctantly but gently places the wiener back on
solid ground. His hockey buddies pout, jeer briefly, then turn
away to look for girls.

The first person to speak is the wiener. "Thank you," he
says, rubbing his body where the thug's pipelike fingers had
dug into him.

Kyle turns a look of scorn onto the thug. "He just fucking
thanked you, Rank."

Who in the universe but Kyle could make a normally
unrepentant thug feel so very repentant — when all he
was doing was acting the way any self-respecting thug was
expected and encouraged to act? *Jeez*. The thug in question
understands what has to happen next.

He turns and addresses the wiener.

"Sorry, man. Just getting a little exercise."

The glasses shift toward him, flicker light into the thug's
eyes. "No problem."

"Now shake hands," says Kyle.

Rank winces. "Kyle, fuck's sake man."

"This is my house. This is the Temple. It is a Temple of
friendship, and it is a Temple of love."

Only Kyle Jarvis can get away with saying this sort of thing. So the two young men roll eyes and shake hands.

"Come with me," insists Kyle, and ushers the two new acquaintances over to the kitchen. Together the three of them stand solemnly before the fridge like it is an altar. Kyle opens it with a somehow ceremonial yank, pulls out a couple of beer, and cracks them for each of his guests before handing them over.

"Now," he instructs. "You two stand here with your beer and get to know each other. Don't come out of the kitchen until you're best friends. I'm serious."

With that, he leaves them.

They regard each other. Rank pushes out his breath, making his lips flap a little. It isn't an encouraging sound, but the wiener doesn't flinch, doesn't make the first appeasing move. Also, he seems to know precisely the right angle to point his glasses in order to make them reflect light into the eyes of the person in front of him. Safe behind his glasses, he gives nothing away. He just waits.

After a moment, Rank speaks.

"Can I say something here, Adam?"

"Certainly, Rank."

"I know we haven't known each other long. But, here it is. You are — bar none — the greatest guy I've ever met."

The glasses shift then, pointing downward at the blackened kitchen linoleum. A silent, sombre nod, followed by a slightly choked-up throat-clearing. "That means . . . so much to me Rank. You have no idea."

Rank begins to choke a bit himself. "And I . . . I just wanna say . . ."

"Just say it, Rank. It's okay. I'm here."

"I'd really like to offer you a hand job."

Adam can't keep it up and ends up spraying beer across the kitchen.

So the ritual was a success. Chalk up another for the magic man.

07/28/09, 12:03 a.m.

I'm sorry but I just have to stop and remark upon what a total trip down memory lane it is, being here, for me. I didn't quite realize it until Owen Findlay came by for a beer the other night. He brought over a bunch of copies of those pics from my hockey days that Father Waugh had mentioned on the phone — one set for me and one for Gord. Neither of us had seen them before. It's weird to see pictures of yourself as a kid that you've never seen before — it's as if there's a version of you, a double, that you didn't even know existed, hanging around somewhere in the past.

So doesn't Gord promptly haul out his own photo album (by which I mean hollers at me to haul it from the top shelf of the bookcase for him), preparing to set sail into Rankin family history.

The moment Gord opens the album, photos cascade from its pages and into his lap because after Sylvie died he couldn't be bothered to maintain it properly. He likes to take the snapshots out of the book to show people and then just shoves them back in the album without bothering to reaffix any of them. I am pretty sure this is not just because he's lazy. It's because he doesn't know how to do it — he's never bothered to figure it out. Keeping albums was my mother's job.

So there's Gord with a crotchful of photos and he makes poor Owen sit there listening to extended narratives about every last one. Here's the boy playing street hockey with his friends — already an enforcer, looka the size a the, etc. Here he hulks in his Icy Dream uniform on his first day of work, all of fourteen years old. Here he is with his lame certificate stating that he has graduated from "Hot Fudge High," which was what Icy Dream Inc. called the weekend training seminar they offered to franchise employees. I remember at the time being pretty excited by the whole thing, because it meant we had to go into the city for the weekend and stay in a hotel, and I was the youngest person in the whole seminar, even though I didn't look it. Gord introduced me to everyone there as his "new assistant manager" and at the bar afterward someone handed me a pint without a second glance.

Owen accepts every photo my father hands over, gazes at it for however long it takes for Gord to unfurl the fascinating Rank-centric anecdote attached, then politely places the photo in a growing stack on the end table beside him in time for Gord to hand him another. I decide that I will allow this to continue for as long as it takes me to hook up the wireless modem I've been fiddling with all day. It might seem a little rude toward Owen, but it's good to have Gord distracted and nattering at someone else for a while. Besides, the modem has been making me crazy, and I can't stand to put it aside until I've got it hooked up. My computer won't pick up the signal. I have spoken, after waiting on hold for two successive eternities, to the tech support people representing both the manufacturers of the computer and the modem — neither party being of any help whatsoever — and I refuse to do it again. If I can't figure it out myself, I am going to throw the computer away and buy another, more expensive one. I don't give a shit anymore.

So as Gord hands over photographs to Owen, I sit there going back and forth between the modem and my computer, checking for a connection, occasionally giving absent-minded answers to Gord's inane promptings, e.g.: "Remember that now Gordie?" "Didn't care for that, much, did he son?" "Guess you showed them, eh, Gordie?"

And I'm muttering, "Yup. Yeah, I remember. *Shit! This stupid* . . . Yeah, I know Gord. *Goddamnit!*"

And Owen is saying things like: "He barely fits into that sweater!" and "That's not the same sign as they have at the ID now is it? When'd you get that sign changed, Gordon?"

And as pissed off as I am at the computer situation I'm secretly very grateful to have something to distract me from the cure for insomnia that's happening on the other side of the room.

And that's when I exclaim: "*You complete and total fucker!*" and notice that I have shouted these words into an uncharacteristic sound vacuum. So I glance up at Gord and Owen who are leaning toward each other like school boys sharing a textbook, only they're not reading, they're looking at a picture together.

And Gord has stopped talking, so I know it's a picture of Sylvie.

What's more, I know what photo it is. I don't know how but I do. Maybe just because I saw it and handled it so many times in my youth — and saw Gord and Sylvie do the same, because everyone in my family always loved the damn thing, were always passing it around, taking it out of the album to show friends and relatives. It was just one of those photos. In these days of digicams you can take a picture a second and delete whatever looks like crap, so a decent snap of someone — where their eyes aren't half closed or they don't look like they have six chins — doesn't have the same magic of really good old photographs. The uncanny luck of a picture that not only gets across everything good in the moment, but somehow composes itself into a representation of something *more*, something beyond that moment — even better than the moment itself.

It's almost like a lie, a good photo. An unbearable lie. Like that moment you feel yourself starting to wake up after the best dream of your life. And you hold your eyes shut and you just lie there; you can't stand it, you're so disappointed to be waking up.

It's the photograph of me and Sylvie after my Confirmation — that's the photo Gord is holding. He took it himself, out in the church parking lot, immediately following the ceremony.

Finally Gord speaks.

"Mother and son."

"That's a nice shot," murmurs Owen. He looks like he would be happy to sit there gazing away at the image of me with my buck teeth and tan corduroy suit for as long as Gord is willing to hold it up in front of him.

Without even thinking about it, I've shoved the laptop aside and am on my feet, reaching out to retrieve the snapshot, which Gord is now holding out to me.

Why did I want to see it again? As I turned it over in my fingers, I could see that I hadn't forgotten a single detail. It was all there, the late morning sunlight, the gleaming cars behind us, the expanse of beige corduroy, purchased in a panic because I'd had the first of my two major growth spurts practically the day before and it was the only thing in the store that fit me. And, oh, it was godawful. And I was godawful. I was a post-growth-spurt mess. My teeth seemed to stick out a mile. My tie, which was Gord's tie, was about the same distance wide and a glaring kelly green. If I had still looked like a child, this clown suit would have been okay, passable, because kids can get away with anything — kids are meant to look ridiculous — but I looked like a young man. A young man with no idea how to dress. Therefore, an imbecile. To top it all off, I still had my pre-growth spurt haircut — prodigious, everywhere, past my ears. Fine on a child, insane on a man in a corduroy suit. Why hadn't Sylvie cut it? Like I said, I had grown up in a day, practically. None of us was ready.

In the photo, I am grinning from ear to ear. Sylvie is also grinning from ear to ear. She is peeping out from behind me, with her arms wrapped around my waist and her tiny hands locked together against my abdomen. There's a slight look of incredulousness on her face, because I remember her exclaiming, as we posed: *I can barely get my arms around him anymore!* And that's when I started laughing, giving the buck teeth a nice healthy airing, at which Gord started laughing, followed by Sylvie, who was also grunting as she reached around me, to indicate what an incredible effort it took.

And then, *snap*. Shot.

We are like — I don't know how else to explain it — Sylvie and I are like two suns in this picture. We radiate.

And then Gord ruins it. As Gord has always ruined it. He nudges Owen.

"Young Gordie was always a bit of a mama's boy, truth be told."

I remember being this angry only a couple of times. Once was in that room at the courthouse with Sylvie, Gord, and Trisha after Gord insisted my suffering mother should absent herself from my trial and I, in turn, insisted I was going to kill him and Trish, in turn, insisted Gord should go get a drink from the water fountain down the hall.

The other time — you remember. You were there. And Kyle was there. And Kyle stood his ground pretty impressively, it seems to me now.

And I think something must happen to my face at that point, because Owen jumps to his feet.

I am talking. In a very low drawl, like a slowed-down recording, I hear myself say: "You know what Gord?"

But Owen won't let me tell him what. His body is suddenly against mine and he is kind of fox-trotting me into the kitchen and out the front door, calling something to my father about us taking a walk out back to see the creek. I can hear myself talking over him the whole time, still in that low-slow tone but getting louder the farther away Owen manages to get me from my father. Have I mentioned Owen is only around 5'11"? So I don't know how he accomplishes this exactly. Years of experience wrangling teenage gland-cases on the ice I suppose.

So we stand on the lawn in front of the house, and I notice

I am still yelling, and as I slow down enough to take actual notice of what I am saying and maybe nuance it a little I also notice that my father's own fulsome shouts are — as always — sounding in vigorous counterpoint to mine from somewhere inside the house. I even hear him bash the crutch against the wall a couple of times by way of emphatic punctuation. Not to put too fine a point on it, but the two of us sound like a couple of raging, incoherent twats. I take a breath and glance over at Owen. His eyebrows are up, his hands in the pockets of his cords.

"Ready?" he inquires.

We take a walk.

07/29/09, 9:14 p.m.

So, you'd think it would be strange hanging out with Owen Findlay after all these years, but in fact it feels as comfortable and familiar as my old bedroom at the back of the house. But when I say *"as* comfortable," you shouldn't mistake that to mean "comfortable," exactly. We head up through the back field and I can't help but be reminded of the walks we used to take together when I was in the Youth Centre. I know I haven't spoken much about the Youth Centre, but that's not because it was such a bad place. The tough-on-crime crowd won't like to hear this, but I was sort of happy there. It was quiet, for one thing — something I never got a lot of, growing up in the house that Gord built — and my days were totally routinized. People told me when to get up and when to eat and when to shower and when to study and when to exercise and when to go to bed. If Owen's social work colleagues ever wanted to develop some kind of ideal mental-health retreat geared toward a sixteen-year-old boy who had accidentally nearly killed somebody and whose mother had just died and who couldn't stand the sight of his father, they would very likely end up with something resembling the Youth Centre. I needed the routine and the quiet but I also needed that over-arching sense of being punished — that every morning when I woke up I could be sure I would go through my day enacting a punishment. Every breath of air, every step taken, every morsel of food ingested — everything punitive.

It was Owen's job to interview me once a week and find out what I thought and how I was doing, but he never wanted to do this in one of the centre's concrete-coloured interview rooms, adorned as they were with industrial seventies-era office furniture, uniformly orange for some reason, and further bleakened by fluorescent lighting. Instead, Owen always insisted we "take a walk" around the grounds, which wasn't bad because the grounds overlooked the ocean. And I know I'm starting to make this place sound like more of a resort than a penal institute, but keep in mind that this was on the coast, so pretty much everything overlooked the ocean — pubs, grocery stores, and Youth Centres alike.

The funny thing is, I remember very little about the talks I had with Owen. Mostly I just remember the sound of our feet in the dirt — the dual rhythm of our footsteps. Being lulled by our shared, repetitive trudge. And maybe that's why, trudging along beside Owen Findlay again after all these years, I can't help but mention this memory to him — or this lack of memory, maybe. The memory of being lulled and not thinking or talking about much of anything, even though we must have.

"That was the idea," says Owen. "That was the idea then and now."

I look over when he says "now," and he's smiling at the oncoming woods in the distance.

"Oh, this is great," I say. "You're using the same therapeutic techniques on me that you used when I was sixteen years old. I thought I'd come so far."

"It wasn't so much a technique as it was just — you know — 'let's go for a walk,'" says Owen.

I remember this from the old days. Owen says or does exactly the right thing and when you point that out, he shrugs it off as common sense — as the obvious move. It took me a while to figure out that this was one of his techniques as well.

"Horseshit, Owen," I say.

He smiles again at the approaching trees. Owen still wears the same round, wire-frame John Lennon glasses I remember from when I was a kid, back when his hair was black with flecks of white instead of the other way around. "I worked pretty intuitively in those days," he tells me. "I thought kids needed to be out and moving around — you in particular. That's why I started coaching hockey. But it makes sense, right? You get upset, you go for a walk. You walk it off. People do it on instinct."

"Yeah," I say, feeling a little bored but also content — again, exactly what I remember from the Youth Centre days. "Gets you out of your head I guess."

"But it's meditative too," says Owen. "It sort of gets you *into* your head at the same time."

And I think he must be right, if only because my memories of being sixteen and incarcerated are so visceral right now. It's as if the steady rhythm of our footsteps has put me in a hypnotic state and shot me back in time twenty-four years. A helpless, pleasant vagueness has come over me too — the same state of mind, I realize, that I inhabited the entire year following Sylvie's death. A sort of contented imbecility. I couldn't focus on anything, had no concentration, yet certain moments could be unbelievably vivid, and a lot of the time those moments took place on my walks with Owen. I remember the thick, living smell of mud thawing in the early spring. That yellow moment of blindness when the afternoon sun hits you square in the face. A black smear of crow cackling at you from a fencepost.

"I just remembered how you used to take us on all those stupid weekend hikes too," I tell Owen. "Like in *November*, even."

"Those were nice! They were good hikes. You would have rather stayed inside playing Atari, I suppose."

"I would have, yeah. I didn't have an Atari at home."

And yes, we talk about other stuff at this point, Owen and I, but it's stuff I haven't bothered filling you in on thus far and I'm not going to start now — life stuff: work, family — none of it pertinent to this project you and I are currently engaged with. (By the way, did you think you were getting the whole story all this time, Adam? A complete picture? Were you even arrogant enough to suppose you could detect psychological subcurrents, underlying motivations that perhaps I'm not even aware of myself? Has it occurred to you that I could be making this entire thing up for reasons of my own — maybe just to fuck with you? Well, let me assure you, I'm not, but let me assure you also that my dealings with you in the past have led me to be very careful with the information I give out. Have you noticed, for example, there are basically no women in this story? Except for Sylvie — but you've already had your way with her. And Kirsten — but really, I've given you nothing about Kirsten except for a name. Believe me, I've learned my lesson. Her name is all you're ever going to get.)

We reach the woods and get on the path to the creek and I can see the splintered ruins of the mini Tarzan playland Gord set up for me back here when I was a kid. Wooden platforms nailed high up in the branches of the best climbing trees, strategic ropes hanging here and there — ancient now, a couple of them snapped off where other kids must've tried to swing from them — hopefully not from one of the tree-top platforms, otherwise Owen and I might be coming across a half-pint skeleton at some point. No tree house — Gord was never much of a carpenter — but a vestigial "fort" sits in the distance. More boards nailed to a circle of trees to form a rough enclosure. I remember feeling invulnerable behind that half-assed barricade, gleefully whiffing one crabapple after another at countless invading enemies.

Finally Owen and I arrive at the creek and we stand there and we look at it piddling away.

"It's shrunk," I remark to Owen.

I think he's going to say something about how I've grown and it just looks that way, but he says, instead, "Not a lot of rain this summer."

I crouch down and let the water piddle across my hand just for something to do. I remember doing the same thing as a kid — just hanging out, bored, by the creek, and reaching out to touch it every once in a while as though it were a friend or a pet.

"Well, this is scintillating," I say, straightening up after another moment or two. "Should we head back?"

"All right," says Owen. "Admit it, though. You feel better after the walk."

"Well I don't feel like I wanna tear Gord's head off anymore, not right this minute anyway, no."

"See?" says Owen. "You doubted."

"I wasn't saying walking is a bad thing, Owen, I didn't mean to criticize you back there, I'm just saying those were some frigging long walks you made us go on. You had us walking all day sometimes. Was that supposed to be part of our punishment? Like did the province order we had to walk a certain number of miles every week?"

We turn and head back in the direction from which we came, and Owen shakes his head.

"Your 'punishment'! You're happy as a pig in shit locked in a room with a television set but the moment someone takes you out for exercise and fresh air it's — Oh my god! What did I do to deserve this?"

"I'm just saying," I say as we crunch our way past my old fort again. "Those were some long walks."

"You know, there are still Catholic pilgrims who'll walk for over a month to reach the holy sites."

"Yes but Catholics are insane," I point out. "They worship martyrs. People who were burned at the stake and eaten by lions and tortured to death. The more you suffer, the more gold stars you get. So of course they're gonna walk for a month straight, that's as good as it gets, that's right up there with self-flagellation. Look at me! My feet are mangled stumps! Look how pious I am!"

Owen, who I happen to know is carrying a set of rosary beads on him at this very moment, laughs his head off at this.

"And besides," I say. "At least the pilgrims have some kind of destination at the end of it. They're not just out there walking around for the hell of it. They're trying to get to Lourdes or wherever."

"I don't know if that's true, now," says Owen, reaching behind his John Lennon glasses to finger a laugh tear out of the inner corner of his eye. "I mean you don't *have* to do all that walking to get to Lourdes or the Shrine of Saint James in Spain, say. You can take a plane, or a bus. The walk is optional. People choose to do that walk for a reason."

"So they can suffer," I explain.

"No," says Owen. "For penance."

"That's what I mean. To punish themselves."

"I don't believe it's the same thing."

"Yeah well walk for a month straight to the Shrine of Saint James or wherever and then tell me you don't feel like you've been punished, Owen," I say.

"Ah dear," says Owen, craning his head back and smiling up at the sky now that we're out of the woods and trudging back across the field. "Whatever happened to that god-fearing young man in his confirmation photo?"

I feel a bit aggravated with Owen now, like it's not very good social worker strategy to bring up the very thing that made me so pissed off I had to leave the house in the first place. Besides, Owen knows as well as anyone what happened to that pious young man.

"He got old," I say.

"Penance," continues Owen, pretending not to notice I'm annoyed. "Is a very deliberate process. It's thoughtful. You engage in it because on some level you need to. It isn't something that's inflicted on you from the outside. You go willingly."

I decide in that instance to get in an argument with Owen.

"Then why," I say, "is it always so repetitive — so, like, mind-numbingly repetitious? It's not about being thoughtful — it's about *rote*, like having to recite the times tables in school — it's about drilling stuff into your brain, precisely so that you don't have to think about it anymore. Or anything. You know what my mother used to do, when she was worried about something? If Gord was off on a tear or something? She'd haul out her fucking rosary and babble Our Fathers and Hail Marys until she was blue in the face."

"Well, maybe that helped her," says Owen.

"It did help her," I say. "It helped her not to think. It helped her to stay put and let herself get walked all over. It helped her to tolerate suffering, like a good Catholic lady, instead of saying, *Fuck this noise!* and putting an end to it. It was a huge help to my mother, her Catholic faith."

Owen doesn't say anything. You have to know Owen as well as I do to understand that Owen not saying anything when it is manifestly his turn to do so is one of the ways Owen goes about "saying" something — usually something really irritating once you settle down to decoding it.

But I refuse to decode. I just let the silence be silence,

ignoring whatever it is that Owen is psychically attempting to beam into my brain.

And after he's finished this silent transmission, he follows it up — as he always has — with a seemingly simple, seemingly innocent question.

"What could she have done differently, do you suppose?"

I guess I should have been ready for it, but I glance over at Owen with my mouth hanging open. The question is so outrageous, and so *Owen* in that shrugging, fake-naive manner I remember from when I was a kid — I can barely even start to form a word.

"I just *told* you," I say after a moment. "Jesus Christ, I just told you what she could've done differently, Owen."

"'Fuck this noise,'" quoted Owen.

"That's right," I said. "Fuck this noise."

"And you think saying 'Fuck this noise' was a realistic option for someone like your mom?"

"Well it was either that or the other option," I tell Owen after a moment, trying not to raise my voice over the loud grind of tooth enamel happening inside my head. "And look where that got her."

Owen's eyebrows twitch behind his glasses. "Seem a little pissed, there, Rank."

"Well no kidding, Owen."

I look away from him, toward the house. Conversation over. Conversation too idiotic to be pursued.

We walk. Our footsteps go out of sync for a moment or two, then gradually fall into pace with one another again. It's impossible to tell if we have made this happen deliberately or not.

"You know," says Owen, "there's still a tradition in Flanders. They release one prisoner a year — this is in Switzerland, now. And they get him to do the walk all the way to the Shrine of Saint James in Spain, carrying a heavy pack. And then when he's finished, once he's reached the Shrine, he's let free."

I sigh.

"Punishment," I say.

"I don't know," says Owen.

I don't feel like arguing anymore — especially if that's the best Owen can do — and we're almost back at the house in any case.

"Have I mentioned how nice it is to see you again?" Owen asks me out of nowhere.

I'm so angry, all I can do is laugh.

14

07/30/09, 10:16 p.m.

HERACLITUS IS SAYING that no man can step twice into the same river and Rank is thugging it up for the boys saying, Yes you can. Of course you can. Duh. Out there is the Saint John River and we could go out and walk to it right now and I would step in it, and then step out of it again, and then step in it again and then I would have stepped into it twice. There. So take that 'Clitus. How do you like that, Captain Clit?

Wade is rolling around on the floor laughing. He's been doing this, at various volumes, for the last hour or so. It is 4:17 on a Thursday afternoon and they are all, of course, stoned brainless. They are doing what they always attempt to do when stoned brainless: talk philosophy. As second-year humanities students, Adam, Kyle and Rank all had to take the pre-Socratics course. Wade is doing a year of sciences in the hope of gaining entrance into the Engineering program at some point, and therefore he gets to refer to the other three as art fags. Rank finds this hilarious — for Wade is the biggest such fag of the bunch of them. Kyle is simply doing whatever he needs to make law school happen. Adam is an all-around grade-maker — a kind of robot who seems to hoover up knowledge and file it away as a matter of protocol, as opposed to deriving any kind of enjoyment or pleasure out of it. And Rank is your average directionless undergrad, hoping one day he'll arrive at a class and the professor will open his mouth and all of a sudden Rank will know exactly where he is supposed to go and what he is supposed to do. Which is to say, none of them come across as particularly passionate about Arts and Humanities — they are all too busy enacting a private duty.

Which makes Wade the only real zealot in the group. If you mention Led Zeppelin one too many times in his presence, he will veer into ecstasy. He'll not only deliver a lecture about the timeless, groundbreaking brilliance of Jimmy Page's guitar — if you let him continue in this vein, he'll actually start in on their album cover art. He'll give you a breakdown of the Arthur C. Clarke novel that inspired the cover for *Houses of the Holy*, and even tell you how the guy who took the photo was a member of some British design group who did album covers for all the big art-rock outfits like Genesis and Pink Floyd back in the day. At which point, he'll be staggering over to his record collection to show you a few pertinent examples, and that's when you'll realize you should have changed the subject long ago.

Captain Clit, wheezes Wade now.

The only time any of them get passionate about what they are learning at school are times like these, stoned brainless and trying to outdo one another.

No, no, no! shouts Kyle over Wade's rug-muffled hee-haws. Kyle sinks from his armchair onto his knees in order to be closer to Adam and Rank — who are sprawled on the Sally-Ann-tastic couch — when he makes his point. As always, he gestures with the spout of his beer bottle for emphasis.

No, Rank. He's not talking about the river, like a river with a name — the Nile or the Saint John or the Thames or whatever. You're thinking about a river as a single, solid object — but he's talking about, like, a moving body of water. It's all a gazillion water molecules right? All different.

Rank knows what Kyle is on about but he's enjoying playing the thick-headed moose to Kyle's impassioned orator.

Bullshit, man, grunts Rank. We go out there, I stick my foot in the water, it's fucking wet. It's wet from the river. I stick my other foot in, it's not a different river that got my other foot wet. It's still the Saint John River, and I'm still wet.

You're getting too caught up in names, man.

What's in a name, really? asks Wade from the floor. Of all things, this is what starts Adam giggling.

Let's say we go out there right now, and I push you in the river . . . says Rank, leaning back against the couch, the more comfortably to spin his scenario.

Rank, huffs Kyle, it's not about getting *wet*.

Yeah it is. That's what he's on about. That's what happens when you step, or for our purposes let's say get pushed, into a river. You're wet and it sucks. So let's say I push you into the river and you flail around and glug for a while but eventually you crawl back out. You're shivering and you're soaking wet. I push you in again. Does it feel any different the second time around? How about when you get out? Still freezing and soaking wet. So, for good measure, I push you in a third time . . .

Rank, you're just . . . this is just turning into a sick fantasy about pushing me into the river. You're not taking the argument seriously.

He's also talking about the man, says Adam, smiling but no longer giggling. Rank and Kyle turn to look at him. You never know when Adam is going to interject. Sometimes he'll just sit there for hours, listening to the rest of them toss bullshit back and forth, and they almost could forget he's there.

Who, says Rank. Me?

No. Heraclitus. Captain Clit. It's not just the river he's talking about; it's the man.

What man?

The man with the wet foot, says Adam. It's never the same man, either.

This stops even Kyle for a moment. The spout of his beer bottle hovers, directionless. Rank can feel his eyebrows begin to pinch together as a half-assed comprehension descends, but before he can call bullshit, a question wanders up from Wade, still flat on his back on the floor.

Is it the same foot?

Ever since Wade became a dealer, they have had far too much access to hash and pot and acid and mushrooms than is strictly advisable for college-aged men. *Particularly if one of those men has a juvenile criminal past*, some all-seeing narrator might observe at this point. But it's hard to turn away from such largesse — they are students, after all. These are supposedly the best years of their lives. They are built to party, just like Wade's T-shirt says, they are kids in a candy store, which means they are helpless not to indulge. This is what happens when your best friend is a drug dealer, Rank thinks in his more lucid moments. This is what happened to Collie Chaisson, I bet. At some point, your brain just falls out your ass.

But they are the popular boys this year as a result — the campus-god charisma of Rank and Kyle in combination with their stewardship of the Temple's weekend excesses, added to Wade's superlative music collection and stereo system, with Adam providing just enough bookish gravitas to keep them from looking like your typical fratboy gang-rape-in-waiting — this, plus an on-site drug connection? They may as well be dipped in gold.

Wade made the connection back in first year. He'd been the only one of them without any kind of scholarship, meaning he had to get a job to see him through. He brooded on this problem as he partied his way through frosh week, when in the middle of a pub crawl it came to him: he could bartend. It so happened that when this occurred to him he was sitting in one of the sketchiest bars in town, a former disco, presently a dive, that nonetheless had retained its Studio-54-era moniker: Goldfinger's. Wade stood up and staggered over to the bar, tended by a woman wearing a kind of corset-tank top who he'd been looking for an excuse to talk to anyway and asked her, "Where can I apply?"

"Apply for what?" she hollered over the music.

Wade could see from her already-wincing expression that she was expecting a sleazy come-on. He tried for a moment to come up with one: *To be your man, beautiful lady.*

"To tend bar. You guys need any help?"

"Right now?" she asked.

"No, not right now, I'm hammered right now."

"That aint stopping *me*," she told him, and winked before downing a shot she'd been keeping under the counter.

Wade shivered with pleasure. Not at the shot, or even the wink. It was his first year away from home and he'd never met a woman who said *aint* without any kind of ironic inflection before.

So Wade tended bar at Goldfinger's his entire first semester at university and quickly discovered that a) it was disgusting work and he hated it and the woman who said aint looked so serious all the time because she was trying not to smile — she had brown teeth — and b) he didn't have it in him to spend three nights a week dodging both punches and vomit 'til one in the morning (followed by another grisly hour of clean-up) while maintaining any kind of GPA to speak of.

The upside? There were drugs at Goldfinger's. But that led to yet another downside of the job — the fact that most of his hard-won tips were going into the baggies he took home with him at the end of every shift.

It took a while for the obvious solution to sink in. In typical Wade fashion, there was no real eureka moment — he simply noticed one day that a great many of his friends — and mere acquaintances even — had come to rely on him for hash and other illicit sundries. His connection at Goldfinger's, a middle-aged paranoiac coke-addict named Ivor who acted as bouncer in addition to his other, more underground activities, mentioned one evening that if Wade "had any kind of brain on ya," he might think about charging his friends a percentage.

And the moment he did was the moment he realized he was crazy to keep tending bar three nights a week.

By second year, Wade was in business.

07/31/09, 10:23 p.m.

And so they party that year, our boys. God love the little fellas, how they party. They bond intensely during those pothead philosophy rap sessions — Cheech & Chong meets Plato's *Symposium* — and consider one another geniuses. They admire and look up to each other, but at the same time harbour their own secret senses of superiority, which keeps them from being too resentful of the others' particular gifts. And they intuit this — that they have one another's respect, but not too much, not enough of it to lead to jealousy or outright emulation. They are each their own man — and, in some kind of shared psychic acknowledgement, each has been deemed worthy of the other's friendship.

They are often seen together as a group, but they pair off just as often too. Because Wade and Kyle have their shared hometown history, they make up one side of the coin, so Rank and Adam come to be the other. Rank and Adam are one of those superficially unlikely-seeming friend-pairings that eventually make a paradoxical kind of sense — in accordance with the eternal principle of "opposites attract," one can only suppose. Rank's big-mouthed bruiser alongside Adam's introverted aesthete are sort of complementary — they click. They tone down what's most provocatively stereotypical about each other. Just as Rank's fellow gland-cases no longer compete to hurl the weedy Adam out of windows, classmates and profs are no longer as quick to dismiss Rank, for all his overgrowth, as a special-needs, Andre-the-Giant goon.

It's a fact that his association with Adam causes Rank to consider that he, Rank, is perhaps a smarter person than he has given himself credit for all these years. People consider Adam deep, if only because he never wastes words — he's not a bullshitter like Kyle, a smart guy who nonetheless believes the only path to profundity is to run off at the mouth until something intelligent inadvertently emerges. Adam just doesn't talk if he doesn't have anything real to say. There are people in their circle who find this annoying, and unnerving, and Rank was for a while one of them, but now he can't help but think that there's an enviable confidence in Adam's zipped lip. He's not trying to impress anyone. Which is a singular thing in a community of twentysomethings.

So when Adam opens his mouth to pronounce, a part of you trembles, thinking: Oh hell, he's going to start quoting Kierkegaard or something and I'm going to have to nod a lot and then maybe pretend I have to go to the bathroom. But Rank found he never had to do that. Rank found he could keep up.

Like the talk they had on the way to the liquor store after Rank had walked out on one of his playoff games, thereby pretty much annihilating his academic future. Rank had gone directly to find Adam because he knew Adam would be the only guy on campus who would not realize that he should be utterly appalled and horrified by what Rank had done. You don't, of course, leave the arena in the middle of a playoff game. Nobody does that. It's not conceivable. But

Adam could be relied upon not to grasp this principle quite as keenly as the other guys in Rank's acquaintance. Which meant that they could just talk about what Rank had done as if it had been a rational, measured decision as opposed to the cataclysmic middle finger to his future — and his current, quasi-respectable college boy existence — that it was.

"Coach was a dick," explains Rank.

"Right," says Adam. "But you've been saying he's a dick all year. Aren't they all dicks?"

"No," says Rank. "My high school coach wasn't a dick."

"So why is this guy a dick?"

"My high school coach would practically stop the game if a guy even got checked. Whereas Francis figured I should be an enforcer. He put me out there to bash the shit out of guys and I wasn't gonna do it."

"Isn't that part of the game?"

"Yeah, it is," says Rank after a moment. "It's everybody's favourite part of the game. So I quit."

"I still don't get why you quit *now*, though. If you knew it was part of the game."

"It's like I said, my high school coach coddled us. He was a social worker. I thought I could just keep my head down here and play defence like I did in school. And, you know, I'm good, so the coach gets pissed off but I figure he's not going to kick me off the team for neglecting to maim people as I was clearly born to do."

Adam just keeps quiet now — listening.

"Anyway, we're losing, is the problem. We're sucking hard. And Francis is practically bashing his head against the wall at half time. And he's got his eyes closed like he's praying to Jesus and he's saying: I'm so sick of having pussies on my team. I'm so sick of trying to coach a bunch of goddamn pussies who don't even have the balls to get out there and *punish* those bastards. And then his eyes pop open and he bulges them at us like he's going to pick up a sledgehammer or something any minute and he barks: I want you to put up your hands. Who hasn't fought all season? I'm fucking serious. Who hasn't got out there and really slammed someone? And of course he's glaring right at me, because I'm conspicuous, right, like he saw me at the beginning of the season and he's been thinking I'm going to crush everything in my wake. But I haven't, no matter how much pussy talk I get from Francis — and I've been getting a lot of it, Adam, and I don't give a shit. And so he's looking at me and we're both aware of this."

"Wait," says Adam now. "Why not?"

"What?"

"You said it was part of the game. So I don't understand. Why not?"

"Why not what?"

"Why don't you want to be an enforcer?"

They are trudging down the hill on their way to the liquor store and Rank stops walking at that moment and he pulls down his scarf so Adam can look him full in the face. Adam finds a patch of ice and deliberately slides a couple steps like a little kid would, until he notices Rank is just standing there on the sidewalk waiting to tell him something.

"Because I could kill a guy, Adam."

Adam's jaw actually drops. Rank can't help but feel affection for him — he's not like anybody else on the planet. He doesn't possess the same frames of reference.

"Seriously?" says Adam.

"Yeah, seriously. Or give him brain damage. It's a very easy thing to do."

"But that's unconscionable — that he would want you to do that."

"Yes — thank you!" exclaims Rank. "But it's like people don't really believe in it. They think death is . . . like a dream. Like it's something out of stories. They don't realize it's . . . always . . . right fucking there. Just hovering over everything we do. It's always waiting for an opening, and this coach, Francis, he's there dying to let it loose."

Adam opens his mouth but instead of saying something, starts walking again, crunching snow. Rank follows him.

"OK — go on," says Adam.

"Well, since he's looking at me, I have to put up my hand, right? I can't just whistle a tune and pretend I didn't hear him or whatever. So it's just me and a couple of other guys, the captain and the goaltender, but it's pretty much all about me at that moment because I'm the meathead, right?"

"Right," says Adam.

"So that's when he says it: Tonight's the night, boys. You either fight tonight or you leave right now."

"Was he looking at you when he said it?"

"Well he actually followed up with: You got that, Rankin? So, you know, not a lot of ambiguity."

"So what did you say?"

"I said: Bill Masterton. Ted Green. Ed Kea."

"Who are they?"

"Those are the names of guys who got their heads bashed in playing for the NHL."

"Did Francis know that?"

"Yeah, I assume, because at this point he goes completely apeshit. Face turns purple. It's like he can't breathe for a second, like he's having a heart attack. And then all of a sudden he starts yelling in this high, really gross voice, like he's trying to sound like an old lady talking to a little kid: Oh! Are we afraid we're going to hurt ourselves out there? Are we worried we might get an owie? Big boy like you, Rankin?"

"So he thought you were worried about yourself."

"No he fucking didn't, Adam, everyone in the room knew I wasn't worried about getting hurt myself, he was just trying to shame me into cracking skulls."

"So what then?"

"So then intermission's over and he drops the old-lady voice, and the purple goes out of his face a little — you know it's all an act, really," says Rank — interrupting himself when this revelation hits him. "On one level, yes it's real, yes he's really and truly pissed, but on another he's just doing what he thinks he's supposed to do."

"I know what you mean," says Adam, to Rank's surprise.

"So he stands aside to let us back out onto the ice and he's just like, All right boys, you have your marching orders. And he points at the other guys, the captain and the goalie and he's like — you guys gonna kick some ass out there or what? And they're like, yeah, sure, even though it's idiotic. Just a stupid way of trying to save face. He's telling the goalie to just grab the first guy that comes anywhere near him, no matter what he's doing. We're gonna go out there and create mayhem boys, he's saying. We're gonna show them well and truly who they are fucking with tonight. Is everyone clear on that? And all the guys are like, Uh-huh, yeah."

"And what about you?" asks Adam.

"No, I'm just staring back at him because he's been staring at me pretty much this whole time. So finally it's: And what about yourself Mr. Rankin? Still worried you might get a boo-boo or are you ready to kick some ass? And I don't say anything. And all the guys have stood up at this point, and they should be heading out onto the ice but they're waiting to see what I'll do. But I don't say anything, because I'm waiting for that ultimatum again. Because we both know, if he restates the ultimatum, what'll happen. I'm positive he knows. And he doesn't have to do it — he could just say something like, Okay, get out there Rank, and I probably would've gone back out and played. So I'm leaving it in his court, right? I'm just not saying anything — I'm waiting. And I can see him thinking about it for just a split second — realizing that if he decides not to be an asshole, I'll go back out there and play and not crack skulls, and he'll be pissed off and we'll lose, but we're going to lose anyway, so big deal in the grand scheme of things right? But no — his pride gets the better of him and he decides to play the asshole card.

"And there it is: there's the ultimatum. Because, he says, drawing it out, Anyone who's afraid to get their knuckles bloody this evening can leave right now. And I have never been more serious in my life, gentlemen. There's the door."

"And what'd you do?"

"Stood up. Opened my locker. Grabbed my shit. Out the door," says Rank. "Didn't even take off my skates. Of course I had to skulk in the hallway for a while until everybody was back on the ice, because I couldn't go anywhere in my gear. Kinda anticlimactic. Then I went back in and showered and came home."

"That's fantastic," says Adam, holding open the door of the liquor store.

And Rank smiles as he crosses the threshold, contrasting Adam's reaction to the sick groans of his disbelieving teammates. To them it had been an experience like watching that space shuttle explosion on TV a couple years back — seeing it combust before it even left the atmosphere, fall to earth in blazing chunks.

"What did the coach say then?" Adam wants to know.

"He was sort of beyond speech at that point."

"You left him *speechless*," says Adam. "That's great."

Of course, none of it is great — it is catastrophic, which is why Rank is now in the process of gathering a potpourri of liquors into his arms, upon which he will spend an allotment of money that was meant to last him well into the next month. But Rank is throwing caution to the wind on this day, in celebration and acknowledgement of his newfound status of Completely Screwed.

But — it's hilarious. He doesn't feel so bad. It's clear now why his first instinct was to dig up Adam and tell the whole story to him before anybody else. He must've known that only Adam would react this way — only Adam would applaud. As Rank rings up his bottles, it occurs to him that this is the first time in their acquaintance Adam has given any indication of being impressed with Rank. Everyone else is impressed with Rank more or less immediately. But this is what it took to get Adam's approval. Upending the contents of his life into a toilet and flushing two or three times for good measure.

"You know, I'm proud of you," says Adam, once they are back outside and making their way toward the Temple. They both live in residence, but Kyle and Wade's has by this time become their default destination after visiting the liquor store.

Rank is pleased to notice they are passing an enormous snowbank when Adam says this, ploughed to towering proportions along the edges of the drugstore parking lot. He takes the opportunity to shove his friend directly into it.

"You monster — you could've killed me!" complains Adam, emerging from the nerd-shaped hole created in the bank. "I could have cracked my skull and died!" he jokes, shaking snow off his glasses.

15 |

SYLVIE USED TO hate it when Gord and I would sit around Sunday afternoons watching the televangelists on the American stations, but now that she is dead and I am stuck here and we have no other means of entertainment in common, we can do this as much as we want. Unfortunately, the heyday of the televangelist is long over. No more does Jimmy Swaggart perform his loony goose step across the stage to the ecstatic howls of his arena-sized congregation. No more Jim and Tammy Bakker swapping earnest platitudes, directing bald-faced cries for money into the camera.

Sylvie refused to watch with us. She had a superstition of evangelicals. But she'd listen from the kitchen.

"Such crooks!" she'd cry after Jim and Tammy's hundredth extortionate demand of their viewers. "How do they get away with it?"

"Americans will believe anything," Gord explained.

But we watched Jim and Tammy only to feel superior. To see what lengths they'd go to — to what money-grubbing depths they would descend in His name. To laugh as Tammy Faye's mascara turned liquid on her cheeks.

We watched Jimmy Swaggart, however, to feel awe — even though neither of us would ever admit it. We laughed at him the whole time — the shameless way he bellowed and bawled — but secretly, he amazed us. He *believed*, was the thing — you could smell the faith pouring out of his sweat glands. It seethed beneath his skin. Every once in a while Gord and I would forget to laugh and just get caught up. Jimmy would be howling his holy ecstasy into the microphone, his audience would have devolved into a shrieking, blubbering human tide, and Gord and I would be silently riveted. *God. God? God!* The way Jimmy spoke the name made you realize that this was the way it was meant to be spoken — in awe and fear and dumb, sub-literate rapture. You should be *shitting* yourself, Jimmy conveyed, at the idea of the Lord. You should be rolling around on the floor in convulsions — it's only *right*. It is *appropriate*. You should be swallowing your tongue in a seizure. The Lord was awesome and terrible. He was pure power. This was the Dude who smashed the planet between his hands and pushed up mountains, exploding them like zits between His fingertips. This was the Guy who turned the earth into one boiling ocean when He was finally fed up with all our crap. Who begat dinosaurs and the bubonic plague. *This* Guy. *Him.* And what's worse, what's most terrifying of all? Dude *loves* you. He loves you like a psycho girlfriend. Endlessly, obsessively, for no good reason. Dude will stalk you to the ends of the earth.

Sylvie had an instinct — a kind of papist radar that alerted her whenever Gord and I were getting sucked in. "Stop watching!" she'd call from the kitchen if we'd been silent before Jimmy a little too long. "It's a cult! They just want your money."

"Oh, Mother, it's not a cult," Gord would say as he came to. "It's bullshit, sure."

"It's witchcraft," said Sylvie, frowning in the kitchen doorway. It seemed to me Sylvie was seeing witchcraft everywhere in those days. She had recently returned from a Catholic women's retreat where she had been taught to identify as witchcraft pretty much everything that was a) potentially more influential than Catholicism, and/or b) something people enjoyed doing. She'd arrived home vowing to never check her horoscope again, for example, or put her feet up in front of the soaps.

"Don't let him watch that," Sylvie would say to Gord, referring to me, her one and only son.

"Witchcraft. You're just as bad as the Jesus freaks with that kinda talk."

"Look at those people, crying and rolling around. Faithhealing. It's witchcraft."

"There's people who'd say the same about Catholics with their body of Christ and whathaveyou," said Gord, putting his feet up and scratching the side of his face theosophically. "Going to some shrine and throwing away their crutches."

A euphoric roar rose up from the television. "Don't let him watch that," repeated Sylvie.

This may well have been the only time I sided with Gord against Sylvie in our entire parent-child relationship. I didn't understand why Sylvie couldn't just ignore what the priests told her, like every other Catholic outside Vatican City, and live her life. Why wasn't she able to just roll her eyes at the priests like she did with Gord? Hadn't anyone ever explained to her about the implicit contract between church and flock — John Paul II hands down completely untenable directives along the lines of *thou shalt not enjoy harmless kicks* and the rest of us ignore them and go to confession every other week in semi-sincere repentance?

"It's okay, Mom," I told her. "It's just fun to watch him — he's crazy."

"That's how they get you," insisted Sylvie. "They make it *fun*."

And it turned out she was sort of right.

And now, as my father and I sit in front of today's pale Swaggart imitators — the televised Christian-industrial complex never did fully recover from Jimmy's fall from grace — Gord cannot help but be reminded of my own brief period of salvation. I knew it was coming.

"Whatever happened to that girl?" he wants to know.

"What girl?" I say, knowing precisely who he means.

"That young one you brought home a few years back."

I know precisely who he means because I've never brought any girl home but her, that single time, twelve years ago.

Of course Gord also knows the answer to the question he's posed. The two of us are camped out in front of the TV on a Sunday afternoon, a tray of tea and ROC Centre cinnamon pinwheels on the table in front of us, watching a Pentecostal preacher rant and weep. In short, Gord is attempting to direct the conversation down a fairly obvious path.

"We broke up when I left the church," I say.

Gord keeps his eyes on the TV in an attempt to be casual. "How long you stick with that stuff anyway?"

"Couple of years I guess."

"She have sex?"

I frown, parsing the question. "What?"

"They have the virginity balls, I guess, the born-agains. True Love Waits they call it — there was a story on NBC. They wear these bracelets . . . "

"Yeah, yeah, no. No. She wasn't like that."

I can feel my muscles reluctantly tense up. Today I have been mostly too tired to keep my guard up with Gord. Two weeks in his presence — not just in his presence but actually catering to the man — will do that. After about the first week my body just sort of collapsed with the fatigue of maintaining a 24/7 fight-or-flight response. It's too bad — I was actually on the verge of enjoying myself, filling up on cinnamon pinwheels in front of the TV. I was up writing to you pretty much the entire night before and up until this point had been sitting here feeling nicely emptied-out — as close to relaxed as I've been since I arrived.

But now Gord is about to say something crass about my former girlfriend. I just know he is — it's an unfortunate habit he acquired around the time I started Grade 9. Except for Sylvie, and perhaps his own mother, Gord has never quite been able to imagine women in anything other than a pornographic milieu. I would get home from a night out at a dance and Gord would be sitting at the kitchen table waiting for me with his tongue practically hanging out, wanting the details of the wild sexual romps he imagined Kids Today indulged in. Because, he informed me, girls my age were now "loose." Every last one of them — it was a well-known fact, he insisted. "Not like in my day," he said with regret. "Not the girls from Our Lady of the Crossed Legs, like I grew up with. These days, they're all on the pill. Anything goes! Tell me I'm wrong!" And he'd lean forward, ready to drink in all the tawdry details of my teenage exploits.

"It's not true, Gord," I'd say, even though in fact I did okay on those weekends. It wasn't exactly porn star time, but it was sometimes, at the very least, furtive hand-job time. That said, I couldn't imagine a bigger hormonal buzzkill than having to detail my activities to the old man. So I'd just shake my head and tell him I got nowhere. Which he never believed.

"Horseshit! Big, good-looking fella like yourself. The young ones must be shoving their panties at ya in the halls."

And I'd grimace and have to go to bed before my dad cured me of heterosexuality altogether.

So here I am, flopped on the couch in front of the TV on a Sunday afternoon, feeling one muscle group after another bunch up in anticipation of Gord saying something gross about a girl I once liked very much.

But all he says is this. "She was nice, that one."

"Yes, she was nice," I say.

"What was her name again?"

"Kirsten," I reply after a moment.

"Kristen."

"*Kir*sten."

"What kinda name is that?"

"I think it's Dutch."

"I liked her," says Gord. "Wasn't always going on about the

blood of the lamb and all that shit, like you were for a while there."

"No," I agree. "She didn't actually like proselytizing very much. You're supposed to try to save everyone you come into contact with, but she didn't like bothering people. She couldn't bring herself to do it half the time."

It's funny to remember this period of my life — how I was secretly still me under all that piety but refused to admit it. I called the secret me Satan and shut it down whenever I could. But you can only shut the real you down for so long. The real you is not having that bullshit, will only abide being referred to as Satan for a short time before it revolts and shows you what true havoc it can wreak. So the secret me, a.k.a. Satan, would watch my girlfriend weep and pray and inside he would be smiling to himself thinking, she's never going to pull it off. At the bottom of it, she doesn't want to. She doesn't have it in her. She's not a social person — she doesn't even *like* people all that much. But you can't be born-again and not be full of love for your fellow man, not be trying to bring people into the fold. It's all about community and fellowship. If you're a natural introvert — if that's the secret you — you call it Satan, and you kneel and try to pray it away. And you fail.

"You ever in touch with her?" Gord asks after a while.

"No — of course not, Gord. I left the church."

"What, the born-agains can't intermarry?"

And now I get it. Now I understand why Gord has neglected this whole time to remark fondly on Kirsten's cup size or recall the tightness of her jeans. Gord saw Kirsten as a potential Sylvie. Kirsten was pious. She may have been the wrong religion, but she was still the kind of girl you marry.

"No, Gord. You don't marry someone who's going to hell. I leave the church, I'm going to hell. I'm hellbound. The whole idea is you'll be together forever in heaven after Judgement Day. You don't want to look down and see your beloved waving at you from a pit of fire."

"Jesus," remarks Gord, impressed at such zealotry. Both of us have barely taken our eyes off the TV during the entire conversation. A woman in a hot pink power suit is swaying and singing into a microphone with her eyes closed as tears pour down her cheeks. I don't know how she can sing and cry at the same time. Kirsten, I remember, could not even verbalize when she cried. She'd just gasp and flop around like a fish on a pier.

Meanwhile, I lean forward to grab another pinwheel off the tray. Gord grunts, so I chuck one into his lap as well. There are only a couple left, but we're not worried about running out because Father Waugh shows up with his baked goods like clockwork every Monday afternoon.

"Maybe you should look her up," suggests Gord at length. "Maybe she's fallen from grace since then."

"Yeah, I'll do that, Gord."

"I'm serious."

"I wouldn't know where to find her."

But then I remember you, and Kyle at Winners, and realize I know exactly where to find her. At least, I have an idea where to start. But I'm not telling Gord that, obviously.

"What's stopping you?" Gord persists. "What else you got going on these days? You're up on that computer surfing the porn or whathaveyou all hours of the day."

Gord's limited experience has informed him that the

internet is basically a Disneyland of porn, and computers are manufactured for no reason but to offer up a sleazy gateway to this magic kingdom. He therefore thinks the worst of anyone who sits all day at a computer unless they work in a bank or office. And even then, he regards them with a suspicion tinged with envy.

"Hey Gord," I say, pushing myself into a sitting-up position. "I have a life, you know? Outside these four walls. I have a job, which I'm going to have to get back to at the end of this summer. And I told you, I'm working on a project right now, and I've got to get it done before September."

"What project," grunts Gord, sullen. "Whacking off to the naked pictures. And you won't even show your old man."

"Dad! I'm not surfing *porn*. I'm writing a — book."

I let this word dangle in the air for a moment. It never occurred to me to call it that before.

"What kind of book?" Gord asks finally, scowling at the still crying, but no longer singing, woman in pink. She sputters praise into the microphone.

"I guess it's a biography or something. My life story, kinda," I say, learning this as I say it.

Gord continues to scowl silently for quite a few moments. I've picked up the remote to channel surf when he grunts, "Is it about that Croft bastard? That's why you were asking me about him back in June, right?"

"It's about that," I say, putting the remote back down again. "And some other stuff. It kind of starts with that."

Gord picks up his crutch. I think he's about to try to hobble off to the bathroom, and I swing around to stop him because he's always trying to get up without my help and practically re-breaks his ankle every time. But instead of struggling out of his chair, Gord smashes the crutch down on the tray of tea and pinwheels. Sylvie's ceramic teapot — a cheerful lavender elephant whose trunk, for as long as I can remember, has provided the spout — implodes, flooding the tray with tea, which is instantly absorbed by the remaining pinwheels.

"Jesus Christ!" I shout.

"Why the *fuck*," yells Gord. "Can't you forgive yourself for that?"

"What the hell are you doing?" I yell back. You would think after so many years of watching my father fly into rages, he wouldn't be able to surprise me like this, but I am near-speechless.

"A *book*! Now he thinks he's gotta write a book! It's not enough that those bastards put a sixteen-year-old boy away for standing up against some drug-dealing *scum*? It's not enough he lost his own *mother*?"

"Cut it out, Gord," I say. "Calm down."

"Oh and I know exactly what you're gonna say. You're gonna let that little bastard off the hook! Just like you always have. Just like everybody did."

"It's not about Croft, Gord."

"And you're gonna blame yourself. And you're gonna blame me. Well you go ahead and blame me, Gordie. You blame your old man all you want in that book. And don't ever call. And pretend I'm dead if that's how you like it. But I'll be *goddamned* [and here Gord bashes his crutch into the shattered elephant twice to emphasize the compound word] if I'll have you in there all hours of the day writing a *god-damn* [elephant pretty much dust now] plea for forgiveness for something that was not your *god-damn* fault!"

And with the final double crutch bash embellishing Gord's last *god-damn*, the tea tray flips over, spewing elephant ash and pinwheel sludge across the carpet.

Before I can react, he swings his crutch to the floor and wrenches himself to his feet.

"*Gord*," I say, reaching for him.

"Get away from me," says Gord, barely managing to stay upright. I see his face contort with pain, and the merciless way the crutch has jammed itself into his armpit. "Fuck off," he adds, pivoting on his crutch so that now I'm facing his scrawny, shuddering back. "I'm taking a piss."

And off he stumps to the toilet.

16

08/03/09, 12:12 a.m.

THE STORIES WADE brings back from Goldfinger's provide them with hours of entertainment. Now that he no longer works there, but only does business, he has enough distance from the place to comfortably laugh off its squalor. Every once in a while, the boys from the Temple will head down for a drink and be welcomed by Lorna of the bad teeth and bruised upper arms, Ivor of the sweaty face and paranoia. They will sit and listen to Ivor's conspiracy theories for what seems like hours, sometimes. And they will notice how the occasional other adventurous clutches of university kids — slumming like themselves — will glance over at their table in admiration. It is one thing to have a beer or two at Goldfinger's, soaking up its reprobate ambiance, but another thing altogether to actually fraternize with its habitants.

What Rank doesn't mention to his friends is how the first time he walked into Goldfinger's a feeling came over him like: *Ah. Home.* Not *home* in the comforting sense of the word, but in the sense of belonging. Which for Rank had nothing to do with comfort.

More than once he thought he saw Mick Croft in the crowd at Goldfinger's. But it turned out to be simply some version of him. Turned out there were countless versions of Mick Croft in the world, countless Collie Chaissons too, countless human riffs on the various personalities Rank encountered in the Youth Centre. There were versions of Rank's dad, even. Not as many of those maybe, but one or two. Tosspot Gords who had never met Sylvies, lacking impetus to morph into upstanding family men.

Turned out these types existed all over the place — not just on the coast where Rank grew up. You only had to know where to find them.

Where you found them in a university burg such as this was at a place like Goldfinger's.

Ah.

Ivor's title was "manager," but he mostly acted as bouncer when he wasn't running shady errands for the proprietor of Goldfinger's, whose name, unremarkably, was Richard, but who looked and acted so much like a gangster the guys could barely suppress their yuks whenever they noticed him slithering into and out of the back office. The boys from the Temple often accompanied Wade down to Goldfinger's early in the evening when he went to pick up his product from Ivor. At eight or so they were practically the only customers, and the place was cavernous. But this gave them time to take in the operation, to chat with Lorna about the military ex-boyfriend who was stalking her and about whom his superiors at the base, when she complained, refused to do anything. To watch Ivor soak through his Motörhead T-shirt as he explained why AIDS was the result of a U.S. government project intended to kill off drug addicts and inner-city blacks.

"Fags was just a bonus!" Ivor would insist, eyes forever bulging. Ivor took the government's crusade against drug addicts personally, for obvious reasons. "They said to themselves, them scientists, 'Fags, blacks and druggies. We scored a hat trick, boys!'"

Wade only dealt with Ivor. Richard didn't as much as look at Wade, although he sometimes eyed the group of them sitting at their table early in the evening and calling flirtatiously to Lorna.

"The term 'greasy eye'," muttered Kyle one such evening, after they'd all sat holding their breaths while Richard appraised them from his doorway, "has never been more appropriate."

When the office door shut they cracked up en masse.

Wade never got invited into the back office, where the boys surmised there was a polar bear rug with the head still attached, a fireplace, a wet bar, a cache of weapons hidden behind a fake bookcase, at least two meth-addicted prostitutes, and an overflowing safe.

Richard would appear in the doorway, cast a greasy eye, then turn to the bar. "*Lorna*," he would say. And he would, no word of lie, snap his fingers at her.

The guys would hold it in until she too disappeared into the office.

Then: "*Lorna*," Rank would say, snapping his fingers. "I got some new product to try out and I need a pair of tits to snort it offa. Chop, chop."

"*Lorna*," Wade would say, snapping. "Blow job. While we're young."

It was all fun and games at this distance. The boys were of the Temple and every once in a while they came down from the Temple to visit Goldfinger's where they would do their best to make Lorna smile and flash her bad teeth, where they would question Ivor about the great AIDS conspiracy, intent on tripping him up with some inescapable nugget of logic (it never happened — Ivor's fantasy was airtight, and arguing with him about it just made it more so, was like slathering it in sealant) but when they had enough they could return to the Temple, down a final beer, snap their fingers at one another for a few final inebriate chuckles before passing out in their respective chairs.

It was all fun and games until Rank lost his scholarship and Ivor, inevitably one night, observed to Rank he was a "big fuckin guy."

"Yes, I am a big fuckin guy," agreed Rank. It was a point in the evening where all Rank was really capable of, in terms of conversation, was agreeing with what was said to him and repeating it back in a mushy voice.

"I can talk to Rich if you want," said Ivor. "Heard you saying you're looking for work."

Rank didn't believe he had said that, exactly. What he remembered was bragging loudly to the patrons of Goldfinger's about how big his penis was and saying he would display it "for a small donation" to any of the ladies present. The music had been very loud and he didn't think anyone beyond his table — and the women at the next table whose attention he'd been trying to get — had overheard.

"Oh gross," says Adam, a few days later when Rank mentions Ivor's invitation to the guys. "Don't work at Goldfinger's, man. You can work anywhere — don't work there."

"You totally have to do it!" enthuses Kyle. "We'll finally find out what's in the back office. You can free the meth-addicted hookers! You'll be their hero! They can stay with us while they rebuild their lives."

"Work at the campus pub," says Adam. "If you want to work somewhere."

"What's wrong with Goldfinger's?" says Rank.

"Yeah," says Wade, offended on behalf of his associates.

"Adam is a class snob," pronounces Kyle. This is a term he's learned recently from a politically active girlfriend who has spent two summers volunteering in El Salvador. "He thinks you're better than Goldfinger's, Rank."

"Trust me," says Rank, remembering the *Ah* feeling when he first walked through the tavern doors. "I'm not."

Let's press the pause button here. An omnipotent narra-tor can do that sort of thing. Let's just stop and, with the benefit of adult hindsight, compare the opposing influences of Adam and Kyle at this moment — their conflicting ver-sions of obliviousness. Because I think we can agree: just because Adam happened to be right, he wasn't any less oblivious about what Rank was getting into than Kyle. True, Kyle was wholly oblivious. He was enthusiastically oblivious, even. It did not occur to Kyle for a second that Goldfinger's could exist as anything other than a joke — that Goldf-inger's was something other than a kind of vaudeville show, a pageant performed for us college kids. On some level, Kyle really believed that Lorna's bruised upper arms were not in fact bruised upper arms — they were an ironic commentary on bruised upper arms, a parody if you will. Kyle had never experienced the idea of bruised women as anything but a satire of a certain kind of lifestyle, and he couldn't get his head around the fact that when they stepped into Goldfinger's, they were face to face with that world itself. He didn't believe that world existed, really. He believed it was a representation. In Richard's back office there wasn't the rug, the weapons, the wet bar, the safe. Not really. There was nothing — that's what Kyle really believed. It was backstage, and Richard simply stood behind the door, adjusting his airplane collar, combing pomade into his hair, waiting for his cue.

Kyle didn't know he believed this, but that's what he believed. Let's forgive him for it. He was barely twenty.

Now how about Adam?

Adam is a thoughtful guy, we'll admit, but he's operating on instinct here. Of all four buddies, he has always been the least enthusiastic about visiting Goldfinger's, even though he's certainly shown no aversion to the product Wade acquires there. But unlike the rest of them, he doesn't care to hang out in the bar. He'll do it, but he isn't keen. He has no interest whatsoever in catching a glimpse of Lorna's teeth. He'll only listen to Ivor's elaborate claims about how the first instance of AIDS occurred in Manhattan as opposed to Africa, like most people have been duped into believing ("Monkeys! How you gonna catch it from a monkey?"), for so long. Is this because Adam is smarter than the rest of them? Is Adam's radar for danger more finely attuned? No. Adam just finds the place distasteful. Simple as that.

Okay, maybe it's not fair to call him a class snob, as Kyle was so happy to do. If we give Adam the benefit of the doubt — which is only fair — we can explain it like this. Adam, like Kyle, is oblivious to a point, but he is also perceptive. Intuitive. He is a future author, you know. Maybe it's not appropriate to reveal this out of the blue. Maybe it's not fair of your humble narrator to jerk you into the future in this way. But, yes. Adam will go on to write novels, or one novel at least, a novel that critics will describe as "devastatingly perceptive." Let it be said: Adam, even now, barely into his twenties, is a perceptive son of a bitch. He perceives something about Goldfinger's — something Kyle is missing, something Kyle just doesn't have enough personal depth to believe in. But Adam does possess that depth. He intuits that behind the joke of Goldfinger's is the reality of Goldfinger's. He doesn't quite grasp what that reality is, but he feels it. He believes in it. Unlike Kyle, on some level he respects it.

Press play.

"You wanna be a bouncer?" says Adam. "At Goldfinger's? Come on."

"I dunno," says Rank, feeling that Adam is being prissy — feeling insulted, somehow. How dare Adam suppose Rank is too good to work at Goldfinger's? Who does he think he is? "What else am I gonna be?"

"Like, anything," says Adam. "Pack groceries. Work in the library. But you wanna get puked on, you wanna wrestle drunks and crack skulls? Be my guest."

Their eyes connect through Adam's glasses when he says the words: *crack skulls.* But it's the way he said that other thing

— like Rank needed his permission — *be my guest*. This is what decides it.

Yes! Rank does it, ultimately, out of spite.

08/03/09, 11:13 p.m.

Doesn't make a lot of sense, does it? Well, it does, a little, when you consider what took place between them only a few nights before. Something both have up until this point pretended not to remember.

It had been sort of a bad day all around. Rank had been in a bit of a state, brooding on the fleshy *smack* that rang out from Kyle's bedroom the night before and the soft grunt of female pain he is pretty sure he heard in counterpoint. Kyle had been in there with Janine, the championship highland dancer with zero chest to speak of. And before that, Rank had discovered a poem by T.S. Eliot in the library which for some reason jacked his stress about school and his irritation with Kyle to unreasonable levels. And before *that*, earlier that afternoon, Rank had met with the registrar to discuss what exactly his status was now that he was no longer the recipient of a hockey scholarship. The registrar — a minty-smelling lady with a *Dead Poets Society* poster on the wall behind her — gave him to understand that everything would be fine, no worries whatsoever, as long as his tuition was paid in full next semester and he kept his GPA up. Easy! At which point Rank decided not to worry about tuition for the time being and sequester his ass in the library to embark on his new career as an academic achiever.

Whereupon he opened the voluminous anthology of English literature — which all by itself had cost forty fucking dollars — and found himself, once again, a trinket of the gods.

Let us go then, you and I.

Whereupon he closed the voluminous anthology of English literature — which all by itself had cost forty fucking dollars — and decided it was time to get drunk.

If Kyle had been home when Rank arrived, it might have calmed things between them. As it was, however, there was only Adam hanging out by himself, using the empty house to study in, and Rank was grateful. He didn't want to think about Kyle, he told himself. When in fact, for some reason, all he could think about was Kyle. Kyle had swelled like a Macy's balloon in his mind, obliterating the minty registrar, the terrifying moment in the library — everything.

Kyle, and the sounds from Kyle's bedroom. The loud noise Rank knows he heard, followed by the soft noise he is almost sure he heard.

The twisting, seething never-the-same river of his thoughts as he yanked Adam to his feet to accompany him to the liquor store and talked a blue streak in order to distract them both, went something like this: Kyle was *such a dick.* Kyle thought he was God's gift. Kyle paraded himself around campus like he owned it. Sometimes, if you hailed Kyle from a distance, he engaged in an elaborate ritual of greeting. He would point to you, then to his own chest, then to his crotch. Nobody knew precisely what it was supposed to mean, but everybody knew approximately. This pantomime all of a sudden struck Rank, who had once laughed at it, as an asshole thing to do. *Me, my dick. Me, my dick. You? No. Me. My dick.*

Kyle was constantly getting laid. Yearning, sometimes sobbing, women were always showing up at the Temple in the middle of the night. Kyle took a kind of pride in this — you could see it. He'd laugh about it with the boys the following day.

He gave girls shitty nicknames behind their back. A girl they knew named Selina, he'd dubbed *Vaselina*. He was the one who started calling Tina *Tiny* once she put on weight. He'd done Tina long ago, way back in first year. He didn't have to be nice to Tina anymore.

Even though he always was, of course, nice to Tina, to her face. Kyle was nice to everyone to their faces. Inordinately nice. He'd maybe talk to you for five seconds, but in those seconds he'd turn his face to you entirely, let it beam his love and fellowship. Every woman on campus was convinced he found her fascinating.

One morning they actually found one sleeping and shivering, curled up outside the back door. This was late October. Kyle had not even come home that night. Wade had given her a cup of instant Maxwell House, which she blubbered into. When do you expect him back? she asked, once she'd regained the power of speech. I have his scarf. And there's this book he said he wanted to borrow. I brought it for him. She held it up. *Anne of Green Gables.*

You could not feel more sorry for a person, yet they'd all laughed once she was gone and teased Kyle about it forever.

But of course Kyle loved to be teased about this sort of thing.

It seemed to Rank, which he did not say or even give any indication of to Adam as they walked back from the liquor store, that Kyle was a bad influence. It sounded very 1950s, but he remembered laughing at and with Kyle about the girl in the doorway, and it made him angry at himself. He was not that sort of guy. You don't laugh at a woman shivering in a doorway, no matter how deluded she might be.

You don't stop your conversation, look at your friends, then look away, moments after you hear the sound of someone getting smacked coming from your buddy's bedroom in the middle of the night. A smack, followed by a groan. Or grunt. A human sound, in any event, of pain. Almost certainly of pain. That is something else you do not do.

But Kyle Jarvis is, after all, a magic man. This has been established. Kyle somehow worked his mojo and kept them in their seats.

So by the time Kyle gets back to the Temple after his late class, his buddy Rank — who has been making innocuous if feverish conversation with Adam for the last three hours and given no indication of his mood whatsoever — is more or less ready to kill him.

17 |

08/04/09, 4:25 p.m.

BRIEF INTERMISSION HERE to relay what I have to contend with now that Gord's ankle is healing and he knows what I am up to in the back bedroom.

Crutch-bash! A nice solid *whack* that vibrates one entire wall of my room. He has to be standing directly outside my door.

"How's it going in there son?"

"Well you just scared the shit out of me and I spilled my coffee everywhere, but otherwise it's fine, Gord, thanks."

"You need any help?"

"You can put on more coffee if you're up to it."

"No, I mean with your book stupidarse. "

A befuddled pause. This is the first time he's even acknowledged what I'm doing since he learned I wasn't in here compulsively masturbating. Since the revelation that provoked his attack on Sylvie's teapot.

"Help?" I say. "With my book?"

"Like when you called me that time. I got a good memory for details. Thought you might need help."

"No, I — not right now. I'll let you know, Gord, okay?"

"Don't forget to tell them about that nice letter Owen wrote the judge."

I'm sitting there in front of the laptop holding the dirty T-shirt I've been using to sop up the spilled coffee. The stench of it co-mingling with my sweat fills the room. Gord is talking about my release at age sixteen, after Owen wrote a letter to the judge to help get me out of the Youth Centre early so I wouldn't have to start the school year midway through. It was, according to the judge, a "glowing" letter.

"Yeah," I say. "Wow. I forgot about that letter."

"This is why you need me. I still have it somewhere."

"How the hell did *you* get a copy?"

"I asked him for one. You want me to dig it up?"

"No, Gord. That's okay. I gotta get back to this."

Silence. I chuck the T-shirt into the closet, read over where I was, am just about to hit a key, and then:

"Make sure you tell them about your hockey scholarship! And that you went to university."

I have to smile at Gord's "them." Who is *them?* Who does Gord think I'm in here appealing to?

"Yeah. I will," I say. "I'll tell them, Gord."

"Don't sell yourself short, son."

"No — I won't."

"I dug out some more old pictures for ya. You gonna use pictures?"

I drop my poised hands into my lap, collapse backward in my chair.

"I didn't plan on it, no."

"You *should*. I hate a book without pictures. Most people don't even bother if there's no pictures."

"Well —"

"A picture's worth a thousand words, they say."

"It's not really —"

"Might help jar your memory in any case."

"I'll take a look at them when I'm —"

"I'll bring em in. Can I come in?"

He's already in.

18 |

08/04/09, 11:58 p.m.

EVERYONE GETS THAT something is wrong practically the
moment Kyle plunks himself down on the couch with a beer
to join them. Who knows what Adam and Rank have been
talking about up until this point. They've been drinking for
hours, playing Century, downing shots, except Adam's shots
have all been beer whereas Rank has at some point switched
to rye. Rank has mostly been trying to get Adam to talk about
himself for a change. Rank wants to know about Adam's
family, his parents, his sisters. He has learned that Adam has
only sisters, two of them, which Rank finds puzzling considering his friend's ineptitude with women. Rank always
figured guys who had sisters totally got the dirt, entered the
world of sexual gamesmanship packing a distinct advantage.
Rank also learns that Adam's parents are divorced, which,
as a Catholic, he finds very cosmopolitan and a little shocking. Not only divorced, but still friends, says Adam. Not only

still friends but planning on getting together with Adam and his sisters for a big two-parent family Christmas. Rank is impressed. Divorce, he thinks dimly. If only. You get a lock, if you're not Catholic, but at least you get the key as well. They don't make you throw away the key. You're not meant to kneel on the goose until it's dead.

"Goose?" says Adam.

"What?" says Rank.

"Statistics," says Kyle, plunking himself down on the couch beside Adam. "Is a bullshit course. That's what I've decided. Why does a humanities major have to do Statistics?"

This is Kyle in a nutshell. He doesn't wait to be included in a conversation that's already taking place without him. This whole "without Kyle" phenomenon is of no interest whatsoever. He simply sits down, interrupts, and starts a new one with himself comfortably at the centre.

"Are Stats some kind of pre-Law requirement?" asks Adam.

"You know what else is bullshit?" Rank mumbles from his chair. "Hitting women in the face."

The other guys laugh, because Rank is so drunk they assume he's approaching incoherence.

"Yeah," says Kyle. "Umm I'd say that's bullshit, Rank. It's a little beside the point, but it's bullshit, sure. What else do we think is bullshit? Adam, care to contribute?"

But Adam does not care to contribute because, as always, he is quicker on the uptake than Kyle, even with multiple shots of beer inside him. He gives Rank a wary look, sensing the change of atmosphere, as if the temperature in the room just dropped several abrupt and inexplicable degrees.

"Compact discs," says Kyle, turning it into a game. "Digital music — all your albums are obsolete overnight, and you have to rebuild your entire collection. Total marketing scam. What else?"

Rank is just looking at Kyle and Adam is looking at Rank.

"Hot chicks who get fat," continues Kyle around a swig. Adam suddenly leans forward. "You fuck em when they're thin, and then they still expect you to wanna fuck em after they're fat."

"You know what, Kyle?" says Adam carefully.

"Like you're not supposed to notice. Like our friend Tiny," adds Kyle.

"Stand up," says Rank.

"Rank," says Adam.

"What?" says Kyle.

"Stand the fuck up," says Rank, standing up himself.

Kyle takes Rank in for a moment.

"You," he says, "are wasted, my friend."

"*Stand. Up*," says Rank.

Kyle jumps to his feet with a sudden, simian instinct, indignation taking shape on its heels. This is the Temple, after all — love, brotherhood, and so forth. This is *his* Temple, more to the point.

Press pause. Let's compare. Needless to say Kyle, in terms of size, is not a grotesque like Rank. But he's doing okay. He plays rugby. He works out, lifts weights; is broad-shouldered and muscularly compact at an even six feet.

Still, Rank looms over him rather nicely. Or, weaves over him, might be the more honest description. Looms and weaves.

Press play. Adam doesn't exactly jump between them. He doesn't have the physical presence to pull that one off. He stands off to the side exactly like a referee.

"Guys," he says.

"What's your problem, Rank?"

Oh and here it gets embarrassing. It just gets so cliché, so guy. Did Rank respond: *You're my fuckin problem?* Yes he did. Did he give his buddy Kyle a shove by way of punctuation? Maybe a little one.

Kyle just stands there once he has regained his balance like he cannot freaking believe what is happening. This is Kyle Jarvis we're talking about, founder and overseer of the Temple. Magic man. Loved by all. Soon to be elected student union president by a landslide.

"Rank," says Adam. "You said you didn't want to fight."

"I don't remember ever saying that."

"In hockey. You fucking walked out because you didn't want to hurt anyone."

"That was different."

"And now you're drunk and pushing Kyle around."

"Stay out of it Grix he can't fucking hurt me," declares Kyle in a gush of outrage and adrenalin.

But already Rank can feel those same chemicals draining out of him, as if there's a siphon connecting him to Kyle who is currently swelling with them — who can barely keep himself from leaping on Rank in response to the shove.

Rank raises his hands and takes a step back.

"Oh, now you're backing off?" exclaims Kyle, his voice seeming to climb in pitch with every word. "How about you back right the fuck out of here?"

"You are an asshole about women," says Rank.

Kyle is speechless. He flails in disbelief. He too has sisters. His mother is a tenured professor of psychology at McGill and has brought him up to be enlightened. He is one of the only guys on campus who dares, and gets away with, calling himself a feminist. When the student newspaper published a bonehead op-ed criticizing Take Back the Night (the only salient point being: did the night really need reclaiming in a town where the streets got rolled up at 7 p.m.?), Kyle wrote a letter of opposition in support of, as he called them, his "marching sisters."

You can see all this, these innumerable defences and justifications, jostling around behind his eyes as Kyle's mouth moves, trying to figure out which one he should articulate first.

"You hit her," says Rank.

"Who?" shrieks Kyle.

"The highland dancer."

"Janine? I did not fucking hit Janine."

"We all heard it. Adam heard it."

They both look at Adam, who has nothing to say on this front one way or another. Rank has an urge to knock him over. Kyle puts his hands on his hips and leans toward them both.

"We. Were. Having. *Sex*."

"It was a slap."

"You're gonna hear stuff, Rank, if you guys are gonna sit out here like perverts while I'm in there with a girl. It's not always gonna be PG. Sorry."

"It was a slap."

"I'm not gonna do this," says Kyle, suddenly in motion. He strides across the room and grabs his jacket. "I'm not gonna go into detail about this with you." Which Rank finds ironic because under any other circumstances Kyle is happy to go into detail about this very thing. Kyle yanks his bookbag onto one shoulder. His ears glow red as if lit from within.

"You think I hit Janine — if you actually believe that's something I'm capable of — I tell you what. Find her and ask her. Check her for bruises."

Rank feels himself losing ground at the same time, and at approximately the same rate, as his anger drains. He hates it. He wants to keep this feeling of being in the right — of being on the verge of righting wrong through sheer force and intimidation. He can't believe that Kyle is leaving, instead of staying and insisting that Rank leave instead, which would make sense. Through his amber fog, it penetrates Rank's brain that Kyle can barely speak. That Kyle will either cry or punch him at any moment, and doesn't know which, and is desperate to leave before they all can find out.

Rank doesn't want to let it go — he's not satisfied. Nothing about the confrontation has turned out the way he wanted. He's about to say something else to Kyle — something that will probably tear them up as friends for good — but Kyle's gone.

So he says it to Adam. "He treats them like whores."

"No he doesn't," says Adam.

"I can't believe you're defending him."

"Because he doesn't," says Adam, flopping back down onto the couch, exhausted from the tension. "He's just a hound, Rank. He's a player."

"He's a fucking sleaze."

"He's a *bit* of a sleaze," Adam allows. "But he's a good guy."

Rank has ducked into the kitchen and returns in the process of cracking another forty of rye, the sight of which makes Adam groan.

"It's like," says Rank, trying to focus his brain. "During the whole Take Back the Night thing last month. There was that poster around campus about virgins and whores. How guys think women can only be one or the other. Remember that?"

Adam's head is cradled against the top of the couch, and his eyes are closed. The dim light of the room hits his Adam's apple in such a way as to make it seem enormous. *Adam's apple*, thinks Rank. *Ha ha.* Adam looks as if he's offering up his throat.

"It's just because you're Catholic," he mutters, eyes still closed.

"What? What's just because I'm Catholic?"

"The virgin/whore complex. The two Marys. Of course that's going to resonate all over the place with you."

"But it's true, right?" insists Rank. "That's what he thinks. My old man's like that too. Virgins or whores, one or the other. Except Kyle thinks they're all whores. It's not a virgin/whore complex it's a . . . whore/whore complex."

Rank is suddenly pleased with himself. If he can't right Kyle's wrong with sheer force, he will do it with the persuasive force of his mind, which seems to be throwing up gems of remarkable lucidity all of a sudden. And he will apply that force to Adam, who for some reason has fallen neatly — in Rank's perception — into the role of judge to whom Rank must appeal.

"That's not what he thinks, Rank."

Rank cannot believe he isn't getting through to Adam. This argument is gold. The moment he spoke it, the truth of it seemed to sing in the air around his head as if someone had struck a tuning fork.

"It *is* what he thinks!"

"It's what *you* think."

Rank has poured them each a fresh shot of rye. Now he puts the bottle down and gapes.

"Adam," he says. "Will you stop lying there with your eyes closed like you're hoping someone comes along and cuts your throat?"

Adam's eyes pop open and he raises his head.

"I do not," says Rank, "have a whore/whore complex."

"You have the opposite," says Adam. And has the audacity to lean back and close his eyes again, resuming the exact same posture on the couch, his Adam's apple towering.

19 |

I HAVE NOT thought about that moment in a very long time. I've thought about that night a lot, yes — what happened later. Because that's the night I told you what I told you as the morning light began to finger its way inside the room, and you put your hand against my head, and after yanking the story from myself like it was a barbed, endless tapeworm I leaned into your palm and, finally, rested. Yes, I've been remembering that night off and on ever since I read your book. And I remembered the fight with Kyle the second I locked eyes with him at Winners. But I'd forgotten all about that in-between time, the calming-down period, your enormous Adam's apple glowing in the shadows, how you told me I had the opposite of a whore/whore complex and next thing I knew I just wanted to open up my throat and down all the alcohol in the world. If I'd thought I could absorb it through my pores, I would have filled up Wade and Kyle's bathtub and climbed in for a soak.

I didn't remember it until I started writing about it.

But what's weird is that I'm sitting here not sure it really happened.

It *seems* to me it must have. I remember how Kyle's ears glowed red. I remember the shove, and how he teetered, his face completely blank with disbelief. I'm sure I remember that. But I don't remember *remembering* it as I wrote it, if that makes sense. I just wrote it — it spilled out of my head like it had been lodged somewhere in there, way in the back. It didn't feel like a memory. It just felt like something that was happening in my head as I was typing.

I want to confess that the longer I do this, the stranger it gets. Half the time, I'm not sure I'm even getting the story right anymore — yet the whole idea of this little project, you'll recall, was to ferret out the truth. To take your bullshit version of me, flush it like the steaming turd of half-truths and oversights it was, and replace it with the glorious, terrible, complex, astonishing truth of Reality. I still feel like that's what I'm doing sometimes. I still find it all pretty complex and terrible. But recently I've been getting lost in it. I forget what I'm about. For example, I know it doesn't seem like it, but I spent about a half-hour trying to figure out the best way to describe your Adam's apple, how it seemed to glow, enormous in the shadows.

I'm worried that this is how the lying starts. You, for example. Maybe you started off writing your book with the noblest of intentions, wanting to get across something real and significant. Maybe you were holding something in your mind — some sacred value or belief — and thinking to yourself: This, *this* is what I want most to articulate. *This* is the most important thing. *This* is what the world must know. Maybe you actually meant to do good.

And what if this same thing happened to you? All of a sudden, you get sidelined. All of a sudden, you need to get the Adam's apple exactly right — something totally stupid and insignificant and beside the point. You let it distract you from your noble purpose. Suddenly people in the story are doing and saying things you never meant for them to do or say — and you're letting it happen, because it's fun. It's interesting. And maybe it's simpler, too. Maybe it's just simpler to say, "This bad guy, this innate criminal? His mom died, by the way. Yeah, so, poor old Danger Man, he's had it pretty rough. Anyway, next chapter . . ." Rather than to sit down with the actual person whose actual life events you're cherry-picking and take the time to peel back his flesh and deal with all the ugly underneath. I get it, Adam. You couldn't bring yourself to break the skin. Who wants to face the mess below the surface, right?

And so you make stuff up. You get sucked into your own bullshit. You want to see where it's all going. You let the story take you instead of you taking it in the direction you originally mapped out. The direction that your noble purpose dictates.

The noble purpose gets lost. And maybe, before you know it, you're screwing over everyone who has ever meant anything to you, without even realizing it. You are changing them, interpreting them, riffing on them, without even asking their permission. Your family, your girlfriends. A bunch of guys you used to be tight with. From any objective standpoint, you're producing what amounts to a kind of slander.

But you can't even see that anymore. You're too busy trying to get the Adam's apple right.

The question is, are you, therefore, an asshole?

Or, let's put it in metaphysical terms. Is this a sin?

I put it this way because that's the feeling it gives me — a feeling like I've sinned. Not the kind of sin I would have reproached myself for in my evangelical days — when, let's face it, anything that didn't serve the greater glory of God was suspect. I'm talking about a deeper, guiltier, Catholic kind of sin. A sort of trespassing.

The truth is, I was as every bit as surprised today, writing about you telling me I had a virgin/virgin complex, as I was when you said it, *if* you said it, twenty years ago.

In fact I think I'm maybe more surprised today.

And now I'm going to do something I never thought I'd do: cite my father's parish priest, Father Augustine Waugh, as an authority.

"God love you," remarked Father Waugh one Monday as I tore the cling-wrap from the Chinet plate of peanut-butter squares he'd set down, "you can't leave the church, son."

It was my first week back in town, and the Father had asked if I would be helping my poor disabled dad get to mass next Sunday. Rather than point out that even at his most sprightly Gord rarely made a point of rushing out to Sunday service, I took a bit of pleasure in painting myself as an apostate.

"Haven't been to mass since high school," I told him. Since my mother's death, to be precise. "I'm afraid I left the church behind me long ago, Father."

And that's when he hit me with his Hotel California-ism.

"God love you," he tittered. "You can't leave the church, son."

Son. I almost laughed down into his four-years-younger-than-me face.

"Yeah, well," I said around a square. They were pure sugar, festooned with multicoloured marshmallows, and the sight of them, accompanied by my immediate desire to inhale the plateful, made me feel about seven years old. I turned to put the kettle on before Gord could yell at me to get the Father his tea. "It would seem you can."

"Nope!" countered Waugh, settling down at the kitchen table. I glanced over at his placid face. Here, too, was faith. Not the raucous, shudder-and-squeal faith of Jimmy Swaggart, but the complacent, immovable dogma of the Catholic Church. Even via Waugh's mild, dumpling-esque visage, two thousand years of papist absolutism projected itself.

"Yep!" I said, getting irritated only five minutes after Waugh's arrival — a new record.

"No sir, you can't. You were baptized, I assume. Took first communion. Confirmed. You're with us for life."

Something occurred to me then. "Hey Gord," I yelled into the next room. "Was I baptized?"

"Of course you were baptized, what in Christ is wrong with you?"

"I'm just wondering because of being adopted."

"You came into the world surrounded by nuns, sonny boy."

I frowned. No getting around it; no escape clause. Father Waugh just sat there turning the Chinet plate of squares, smiling liplessly.

And the lousy thing is, he was right. You don't just decide not to be a Catholic anymore — it doesn't work that way.

Catholicism is something that soaks into your skin like vitamin D. You can't just stand there as the sun pours down upon you, saying, *None for me, thanks*. It seeps into your world view; it dictates how you act and everything you think you know. I see this now — thanks to writing down what you told me twenty years ago.

So you were right too, Adam — you're up there in the Paunchy Sages Club with Father Augustine Waugh. I see it. I admit it. I had then, and have now, a virgin/virgin complex when it comes to women. I had, and have it, because I am, and will always be, a Catholic boy at heart.

There is only one person I can really blame for this.

I can't believe I tried to depict her to you as a glimmer of light. I'm embarrassed about that now. It's so obvious. I am very nearly forty years old, have not been inside a Catholic church since 1986, and I'm still as conditioned as a Pavlovian dog. Holy Mary Mother of God. Why didn't I just put her in virginal robes, describe her ascending into heaven, hands over heart, eyes in the clouds?

All my girlfriends too, every last one. I see it now. You don't know about them, because I figured I was being a hero. Protecting them from you, and making myself sound like some kind of holy celibate along the lines of Father Waugh in the process, when needless to say — you knew me in school — I'm not. But also, needless to say, Gord wasn't the only one who considered Kirsten — a girl so inflated by the holy spirit her feet barely ever touched the ground — marriage material. And it's no accident, I realize now, that she was the only one I ever felt that way about with total certainty.

I can't remember much about the girls we knew in university. I remember the night we both had sex with whatsherface, and I remember being angry, and I remember you brushing it off with Kyle's "Paris in the twenties" line although I could tell you were a bit freaked out yourself. But I can't remember which one of you, exactly, I was pissed at. I can't remember what I might have done or said or how I might have acted with women to lead you to the conclusion that I had a virgin/ virgin complex.

Truth be told, and I never would have admitted this that night, I considered myself at least as much of a player as Kyle. But that's not how you saw me, clearly. Somehow, before I'd even spoken one word to you about Sylvie, you called it. You had me pegged.

Even now, speaking to me from twenty years ago, you have me pegged.

Which makes no sense when I think about your book. How is it you could have me so nailed down, and still get everything so wrong?

08/05/09, 2:31 p.m.

Okay so, fuck it. Here's Kirsten.

Kirsten had her own curse word, tailor-made to be inoffensive to the Lord, which nonetheless she used only in moments of supreme agitation. It always made me howl, reminding me of my mother's little-used cache of Franco-Ontarian curse words, which in English translation sounded ridiculous, not to mention utterly inoffensive: *chalice of the tabernacle!*

Kirsten's preference was to take four innocuous "curses" and smash them together as if to enhance their execratory power. *Darnfriggerbumheck!*

She had dark hair, enormous blue eyes, and long bangs that stopped precisely at her eyelashes. She cut them herself about once a month, and I don't know how she got them so straight and perfect every time. They were fantastic bangs, childish and sophisticated all at once. They were also a little naughty, a little Bettie Page. No other girl in the church wore bangs like that, except for some of the younger ones, who wore them with braids. When Kirsten wore them with braids, I'd go a bit nuts.

Kirsten grew up in the prairies and had been saved since the age of eleven. Her parents divorced due to her mother's whirlwind, torrid infidelity with Jesus Christ. Kirsten's father was a town engineer who worked practically all the time, and her mother had been lonely, and initiates of my former church, in the small prairie town of Lacombe, Alberta, happened to be practising their guileless, welcoming faith nearby. They held a revival meeting one weekend, featuring a charismatic preacher from the States, and because it was a small town, even the irreligious were interested in coming out to see the fundies roll around. It seemed so deep-south, so voodoo. It was rumoured there might be laying on of hands and speaking in tongues.

People like Kirsten's mother didn't show up just to gawk, I am convinced. They might have told themselves that — I know, because I told myself that too, when I got around to sticking my own head in the proverbial tent: *Should be good for a laugh.* The truth is, you go because you want to be persuaded. After all, who can deny the power of God? Who *really* wants to? The truly religious are never entirely dismissive of other religions, no matter how whacked out — a believer's a believer. Just look at Gord and me, camped out in front of Swaggart every Sunday. Even Sylvie sometimes used to speculate about her "past lives," an idea that was in no way Catholic. But she had heard it on TV or read about it somewhere and she just liked the thought of it, of karma: returning to earth for a do-over. It sounded fair to her.

I think now that anyone who believes in God, even a little, can't help but yearn toward the evangelicals. Let's face it, theirs is the church we really want. We want to be swept up. We want to sob and roll around on the ground. We want to feel the Holy Spirit as a real living force and we want it to swoop down and kick us in the ass. We want it to heal our souls. We want it to remove every last doubt we ever entertained about our randomness as creatures of the earth. We want certainty. We want to see the face of Jesus in a grilled cheese sandwich. We want to throw away our crutches. We want Satan, and we want him to want us too, so we can always be at war, because war makes our daily bullshit righteous and significant. We want to hear the voices — the ones that tell us what to do, and tell us how we're loved. We want to be as little children and believe.

And Kirsten *was* a little child, so it was easy. She took one look at her mother's rapturous face, and she believed. She was on board.

The town engineer sued for custody on the basis that his wife was actively engaged in sculpting religious fanatics of Kirsten and her brother. The family court of small-town

Alberta, however, didn't see excessive piety as a problem worth separating mother and child over. So Kirsten's mother won custody and promptly headed east, away from the unholy "contaminating influence" of this godforsaken engineer, a man about whom Kirsten hardly ever spoke, of whom she had no pictures, and who I thought about a lot for some reason. I imagined him abandoned on the prairie, squatting like Job, befuddled in the dust.

20

08/06/09, 11:15 p.m.

APPARENTLY, it can all be traced back to Nixon. In the guise of conducting cancer research, the Nixon administration was actually neck-deep in biowarfare. Genetic engineering of viruses became a common practice under Tricky Dick. Sure, says Ivor, everyone these days thinks Nixon was a "total cock." And he was, no doubt about it. But Watergate? Tapping a few telephone wires?

"Tip a the iceberg," says Ivor, wiping his forever-running nose on his forever-crusted sleeve. "How about unleashing a plague that sweeps across the planet, killing millions? How many people did Hitler kill? Well, how many people did *Nixon* kill — how many people did the *American government* kill, Rank?"

"I don't know," says Rank, wishing some redneck Goldfinger's patron would attempt to kick in the teeth of another so that he and Ivor would have something to do besides shoot the preposterous shit. "I don't have those numbers on me, man."

"More than six million, I'll tell you that."

"Yeah," says Rank, scanning the thin early-evening crowd of Goldfinger's die hards. Rank so far only works weekends, when the bar is at capacity and the crowd at its most unruly. He gets to split bullshit tips with the coat check girl at the end of every evening, and so far it sucks. He needs to get more hours if this is going to be worthwhile, and he needs to tend bar, because already he can see behind the bar is where the real tips happen. Lorna's tip jar is insane. Ivor has explained, however, that Rank must "work his way up" in the Goldfinger's hierarchy before Richard will even consider putting him behind the bar. Which is a blatant lie, because Rank recalls how Wade was stuffed back there with Lorna only a few days after inquiring. But Rank is in no position to complain.

After a handful of nights on the job, Rank has already broken up a fair number of fights with relative ease. Non-events for the most part, men too drunk to even see, except for the occasion when a couple of girls called him outside to stop some tosspot from trampling an elderly cab driver. Rank arrived in the parking lot just as the old guy was being slammed against his car. His false teeth went flying, startling everybody. The drunk loosened his grip on the cabbie's jacket, eyes following the airborne teeth in confusion, and it was just the opening Rank needed to pull him off the driver and shove him into the street.

"Don't come back," said Rank, feeling mildly heroic.

"Pardon?" said the drunk, looking around him and patting his jacket. "I need a taxi."

"You don't have to bother with what's going on in the parking lot," Ivor told him when he was back inside. "Once they're off the premises they can shoot each other in the face for all that Richard gives a care."

Rank was about to say, The parking lot is still our property, like he used to recite to the punks at Icy Dream. *And we want you off it.* Instead he shrugged. Goldfinger's was clearly a different sort of establishment.

"What makes me sick," says Ivor now, "is how the government covers it up. One administration after another. When Ford pardoned him for Watergate, what most people don't realize is that it was a blanket pardon. It pardoned him for anything and everything the law might eventually dig up on him — and those bastards knew it. They are all complicit, Rank. Bush, Reagan — all the way back to Carter, even."

Complicit, thinks Rank. Ivor recited the word with care, as if he had practised it. It makes Rank feel depressed. He doesn't know if he can continue having this conversation night after night. Back when he and the boys would accompany Wade to Goldfinger's for a quick beer, it was entertaining to have red-faced Ivor plunk himself down and sweatily expound upon his alternate reality. A few minutes of this was one thing, but it was sort of disturbing to realize that Ivor never changed the subject. His mind was stuck on this particular track, and there was no getting him off it.

Rank had tried one time.

"You got a family, Ivor?"

"No, I. Well, yes, I have a family, I have a mother and father and sisters and that shit. I had them, growing up. Now I work for Rich."

"But you don't —"

"When you are poor, Rank, when you spend your life hanging out on the wrong side of the tracks like yours truly, you don't get many breaks in life."

"Yeah, but I'm just wondering —" Rank didn't want to push the matter, but he could already see, after only a handful of conversations, where Ivor was leading this one — the same place as ever.

"And you are lucky, if you are someone like me, who has had the kind of life I've had, if you can work for a man like Richard. You know, maybe I got nothing but I don't drink and I haven't used needles for over a decade and I hold down a job and I'm good at it. And when the government of the most powerful nation on the planet is dead set on the extermination of people like you — because you're poor, and you're *scummy*, and you've got a single possession charge on your record — it doesn't make existence any easier."

Rank was a little dumbstruck by the word *scummy*. He had never heard a man describe himself as *scummy* before.

"You're not scummy, man," said Rank, after a moment of singing along with "Heartache Tonight."

"It doesn't matter how I see myself," explained Ivor, scanning the crowd. "The point is, the most powerful people in the world think I'm expendable. They have me in their crosshairs, is the point. I have to live with that. Every day."

"Jesus," said Rank.

"Yes, it's very stressful," said Ivor.

Things were different with the guys from the Temple. They were still friends, of course. Rank still went there all the time, often after his weekend shift, to wind down with a beer. And they came sometimes to visit him at Goldfinger's. But it was different. When they left, usually around eleven at night, which was practically like Sunday morning at Goldfinger's in terms of the comparative drunken mayhem to come, Rank had to stay and see the mayhem through. Rank was stuck there, and the novelty of Goldfinger's — which for him had never been that novel in the first place — had worn off entirely. Even Richard in his back office no longer seemed like much of a mystery. He'd spoken to Rank a couple of times since Rank's hiring (if you could call getting a few twenties shoved at you at the end of every shift being "hired") and both times hadn't met his eye. It occurred to Rank that Richard simply didn't have a lot of social skills — that Richard hung out in his office night and day, cracking the door only to grunt at Ivor or snap his fingers at Lorna, because he was, in fact, shy.

And Rank had seen inside the office. It held filing cabinets mostly, had fluorescent overhead lighting. In its glare, Rank had noticed Richard's acne scars.

He had apologized to Kyle immediately and unreservedly. Rank spent the whole day following their dust-up sleeping off the rye, groaning his way through dreams of satyrs in hockey skates, and by the time he got up it was suppertime. Supper was out of the question, needless to say. He headed to the Temple. There, he found Kyle practising guitar tabs with Wade, and didn't beat around the bush. Kyle stood, grave and respectful as the apology unfurled. He allowed Rank to stand there for only a single sadistic moment of silence before responding with predictable Jarvis magnanimity, even going so far as to insist that they hug.

Rank (stepping back): That's okay, man — as long as we're good.

Kyle (stepping forward): Let me love you, my brother. Then we'll be good.

So they hugged, Rank rolling eyes, Kyle closing his in reverence of their ongoing brotherhood, Wade clapping and grinning like a chimp in the corner.

It was a slap, thought Rank.

Where was Adam that day? Rank didn't see Adam for a while after that, not for about a week, not until the evening at Goldfinger's when Ivor pronounced Rank a "big fuckin guy" and a job offer was on the table. Rank had been disappointed not to find Adam at the Temple when he arrived to apologize to Kyle. Adam had witnessed the altercation, it seemed right that he should witness the reconciliation too. The result was that it didn't feel complete to Rank.

Strange to say that even though he knew he was right with Kyle after that, things never quite felt right again with Adam.

———

It makes Rank feel panicky to remember what he'd confessed in those seasick morning hours. He trudges the campus wondering what Adam must think of him. It makes him resentful. He imagines a slow crust of loathing hardening over Adam's perceptions now that he knows what he knows about Rank. Adam had barely said anything that night. He couldn't find the words, he'd been so revolted. He'd put his hand on Rank's forehead, but what did that mean? At the time, Rank didn't care. He took it kindly. He took it kindly because he needed kindness. But, in retrospect, a hand on the head at such a moment could mean anything. It could mean: *Jesus, stop*. It could mean: *Ew*.

Or maybe he had genuinely meant it kindly at the time. But even if he did, he's had time to think about it since. He's had time to turn it over in his mind and draw conclusions, adjust his view.

They didn't talk about it afterwards, though — not at all. There'd been little opportunity. Adam isn't around as much, and when he is, the other guys are there. So Rank and Adam never get a moment to discuss it much further. They only communicate obliquely, via the usual drunken and/or hungover half-assed, semi-serious bull sessions with Kyle and Wade.

You want to crack skulls? said Adam during one such conversation. *Be my guest*. Their eyes connected through his glasses. It felt like the first time they'd looked directly at each other in a while.

Fuck you, thought Rank.

It makes no sense but they are angry at each other now.

08/07/09, 3:16 p.m.

"Ivor has a gun," says Wade.

It's a Thursday night, and the three have been sitting around eating pizza waiting for Wade to return home with what Kyle likes to call "party favours" from Goldfinger's. The Temple will be hosting a Christmas bash tomorrow night and Kyle has put in a special order for tabs of acid in the shape of

Santa hats and a few bags of mushrooms. Kyle is all about the psychotropics of late. He has been listening to a lot of Grateful Dead and even getting into tie-dye. Rank himself would sooner self-flagellate than succumb to hippiedom, but he understands the draw of the psychedelic. One of the best times he's ever had with Kyle was in the early fall when they ate mushrooms and lay down on their jackets by the duck pond to look at stars. The mushrooms were taking forever to kick in, and they began to worry they'd swallowed duds, so they focused their minds on the stars and tried to talk themselves into a trip. A few minutes later, the stars began to pour from the sky. Kyle and Rank held their heads and moaned at each other in disbelief. It turned out there'd been a meteor shower that night, but the magic of the moment was all it took to switch the mushrooms on and for the rest of the evening they saw beauty everywhere they went.

Kyle has been playing inept guitar as they wait on Wade's return. Rank has been amusing himself by rifling through Wade's record collection and putting aside a few of what he knows to be Wade's favourite albums. Rank plans on trying to convince him that each contains a secret, coded pro-homosexuality message. Ever since the revelation about Freddie Mercury and Queen, Wade has been in a homophobic tailspin and doesn't know what to believe about his favourite bands anymore. For the *coup de grâce*, Rank is preparing a bombshell having to do with a sordid songwriting ritual regularly indulged in by Robert Plant and Jimmy Page.

He's rehearsing some of what he's going to say out loud, to Adam, in the hope of making Adam laugh. He keeps trying and Adam is laughing, it seems to him, politely.

And otherwise what is Adam doing? Adam is just sitting there on the couch doing nothing, staring into space like a malnourished, bespectacled Buddha. He has stayed for pizza, but turned down an offer of beer. He says he has to get back to residence and write a paper on the idea that Satan is the hero of *Paradise Lost*. Neither Rank nor Kyle has read it, so neither can weigh in.

Wade comes in and tells them Ivor has a gun.

"Ivor doesn't have a gun," says Rank instinctively. "Get serious."

"He has it! He showed it to me."

"What kind of gun?" says Kyle, putting the guitar aside.

Adam leans forward at the same time and says, "What were the circumstances?" Rank wants to laugh at this lawyerly question. Wade doesn't even hear it.

"I don't *know* what kind of gun. I've never seen a gun except on TV."

"Was it, like, a handgun?"

"Yes! It was a handgun."

"Was it in a holster?"

This was Kyle. These were very Kyle questions. Kyle was excited by the news. He wanted Wade to paint a picture for him. Kyle didn't get it.

Of course, it's probably fair to say that none of them did just yet. Maybe only Wade, a little, because he had actually seen the thing — seen Ivor with it — and his eyes still hadn't quite returned to their sockets. It was pretty clear he had run the entire way up the hill from Goldfinger's to the Temple. Now, he whipped off his jacket but didn't sit down.

"What were the circumstances," repeats Adam.

"What?" says Wade, panting a bit.

"He's asking," says Kyle, "Why was he showing you a gun? Did he, like, threaten you?"

"No," says Wade, diving onto the couch beside Adam. "I think he was kind of showing off. I think Richard must've just given it to him or something."

"Was it in a holster?" repeated Kyle.

"No! He had it in his jacket frigging pocket like it was, like it was one of his *mittens* or something."

They all start laughing at the word *mittens*. The idea that someone like Ivor would have mittens in his pockets.

"There's no way Richard would give Ivor a gun," says Rank. But as he says it, Rank realizes he knows no such thing. What he meant, when he said the word *Richard*, was "anyone with any sense." You would have to be crazy to give a paranoiac cokehead a gun. But Rank knows nothing about Richard, really, except that he owns Goldfinger's, sells drugs from his morose, fluorescent-lit office, and suffered raging acne is his youth.

They're all silent for a moment. Wade leans over to retrieve the remaining slice of pizza sitting lonely in its box. Solid, miniscule beads of grease have formed across the pepperoni.

"Should we call the cops?" says Adam, and everyone laughs again.

21

08/08/09, 10:36 p.m.

FOR A FUNDAMENTALIST, Kirsten was remarkably easygoing
about sex. I saw a lot of this sort of thing after I joined the
church. The most faithful people on earth are able to be so
abstemious and upright all the time because when it comes to
what they really want, they manage to convince themselves
that Jesus wouldn't mind. I might mention that Kirsten had
been married before — at eighteen years of age. "Too young,"
she said. "But we were dying for sex." By the time they reached
twenty-two, the dude in question was on his knees snivelling
and praying every night until one such evening he raised his
leaking face to hers and confessed, "I am so afraid that this is
all there is." Long story short, when Kirsten and I met up the
husband was long gone but the pleasures of the flesh were by
no means unknown to her. And she wanted more of them. But
she had learned an important lesson about tethering yourself
to another person for life just to get a little action.

I made the mistake of joking to her about Swaggart once. In fact, I compared her — in her okay-ness with illicit sex — to Swaggart. This was a mistake.

"Jimmy Swaggart was a *liar*," she barked at me. I had only made her bark in the nicest way thus far in our relationship, so was taken aback. "Jim Bakker was a *liar*. Nobody cared that they were sex fiends — everyone's a sex fiend. That's what it is to be human, to be fallen creatures, it's who we are. The sin is the lie, Rank. The hypocrisy. I don't lie to myself about who I am and I don't lie to you and I don't lie to Jesus. I *can't* lie to Jesus. The difference between me and Jimmy Swaggart is that I'm not so arrogant I'd even try."

It was lying that was the ultimate trespass to Kirsten, so no surprise that it was lying that broke us up. I wasn't cheating on her, if that's the conclusion you just leaped to. Eventually she just came to see how I was faking my way through faith — characteristically, she saw it before I did. Don't get me wrong, I had no desire to leave the church. I loved the church. I just didn't buy what they were peddling anymore. I still loved it; I *wanted* to buy it. I would have done anything to buy it. But I didn't. Every time I closed my eyes and tried to feel the Holy Spirit bearing down on me like a typhoon of love and terror, all I'd get was Zeus, aiming drunken thunderbolts, sticking it to nymphs. Other times, I'd picture Kirsten's father in the dust. She saw through me, somehow. And she would be damned, literally, if she was going to let me keep pretending otherwise.

"My husband," she said to me at one point very close to the end, "was less of a coward than you."

So that was it with me and Kirsten.

But that's not really enough for you, is it, Adam? I'm starting to figure out how it works. I remember the details in
your book that freaked me out the most — it was the minor
stuff, those dead-on grace notes that no one else would
notice. Some tiny, throwaway item like how every once in
a while I used to shave between my eyebrows — I'd inevitably use dirty razors and give myself a rash. There it was,
between your pages. I cannot believe you wrote about my
eyebrow rash, Adam. Or the time during one of our parties
when Wade walked into the kitchen with an enormous zit
on his chin, moving me to quip: "Who's your friend?" It got,
needless to say, a huge laugh, from Wade as much as anyone,
and I never gave it a second thought. Until I read the same
line, delivered in almost precisely the same context, meant
to demonstrate to your readers what a mean-spirited asshole
the guy could be.

It's like seeing pictures of yourself that you didn't even
know anyone was taking — candid camera — a whole album
of worst-moment closed-circuit stills. There you are taking
a dump. There you are saying precisely the wrong thing at
the wrong time. There you are stepping on someone's puppy
while scratching your crotch.

So I get you now, is what I'm saying. I understand how you
do it — I know what kind of food someone like you is scroun-
ging for when it comes to the character of Kirsten.

1) She used to like to eat in the bathtub. She'd bring apples
in there with her. Milkshakes. Bowls of cereal. Even stuff that
could get soggy — I think she liked the challenge of it. Toast
and peanut butter; crackers. Once I heard the long plop of a
banana fallen from its peel.

2) Sometimes, when she was overcome by the holy spirit, I recognized the expression on her face from her orgasms.

3) She would also, sometimes, when we were sitting together chastely side by side at worship, wrap her entire hand around my index finger. We'd just sit like that. My finger totally encased in the warmth and darkness of her palm.

(This was probably the sexiest time of my life.

"I'm not faking *this*," I remember pleading with her near the end of everything. "You and I."

"You and I are not what matters," she said. Her eyes had begun to puddle up. Her chin was vibrating as if at any moment it would lose cohesion. I could see that pretty soon the conversation would be over; she would begin to flop and gasp. "You and I are *nothing*."

This was where we parted company, theologically speaking.)

4) Whenever someone asked her to do something social, go shopping or out to dinner — even people she liked — it made her feel flustered for the rest of the day.

5) I think she liked prayer meetings so much because they let her have the experience of community without having to actually interact with anyone. Together we'd all raise our hands in the air, palms forward — as if to say, "Over here, Lord" or "Stop it, Lord" — together we'd cry, together we'd call on Jesus. It was powerful stuff. But you never had to have a conversation. You could just roll your eyes back into your head and let the spirit overtake you.

6) She liked it when I cooked, even though the only thing I ever did was fry steak and boil pasta.

7) Whenever she spoke with her mother on the phone, she always ended up screaming, and a lot of the time, after

she hung up, didn't seem aware that she had done this. She seemed refreshed, edified. Like she had just come back from a run or stepped out of the shower.

8) There was a radio program on the oldies station called *The Disco Diner*, which played old Wolfman Jack broadcasts. She listened to it every Saturday while she did the dishes. She liked the Bee Gees, because she could sing in the exact same key as them. She actually referred to this habit as one of her "vices."

Kirsten didn't realize that Wolfman Jack had died back in '95 and the broadcasts were repeats. When I mentioned this one Saturday during the program, she stopped what she was doing, turned from the sink, and I thought she would come after me with the meat fork she'd been cleaning.

08/09/09, 12:46 a.m.

So it only seems fair to confess that immediately after writing that last email to you I went looking for Kirsten on Facebook and there she was, flanked by children and still — miracle of miracles — sporting her Bettie Page bangs. I clicked on her name and started writing her a message without even thinking about it. I wrote: Kirsten, I can't believe this is happening. I can't believe that I am thinking about you one minute, writing about you — dreaming you — embellishing you as if you are a figment of my imagination or a creature out of mythology, and then the next minute typing your name into a website that delivers a photo of you twelve years later and an actual portal of contact. You are out there, apparently, and you are real. I am writing for confirmation. Are you out there? Are you real? My whole summer has been one long surreal dream, and now you are a part of it.

Then I deleted that. I wrote: Dear Kirsten. Hey! Don't be fooled by my internet moniker, it's me, Rank. How are you? Wow. Are those your kids in the photo? Nice job, if so. Nice cat, also. Looks like you are living a very rich life these days, which is great to see. I just discovered Facebook recently and thought I'd look you up. And there you are. It's kind of amazing.

all best,

GR

Of course what I wanted to write was, I am so glad you haven't let your bangs grow out. Are you still into Jesus? Do you still go in for the occasional light spanking pre-intercourse?

And she wrote back.

Dear Rankenstein,

I see you have no friends. Way to go! It is so nice to hear from you Rank. Yes, I have kids and a cat. Am living the dream. Thank you for telling me exactly nothing about how you are or what you're doing these days. Wonder why you're friendless. Get with the program!

xo,

K

Adam, it is Kirsten. It is so, precisely Kirsten, ascending from the muck of my afflicted dreams and persecuted memory, clean as a whistle, entirely herself despite my guilty distortions — hands over heart, rolling her eyes sarcastically toward heaven.

So now I have a friend on Facebook. And now I have to write to her and tell her how I am and what I'm doing.

Then I went a bit nuts thinking to myself if Kirsten is on Facebook, everyone must be on there. All the ghosts and figments — all people I thought I had successfully kept to myself for so long. I typed in, for example, *T.S. Eliot*, and do you know what? He was there. He has a fan page — a couple of them. It sounds stupid, I mean I realize he's famous and everything, but it freaked me out. I typed in *Ivor Breese* — no Ivor. I mean, lots of Ivors, obviously — there's lots of everyone on Facebook — but no Ivor from Goldfinger's. I typed in Richard's name and a bunch of Richards came up with the same last name, but none of them were the greasy, pit-faced son of a bitch in question.

I typed in *Sylvie Rankin*. Five names came up but, I was relieved to see, all of them called themselves Sylvia, which my mother never had.

Then I tried *Sylvie Le Blanc*. There were five again, all of them younger than me, except for one I couldn't see, one who hadn't posted a photo. There was only an empty square containing an androgynous silhouette where her photo should have been. I was tempted to drop that one a line.

To keep myself from doing this, I typed *Kyle,* and Kyle was there, in hiking clothes and sunglasses with a mountain lake the colour of a swimming pool behind him, just as he'd been the first time he contacted me after I'd signed up to find you. And Wade was still there too, perched atop a Harley-Davidson motorcycle, giving the photographer a hearty thumbs-up, sporting an ill-advised Vandyke beard to camouflage his double chin — everything but a banner proclaiming I CAN'T STAND THAT I AM MIDDLE-AGED fluttering in the background.

But where was Adam? There weren't even any versions of Adam, with his weird last name, hanging around Facebook. No teenage Adams giving gang signs in Etobicoke, no corporate Adams with their bland headshots looking to network with fellow drones. No photo-less, phantom Adams, even — and no fan page touting the Respected Author, I might point out. No vestiges. Adam was hiding out. Adam remained solidly nowhere.

I typed in *Mick Croft*. Three Micks, two Michaels, none of them the man whose head I crushed. Then it occurred to me if I wanted to get a glimpse of Croft, all I'd really have to do was head downtown and ask around.

Or I could just call Owen Findlay.

Or I could type in *Colin Chaisson,* which I did, and there he was — same photo as when he sent me his ignored friend request — fat and old and freckled like a dissolute leprechaun, smilingly giving me the finger from his living room couch. No mountain lake backdrop for Collie, surprise surprise. And where is Collie keeping himself these days, you might ask? Only five miles up the coast it would seem.

I am starting to view my past in a different way these days. Strange to say under the circumstances, but I think now that I used to see my past as a book — a story with a beginning, middle, and end, all of which I knew by heart, and therefore had no reason to even crack the spine. But now I'm starting to see it as something more like a frontier — a landscape I have spent my life cultivating, fortifying against the random elements. But the landscape is alive, is what I'm realizing — is a thing unto itself — and if you're brave enough to ever leave your house you start to see this. In fact, the landscape consists of multiple things, multiple wills that shift and change and occasionally assert themselves in force. None of this, you eventually understand, belongs to you — not a rock or flower a broken branch — no matter how you work it, no matter how much scrub you clear. The ground could decide to open up beneath your feet. The sky could decide to open up above your head.

The world is independent. It moves, and moves on, with or without you.

Everything, that is, except that which you make die. What you've killed is yours, forever — a trophy picked off from the landscape and hung up on your wall.

So you can greet one another each day.

I write: Dear Kirsten, looking around me I see to my chagrin that it is 2009 and I am nearly forty years of age and staying with my father in the house where I grew up while he recovers from having fallen off the roof like an idiot. You remember Gord, right? He kept trying not to say "goddamn" when you visited that time, which for Gord is like trying to keep from drawing breath. He liked you: would you believe he said that to me just the other day, out of the blue? And you liked him, I seem to recall.

Since we last spoke, which was an unbelievably long time ago, I managed to graduate. Now I teach Grade 7 and 8 History and coach soccer. I stayed in Hamilton after getting my teacher's licence, believe it or not. I bought a house a few years ago just off Barton, so you'll be disappointed to learn that I no longer have that elegant bachelor suite that overlooked the slag heaps.

Hobbies: trying not to kill Gord, eating church-bake-sale confections in front of the TV, getting fat, not preparing for the upcoming school year, cyber-stalking a friend from twenty years ago.

You?

22 |

08/10/09, 4:32 p.m.

WHAT DID YOU THINK?

I figured I'd just let that information sit with you for a bit.
I thought you might even be moved to drop me a line now
that you know I'm not a drug kingpin or mob enforcer. Guess
not, though. I guess you're thinking even history teachers can
be psychopaths. It's always the quiet ones, after all. But I just
want to point out, maybe you don't quite realize it, but you've
got something on me now. You know what I do and where I
live. You even know my neighbourhood — you could send
the police to my door if you thought you had cause. Okay?
You can relax, is what I'm saying.

Throw me a bone, is what I'm saying.

But really: what *did* you think? What did you think happened to me after I disappeared that night? Into what corrupt
underground existence did you suppose I, with my "innate
criminality" and everything, allowed myself to sink? It might

surprise you to know that, as much of a mystery as I left in my wake, I was hauling as big a mystery into the darkness with me. That is to say — you guys didn't know where the hell I went, but neither did I ever find out what the hell happened after I took off. Was there a police investigation? Did cops swarm the Temple like locusts? Did you guys get questioned? What happened to Richard? I imagined it all — I imagined a rectangular army of Constable Hamms kicking in the Temple door and throwing you guys to the ground. Poor Adam, glasses flying across the room. Kyle, pleading in handcuffs, fearful of his future political career. I imagined Richard — who in reality that same army had to have been watching pretty closely all along — being dragged in for questioning, his whole half-assed druggie empire crumbling in one raw night, Goldfinger's with a padlock and sign: *Closed until further notice.* My imagination went wild with the possibilities, scrolling through every worst-case outcome there could ever be for you, my friends, my sullied associates.

Needless to say, I wasn't all that keen to learn the real truth, but all and all it constitutes a pretty big question mark to be carrying on your back for the rest of your life, wouldn't you agree?

Speaking of cops at the door — I expected it myself any day, every day. I travelled all over the country doing the kind of work that didn't require identification. Shit work, that is. It was easier to do in those days, there were a lot more of the kind of construction projects that happily paid under the table and didn't ask questions. I even — this is kind of embarrassing — worked under an assumed name for a while, which I was not very good at. I'd tell the boss my name was Joe Smith, and

then after a day or so of ignoring everybody calling me Joe,
I'd explain that my nickname was actually Rank, and would
they please call me Rank.

Which is to say, if the police had been looking for me, I
may as well have been walking around waving a *Come and
get me* sign.

And I kind of think I was. I dropped the assumed name
pretty quickly, got tired of working shit jobs for crooks like
Richard, so pretty soon I was signing my own name to EI
forms and rental agreements.

Come and get me! Come and get me!

But as a nominal precaution, I kept moving around. This
helped me to feel safe but had the additional merit of pre-
venting me from making any more close friends. I would not
be making that mistake again. I read the papers from out east.
I watched those true crime shows about unsolved murders
and criminals at large. Nothing about Goldfinger's, nothing
about a goon of a bouncer with a juvenile record wanted for
questioning. Nothing about anybody dying under suspicious
circumstances.

Nothing about it, ever. Not a trace, not a word. Can you
blame me that I stopped believing in it, Adam? That the
world seemed so eager to accommodate my most urgent,
desperate wish? There was nothing I could do about Croft,
or Sylvie. That stuff was on the record, written in stone — it
had repercussions is what I'm saying — sent ripples throughout the cosmos. I had been on my way to living a certain
kind of life and those two incidents blew me completely off
course; made me the man I am today, whatever kind of man
that is.

But what happened at Goldfinger's — it was like it hadn't happened. Which is exactly what I wanted it to be like but couldn't dare hope. For a long time, I didn't let myself believe that such could be the outcome. It was uncanny. It was miraculous.

It could only be, I realized, the gods, at work, again.

Which meant I couldn't trust it. So I moved again, for what had to be the fifteenth time, this time to Ontario, knowing as I crossed the country in what had to be the fifteenth U-Haul that somewhere up there a bunch of jerkwads in togas were drawing their heads together, snickering down from their gilded cloud and just waiting for the moment I relaxed. Waiting, maybe, for me to find a wife, have a couple of kids, buy a house, set up a hammock in the yard, kick back, breathe the fragrant summer air and tell myself: I'm happy.

And only then, of course: the knock on the door.

So I didn't. I refused. I was not going to even make the attempt to gear my life toward such an obvious outcome. I would show those bastards — I would be lonely. I would live in basement apartments. I would be broke. I would render myself repugnant to the opposite sex. I would drink! I'd be one of those smelly, belching assholes that hangs around in bars that cater to smelly, belching assholes, with other smelly, belching assholes because like attracts like. I would grow crude from my proximity to such company. I would end up slavering at any woman who crossed my transom, because I saw so little of women as a rule, thereby rendering me as repulsive in terms of personality as I was physically. Oh yes, I was winning this war. I was deteriorating nicely. I was one in a long line of mythic heroes acting in defiance of the gods.

When one day she appeared to me. The fat lady.

I felt a distinctive shift in the booth where I'd been sitting playing bar trivia with my usual drunken rabidity. A heavy shift. A protesting sort of creak. I looked up and I thought: Oh no. *Mon doux*, as Sylvie used to say.

Well hello, she said to me.

This, I thought. This is the kind of woman you attract now, hotshot. This is where you find yourself at twenty-six.

I just saw you sitting here all hunched over, she explained, and I thought you looked a little abject.

Ab-ject, she pronounced it. It was jaunty, her pronunciation; it made me smile. *Abject* was not the kind of word I heard a lot of lately, even as an obsessive player of bar trivia — my single intellectual pursuit.

She smiled back. Her lipstick was bright pink — a shade you might see on twelve-year-old girls in plastic barrettes. Her hair, like her lipstick, was frosted, sprouting stiffly from her scalp in aggressively gelled tufts.

She liked gold, the fat lady. Her wrists jangled with bangles. Her earlobes drooped with hoops.

She was wearing a velour purple hoodie, the luxuriant and authoritative colour of Monsignor's robes.

The overall effect was queenlike.

I'm Beth, said the fat lady.

I'm Rank, I said.

You are most certainly *not* rank, replied Beth, folding her hands (the mere act of which caused an unholy racket of jangling bracelets). I'm sitting right across from you. I should know.

A thin, frosted smile.

She was quick, the fat lady. Most people just frowned and asked me to repeat myself a couple of times when I told them my name.

Ha ha, I said, to show Beth my appreciation.

Now tell me your name, insisted Beth.

I'm Rank, Beth. Rank is my name.

Rank is *not* your name.

She lowered her head as if peering at me over glasses. But she wasn't wearing glasses. I shrugged: *What do you want? It's my name.* But she continued to peer like a schoolmarm waiting for a math lesson to sink in. This was an very odd mode of flirtation.

Gordon, I said at last.

Her face expanded — beyond even its current expanse — in a beatific smile. She spread her hands and her bracelets clattered, sliding down her thick wrists.

Now, see? said Beth. That's a perfectly lovely name.

Oh what the hell, I thought, draining my rye. Let's have sex with the middle-aged fat lady. It'll be freaky. It'll be one for the books.

Can I buy you a drink? I asked, waving with both hands at the bartender.

No thank you Gordon, but that's very kind. I didn't come here to drink. I came here to talk to you.

Beth. I'm flattered. You don't even know me.

I knew you, Gordon, the moment I saw you.

Over at the dartboard, a couple of my buddies had been entranced by the situation from the moment Beth sat down. Every once in a while I'd shift my eyes and see them performing various obscene pantomimes for my benefit, but now that the glee had worn off, they shot me more serious, questioning looks to ask if I needed a little conversational interference run. I leaned back and gave them a *no-worries* wave.

Beth glanced over her hulking shoulder when I did.

Your friends?

My friends, yeah. Best there are.

You know, Gordon, I've only caught a glimpse of them, but I find I really doubt that.

I'd been waving my arms at the bartender again when she said this. Now I stopped and dropped my hands onto the table.

You know, this isn't a criticism or anything, Beth, but you're very direct.

(Of course it wasn't so much that she was so direct, but that she was so accurate. They were by no means a quality pair of friends. They were sort of thick and irritating. One of them ingested nothing but creatine shakes three times a day in an eternal obsession with "getting big," and clearly hung out with me in the surreal hope of somehow absorbing a percentage of my body mass. The other one had a creepy obsession with World War II, collected Nazi memorabilia, and when drunk would expound upon how what we needed in this country was another "good war" against a nation of "truly evil fuckers" like the Nazis so that we wouldn't have to feel bad about completely annihilating them. "All this country needs," he would explain, "is someone to annihilate. We've never just totally annihilated anyone before, and that's why we get no respect on the world stage.")

Beth multiplied her chins in a serene, fleshy nod.

Yes I am, Gordon, she agreed. I am direct. That's something

I've learned to be over the years. There's not much point wasting time being anything else.

For all the cacophony of her appearance, Beth possessed a low, pleasant voice and the sort of gaze I can only describe as quiet. Not quiet in the sense of being subdued, but more along the lines of intensity and concentration.

It's sort of fascinating, I admitted.

Has no one ever spoken to you like this before, Gordon?

Not really. And no one ever calls me Gordon, either, so that's weird too.

Are you finding our conversation a bit weird?

Yeah, quite weird actually, considering I don't even know you.

But like I said. I knew *you* the moment I saw you.

At that moment, I stopped smiling. I didn't like the idea of that so much. Beth's smile dropped as if to mirror mine, but not quite in mockery.

Did I say something to upset you, Gordon?

My rye arrived and I wrapped my hands around it.

I'd like to know what you meant by that, exactly, I said.

Exactly? All right. I meant that I came in here tonight looking for someone who needed my help. Someone who was lost. And that was you.

That was me, I repeated. I'm the lost guy.

You are the lost guy, Gordon.

Beth's smile began to resurface, but mine stayed buried.

What makes you say that? I said, looking around the bar in affront. Me? I was the lost guy? What about the guy in his seventies with hair past his shoulders who could be counted upon at least once a night to shamble across the room and start humping the jukebox? What about Lingering Steve, who stank so badly that even when he was hustled outside after only a moment in the foyer, his olfactory signature would hang in the air long into the evening? What about my loser friends, for that matter — Creatine and the Annihilator? I was no lost guy. *They* were the lost guys, rambling and hovering around the bar, ricocheting against the VLTs, the tables and waitresses like sluggish pinballs. Whereas I, unlike maybe 90 percent of the soused clientele, was young and fit and winning. And I kept my mind sharp playing bar trivia, was in fact the reigning tournament champion, and had taken home my share of cash prizes.

I was, if anything in company such as this, a prince among men.

Why do you say that about me? I demanded again of Beth.

The fat lady leaned forward, bracelets clattering as they collapsed across the tabletop.

Gordon, she said, you *wear* it. It's *on* you, from top to bottom. Like a rash. Or should I say: it's wearing you.

Hey Beth? I said after a moment of just sitting and looking rudely around the bar, as if bored — as if to look at anyone but her. My buddies, I noticed, had long since lost interest in our unlikely tête-à-tête and returned to their game of darts. It's been nice talking to you, I said.

You didn't mind talking to me, replied Beth, when you thought I was just some silly old fat lady. But now that you intuit who I am, you find yourself uneasy.

It's just that you're getting a little personal.

Yes, agreed Beth. This is getting very personal, isn't it?

We sat and looked at each other. I noticed then that I was

feeling cold. I was feeling cold, but I was sweating. I had been about to bark, *What?* at Beth with her implacable gaze. But the moment that basic, belligerent question arrived in my mind, it was answered by a voice I hadn't heard in years.

You *know* what, replied Constable Hamm. We both know what.

Gordon, said Beth. You're perspiring, I see.

And then I was doing more than perspiring. I was crying. I was crying in the booth with the fat lady.

Oh, Gordon, she said. Dear.

Who are you? I said.

Her braceleted arms shot forward and noisily she took my hands in hers, which I allowed. Her palms gave off heat as if fresh-baked.

I'm an envoy, Gordon.

Of God, I said a moment later.

Our whole booth was shaking. Even with Beth's weight to steady it.

He's here now, Gordon. You think he hasn't been but he's always been. All you had to do was lift your gaze.

She closed her eyes and leaned her full mass toward my hands, the knuckles of which she kissed.

Part Three

23

RANK NO LONGER answered the phone in his dorm — even when called to it, even when it was specifically for him — because whenever he came to the phone it was always his father, and ever since he quit the hockey team, Rank and his father did not so much converse as rail at each other. And because the phone was in the hallway (Rank's school was old-school — it would be another year until phones were installed in individual student rooms), his dorm-mates would often congregate when these calls took place in the shared anticipation of seeing Rank completely lose his shit.

It wasn't that Gordon Sr. was angry at Rank for having quit the hockey team. Indeed, he lauded his son's decision. He thought it was the finest thing a boy could do.

"Just like your old man!" he'd crowed at the news. "Don't take any crap from no one! You march to your own drummer, Gordie, and that's a fine thing."

"Yeah well I probably marched myself right out of an education if I can't pay tuition next semester."

Rank had said this a) because it was true but, also b) out of a vague, fantastical hope that somewhere Gord might have a cache of money tucked aside for precisely such a rainy day as this.

Gord, however, had other ideas altogether. "Forget it, son," he said. "And come on home."

"Come on home?" repeated Rank. "That's what you want me to do?"

"Come on home, live rent-free for a year, earn some money. You can always go back to school after a year."

"What am I gonna do?" demanded Rank. "You want me to work at SeaFare?" He could feel his grip on the receiver tightening and gaining heat in anticipation of what his father was about to suggest.

"Come on back to the ID! I'll make you assistant manager. Nice pay bump for ya. Shelly's not working out anyhow, keeps having to run home to her consumptive crew a kids. One of them down with the flu every other day."

Even when Rank returned home for summer vacation after his first year, he hadn't gone back to the Dream. He opted for a government grant requiring him to mow the lawns of every municipal building in town and, when all the lawns were mowed, walk up one side of the highway and down the other picking garbage.

"You want me to work at the Icy Dream. This is what you're suggesting to me."

"Oh for the love of Jesus, Gordie, it's a job. What's past is past. When are you gonna put all that shit behind you?"

"All that shit," repeated Rank.

"Well I can see where this is going. I can see there's no talking to you about this, as per usual."

At which point Rank began to shout into the phone, and the phone immediately began to shout back. Which sounds bad, but actually was good, because it attracted enough of a crowd that when Rank commenced his eventual attempt to wrestle the unit from the wall, enough guys were present to dissuade him.

End-of-term exams were looming in the distance, radiating menace, like Dracula's castle. Rank had no idea what to do about them. Why write exams when he was about to get kicked out on his ass? Wouldn't it just be adding insult to injury? Then there was the question of Christmas break. Gord had kept asking, between bellows, sometimes via bellows, when the Jesus was Rank coming home for Christmas? Ivor, meanwhile, wanted to know if Rank would be around throughout the holidays. Lorna, he said, had kids and was looking to take some time off from behind the bar. If he could come a couple of extra nights over the next two weeks, she would train him, and he'd get a percentage of her tips.

Having embarrassed himself in the dorm, Rank started pinballing in earnest back and forth between the Temple and Goldfinger's. Often at two in the morning after his shift he'd head straight to the unlaundered squalor of Wade and Kyle's crash pad as opposed to going home. Still, undergrads gossiped worse than bridge-playing grannies, and word spread fast about what he tried to do to the payphone. Wade made fun of him for it.

"What the fuck, dude? Were you drunk or something?"

"No," said Rank. "Just my dad on the other end. Pissing me off."

"I can't picture it," said Wade. "You get crazy, but you don't usually get violent and shit."

Kyle and Adam traded a look then that was not as surreptitious as they probably thought.

Rank's emotional spectrum during this time ranged from panic to anger to drunkenness to boredom (and yes, drunkenness can be described as an emotion in this instance, considering Rank experienced so much of it). First, there would be the panic of the realization that he was expected to write exams and papers by end of term. Then, the anger quick on the heels of this, knowing there was no point to worrying about his academic obligations since he would not be able to continue next semester anyway, swiftly followed by the drunkenness he used to alleviate both these sensations. The emotion of drunkenness, if Rank had to write a paper or an exam on it, say, could be described thusly: it was similar to relief. It was similar to the sensation of kicking back in front of the TV on a Sunday morning and letting Jimmy Swaggart experience fear of the Lord on your behalf. Watching some other guy rail and blubber and holler in love and terror as you stay calm and feel somehow edified by proxy. It was similar to relaxation — in the same way TV is similar to real life. It allowed you to delude yourself, to pretend and then forget that you're pretending.

And then boredom. It turned out that if you spent a lot of time inducing the emotion of drunkenness, the emotion of boredom would station itself just around the corner, just on the other side of sobriety, and wait — not to pounce, exactly, boredom wasn't an emotion that *pounced* — but to sort of collapse against you and hang on, like a girl at a party late at night.

Speaking of girls and speaking of parties and speaking of boredom: the night before had been Kyle and Wade's Christmas hoedown (on campus, holiday parties inevitably took place in early December, since everyone but Rank would be heading home to their loving, gingerbread-scented nuclear families by mid-month). So Rank had experienced the party and the sloshed, clinging girl the night before, and presently, standing aching in the Temple's annihilated kitchen as he squints at the inside of the fridge, Rank is experiencing the boredom full-throttle. He is a bit worried about the boredom. The boredom has taken on a kind of desperate intensity of late. The boredom seems to be the only thing waiting for him these days on the other side of drunkenness. Even panic and anger have retreated as if in deference to boredom's sudden domination. Rank has never experienced a boredom like this before. This boredom has edge; it has teeth. It's like waking up every morning to discover the colour has been sucked out of the world, and finding this insufferable, but also not having the energy to do anything about it except sink angrily down into the grey.

Rank is the only person awake, and ready to die of thirst. His insides throb and shudder. He's wishing there were some way of removing his entire nervous system and sending it out to be laundered. The kitchen's overhead bulb hangs bare and unspeakably bright. It is nine o'clock in the morning. It is disgusting to be awake at nine o'clock in his state. Nobody should be awake at nine o'clock in the morning under such harsh light. He feels exposed, like a beetle. He has stuck his head under the kitchen sink tap and drunk a few gallons of water because there are no clean glasses anywhere in sight. Now he is looking for orange juice. He feels he could use a little vitamin C. There is a carton in the back, which he grabs and drinks from, discovering too late that it is mostly vodka.

Adam enters the kitchen to find Rank retching gallons of water into the sink. He announces himself with a sigh.

"Hey man," glugs Rank, glancing up.

"Paris," says Adam, "in the twenties."

Rank holds on to either side of the sink and wonders, not for the first time, what the quip is actually supposed to mean and why they all find it so uproarious. Paris, okay. Land of elegance and cheese and, well, the French. *Real* French, not Canadian French, not hip-wader, goose-squashing chalice-of-the-tabernacle French. French *perfume* French. French *bakery* French.

But what about the twenties? Rank knows nothing about the twenties. He racks his brain, hunched over the sink. Flappers. Titless women dancing the Charleston. He doesn't fucking know. What is he doing here, with guys like these? He is a hulking, heaving hick. He is good at drinking, and lifting his fellow man over his head, and throwing up. Also, destroying lives. That's why the not-so-good Lord placed him on this earth.

Rank straightens up. "Sorry." He wipes his mouth on his bare arm. "That was gross."

"No problem," says Adam. "I just came to get some juice."

"Don't drink the OJ," advises Rank. "It's all vodka."

Rank runs the tap to clean out the sink, grateful he had hardly eaten anything the night before.

"No chunks," he remarks to Adam.

"Nice," says Adam, pulling an unopened two-litre bottle of cola from the fridge.

Rank watches as Adam slowly unscrews the cap, careful not to let the carbonation out in one fizzy spew. All at once he remembers they had sex with the same person the night before, a girl named, Rank is pretty sure, Jennifer. Yes, because she said she spelled it with a *V*. He remembers now. He remembers laughing and saying, You do not. No one spells Jennifer with a *V*. And she pretending to be miffed, going, That's how it's spelled. You made it up, insisted Rank. You made up this lame spelling because you wanted to be different and special. It's on my fucking driver's licence, replied Jennifer. You want me to show you? And then Rank recalls being a little chastened. He has met people with names like Zoltan and Paco and Mercedes since arriving at school and it didn't take long for him to realize that his knee-jerk urge to laugh in these people's faces when they introduced themselves did not make him the most sophisticated of men.

Anyway: Jenniver drank like a linebacker. She had been all about the Jell-O shots the night before — had an endless repertoire of shooter-based games she insisted everyone play. Afterwards, Rank had found himself fiddling with her wiry black hair as they slouched side by side on the couch, twirling the curls around his finger, to which they clung as if having been cultivated for this very purpose. And then he and Jenniver stumbled into the crash pad and had the kind of sex that Rank can barely remember. He mostly recollects trying to stuff both her boobs in his mouth and a distant gratitude that he'd been able to get it up. And Jenniver leaving to pee every five minutes. And then taking a long time to come back — in fact not coming back. At which point it was about four in the morning. And Rank, on the verge of passing out, suddenly brought around by an image of Jenniver lying on her back in the bathroom bubbling vomit through her nose. So getting up to check on her. And Wade passed out on the couch. But noises coming from Wade's room. And, after finding the bathroom empty, going to see what those noises were.

So. That had been awkward.

Now Rank and Adam blink and wince and each other at 9 a.m. in the Temple's kitchen with its screaming white overhead bulb practically bleaching them out of existence. Rank is only wearing shorts and Adam only jeans and they face each other bare-chested like boxers.

"Hey," says Rank, leaning against the counter. "I get that we're being ironic when we say it — I understand that much. But what was supposed to be so great about Paris in the twenties anyway? I mean in all seriousness."

Adam takes a swig of cola, but the carbonation invades his nasal passages so he ends up having to spit it into the unfortunate sink.

"Ernest Hemingway," he says once he has recovered.

"Hemingway? That's it?"

"Well, you know. Paris. Everything Paris implies."

"Yeah, yeah. But what about the whole twenties thing. Why is that a big deal?"

Adam takes another, more careful swig, thinking about it. Eventually he shrugs.

"You don't know?" says Rank, delighted.

"Why am I supposed to know?" says Adam.

"Because," says Rank. "What's the point of having guys like you around if you don't know that stuff?"

Adam blinks at him a few more times, trying to gauge the atmosphere. It's tricky, because everything is slightly off. The fact that it is nine o'clock in the morning, the fact of the operating-room light bulb overhead, the fact that they are half naked and semi-crippled by hangovers, the fact that they just had sex with the same girl, the fact that they haven't had a real conversation since the night Rank delivered to Adam his grotesque confession.

And, needless to say, Rank has insulted and ridden his friend Adam many times in the past — for being pretentious, for being fruity, for being slight of frame, for wearing glasses, for being overly interested in school, for doing poorly with the opposite sex. Yes, this is standard operating procedure as far as their friendship goes. But there was something in Rank's tone just now — *what's the point of guys like you?* — that can't be ignored. Rank is ready to deny it, but he knows it was there as well as Adam does. He'd been helpless to suppress it. It had something to do with this new, improved version of boredom he's been experiencing of late: the edgy boredom, the boredom that doesn't seem to give a fuck one way or another.

"I'm going back to bed," says Adam, turning.

"Hey!" calls Rank. "Is Jennifer with a *V* still around? You finished with her yet?"

It has to be understood at this point that Adam is entirely the kind of guy who would wave a dismissive hand — or finger — at this comment and continue on his way back to bed. Adam is a high-road kind of guy, the object of macho taunts and tough-guy jeers his entire life, one can only assume.

So this kind of remark could typically be counted upon to bounce right off him for the most part.

Rank, therefore, is surprised to see him stop and turn back.

"If you're pissed off at me," says Adam, "just say it."

"What," says Rank. "Share and share alike, right?"

"She was completely shitfaced, Rank."

"So you figured the gentlemanly thing to do . . ."

"A woman climbs on top of me in the middle of the night . . ."

"Look I'm saying I don't care, man."

"Okay, fine. And I'm just saying, if you do care I'd like you to tell me now because I'd rather not end up getting shoved across the room like Kyle some night when you're pissed out of your head."

Rank pauses to grind his molars. He's at a loss for words due to the fact that his feelings are hurt. He certainly didn't *shove* Kyle *across the room.* He knocked him off balance a little, yes. It was barely a shove at all — it was more of a *gesture* of aggression than an *act.* He is hurt that Adam could consider it otherwise, that Adam would portray his friend Rank as some kind of ongoing threat.

"Maybe," says Adam, after Rank's silence has entrenched itself, "you shouldn't hang around here so much right now, you know? It's almost exam time and you seem kind of out of control."

"I have nowhere to go," says Rank.

"Like . . . go to the library or something."

Rank snorts so that Adam won't notice him shudder. There's no way to explain that the library is haunted for him now. T.S. Eliot lies in wait, crouched somewhere behind the stacks with a protective arm around his unfortunate friend Croft — still weeping angelically, still bleeding from the ears.

"Go to bed Adam," says Rank. "Nighty-night."

Instead, Adam takes a step closer and scratches his scalp in such a way to make his already preposterous bed-head even more mad-scientist than what he walked into the kitchen with. He now looks like he's stepped out of a wind tunnel.

"Are you going home for Christmas?" Adam wants to know.

"No. I'm gonna work through the holidays. Make some money."

Which, he knows, is stupid. What he'll make over December working at Goldfinger's, even behind the bar, won't be anywhere near enough to cover his tuition next semester. At the same time, he doesn't have to worry about his living expenses, because he'd paid for the room and meal plan in advance at the beginning of the year. So really, there is no compelling reason whatsoever to work at Goldfinger's over Christmas break. And there is no good reason for him to stay on campus by himself in an empty dormitory over the holidays, with no one but a handful of lonely, language-challenged Chinese and Middle Eastern students to keep him company. He is just being perverse, and Adam seems to know it.

"You could come to my house," suggests Adam, and Rank realizes something all of a sudden. The reason Adam looks so squinty and diminished this morning. It's not the hangover, or the glaring overhead bulb.

He's not wearing his glasses, is the thing.

"My folks are only three hours away," he adds. "I'm taking off next week."

Right, Adam's "folks." Adam's folks, who are divorced, but still "friends." *Still* friends. As if marriage and friendship are of the horse and carriage variety. Imagine having "folks," and they are "friends": chucking each other on the shoulder, getting together in bars to shoot some pool. Rank opens up the fridge again and sticks his head inside because he doesn't want Adam to see his face. He has to appear to be looking for something, so he grabs the bottle of cola.

"I told you, man," he says, staring down at the cap as he unscrews it. "I gotta work."

Some of us, he wants to say, don't have "folks" waiting three hours away. Some of us have tiny screaming lunatics instead, waiting in an empty house with a fresh-dead mother congesting every room.

Adam is just standing there and even though Rank has already unscrewed the cap he finds he is too sickened to drink. He stares at the bottle in his hands. If Adam doesn't go back to bed soon, Rank is going to say something shitty to him. He can feel it creeping up his esophagus and filling his throat with sour. Something irrevocable.

24 |

ONE BIG BLOWOUT before they go their separate ways for Christmas, Kyle insists. Just the four of them. The Boys. The Overseers of the Temple. Kyle is a young man of acute social instinct. It could be that he senses the group has lost cohesion in the past month or so, that the guys are not as tight as they once felt themselves to be. Kyle is not having it. Kyle, at heart, is a sentimental goof — having grown up with only sisters, he calls the other three his "brothers," insists they'll be together unto death. Sometimes he rhapsodizes about the four of them going into business together, assigns them each a role based on their diverse talents and gifts (Rank always seems to end up doing the heavy lifting in these scenarios), making scads of money, buying real estate, Italian suits, vacationing with their supermodel girlfriends and, eventually, once wild oats have been thoroughly sown, their children — so beautiful and gifted you'd think they'd been engineered in labs.

Maybe Kyle intuits that these rhapsodies of his — these fantastic future scenarios he's mapped out for the four of them — are not as heartily indulged by his compadres as once they were. It used to be the boys would join in. Wade would mostly grin and nod while trying to weave a rock star subplot into Kyle's reverie, and Adam would shake his head and try to explain to Kyle that four guys can't just start their own business out of the blue ("You need *capital*. And you need, like, an *idea* other than just 'a business'") and Rank would tell Adam to shut up and insist that they should locate their offices in Trump Tower in New York City. Or, if not Trump Tower, then directly across the street in order to draw inspiration.

"We'll get an idea, eventually," Kyle always assured Adam. "An idea will come. What's important, right now, is the concept. And the concept is *us*. The four of us are a winning proposition, my brothers, no matter how you slice it."

Except that lately when Kyle spoke this way, the only one to react with the old enthusiasm was Wade with his reliable grin and nod. Adam would look at his lap. Rank would tilt his head back and finish whatever he was drinking.

And so the boys needed to get together before Christmas, Kyle decided. The boys needed a night on the town, just the old crew — the original four.

"I gotta work," said Rank.

"I need to study," said Adam.

"Guys, don't be dicks," pleaded Kyle. "When's everybody's last exam?"

Everyone but Rank already knew their schedule by heart. Rank was in the process of deciding whether or not to even write his. On the one hand, there was no point; on the other, if he didn't, it would raise the kind of questions among his friends he wasn't prepared to face just yet.

Besides, what was wrong with indulging in his college life a little longer, even if it meant the hassle and needless stress of sitting down to write exams, even if he was only going through the motions at this point? After all, who knew how many weeks of higher education he had left, how long he'd be left to linger in the dorm before the university bureaucracy roused itself to inquire as to the next instalment of his tuition? Being left out of exams — leaving himself out — would, he knew, make him sad. Would be an acknowledgement. He would be nostalgic for the experience of exams all too soon — lonesome for that sense of harassed community and beleaguered fellowship.

Truth be told, he'd already spent the past month floating around campus in a fog of pre-emptive nostalgia for this time, this place, these people. Now all that was left was to set about hardening himself against all three.

Which would not be an easy thing to do with Kyle and his soupy talk of brotherhood growing faggier by the moment as the holidays approached.

We'll get it over with, thought Rank back at the dorm, dutifully tearing apart his sock-smelling berth in search of his exam schedule. Screw it: one last night out, one big blowout with the boys. Raise glasses, toast themselves, cut each other's palms and mingle blood like kids in a clubhouse, let Kyle spin his future dreamscapes, utter vows and proclamations, bestow hugs, brand their asses *Brothers of the Temple*, give them all fucking pet names if he wants to. Get it over with — one final time, and then.

And then: what?

And then the black hole of the future that was Christmas/ New Year's '91. The other side of which remained unfathomable to Rank.

———

Lorna could not grasp the simple fact that patrons of Goldfinger's responded differently to a bartender like Rank than they did a bartender like Lorna. She noticed how the ancient, ruined regulars — who usually liked to linger at the bar after paying for a drink, hacking up bon mots along the lines of *Boys oh boys I wuz so fuckin hammered last night* — tended to just mutely accept their drinks and change and shamble back to their table when dealing with Rank. It concerned her. She didn't like to see the Goldfinger's customer-service dynamic thrown off.

"The regulars," she explained to Rank, "they like to joke around, you know? Like to chat with us up here at the bar. Makes them feel they belong."

They like to chat up here at the bar, Rank wanted to say, because you wear that corset thing and have dyed blonde hair that you have grown down to where the cleft of your ass begins. Which I can see, by the way, emerging from your pants every time you bend even the tiniest bit forward.

He told her, "I am always very nice to the customers."

"I know you are, lovey, but you're a big fella and maybe you scare them a little."

"I'm as nice as I can be," protested Rank.

Truth be told there was nothing he was less interested in

than chatting up the regulars. He didn't find them lovable or endearing the way Lorna pretended to. They were last-stage alcoholics, ageless in their decrepitude, shaking, stinking, their shrivelled grey heads sloshing with permanently pickled brain cells, only able to make conversation on the off-chance that one such depleted cell happened to slosh against another somewhere in the depths of their cerebral brine.

Oily ol' fuck so I get home last night and I get outta bed to take a piss and don't he forget he's wearing pants! So I'm standing looking down at the toilet thinking: Where's it goin? It's gotta be going somewhere. Well it's goin down my leg is where its goin! Har har hagh . . . HAUGH! Hwack hwack hagh . . hagh . . ugh. S'cuse me Lorna darlin.

More importantly, they rarely tipped. They were drink-cagers by and large, relying on the kindness of strangers. Why indulge them? Why did Richard even let them in the place? He could readily imagine how Gordon Sr. would respond to such a customer base. But when he pointed this out to Lorna, protesting that the barflies contributed nothing but a frankly scuzzball ambiance, she shook her head.

"You're not here on Welfare Wednesday, lovey." She tapped the tip jar with a turquoise fingernail. "That's when Santa comes to town."

Okay, so Lorna was worried for her welfare tips. That explained it, but didn't particularly prompt Rank to take her advice seriously. Heaven forbid he not endear himself to the pub's incontinent habitants. Besides, he was perfectly civil — he just wasn't a blonde in a corset who called them "lovey." Why would the alkies stay and talk to Rank? Swap weight-room stories? Compare how much they can bench?

It was only after Ivor approached him on the same matter that Rank started to think perhaps he did require an attitude adjustment.

"Rich," Ivor said, "is thinking maybe you're not having such a good time behind the bar."

Rank hesitated, before responding, in a moment of startled respect for Rich. Rank scarcely ever caught a glimpse of the guy, yet somehow he had managed to attune himself to the mood of his most insignificant staff member.

"No," insisted Rank. "I really like it, actually." And in fact, when the place was busy, he did. It was a million times more diverting than standing around with his arms folded scanning the crowd for violence. When things got cooking, three hours could pass in an eye-blink, Rank bouncing back and forth from the bar to the till to the beer fridge, serving a steady stream of hoarse, happy revellers who tipped bigger and bigger as the night wore on.

"Rich says you come off a little tense."

Rank did his best to clamp down on a smirk. This coming from a man so coked he practically vibrated.

"No, you know what it is, man," said Rank. "Exams. Stressing me out."

"Fuckin exams," commiserated Ivor, nodding as if in perfect understanding, like a departmental chair.

"You know," continued Rank, "I should be studying, but I gotta work. I need the money for tuition next year otherwise they'll kick me out."

It was weird, Rank reflected later, how in the Goldfinger's environment he was able to articulate the worst thing going on in his life with such a casual air. Of course his excuse was more a version of the truth than the truth itself, but the fact remained he had just confessed something to Ivor that he'd spoken not a word of to his friends, or anyone other than Gordon Sr. He'd spoken it like an afterthought: *otherwise they'll kick me out.*

He'd told his friends he needed money for tuition, but that was all, and to them it was a statement so obvious as to be unremarkable. After all, they were students — everyone was living on a shoestring. If he'd said the same to Kyle, with his two professor parents at McGill, Kyle would have responded, Oh yeah, me too man, I'm so screwed for money.

Ivor leaned, placing his bloated forearms on the bar, and then reached up to scratch his entire head, starting with either side of his chin and working his way up and back. It came across as a kind of frantic thinking ritual, so Rank politely stood and waited for it to be over.

When it was, Ivor dropped his forearms back onto the bar where they landed like pair of immense sausages. He looked up at Rank. "You gonna be able to cover it?"

"Cover what?" said Rank, who had become a bit lost in Ivor's head-ritual.

"Your tuition."

"Um," said Rank. "No, actually. There's no way I'm going to be able to cover it."

"How much is it?" Ivor wanted to know.

As Rank stared into Ivor's bulging, frankly inquiring eyes, he understood what the deal was with Goldfinger's. Ivor felt no shame in asking such a question — as anyone else in his circle would — because such questions were the foundation upon which the establishment he stood in was built.

Goldfinger's was after all about the numbers. Goldfinger's was a counting house done up as a pleasure palace. Up the hill at the university there was Milton and Heraclitus, Take Back the Night, Evolutionary Biology and the Western Canon. Here, it was Basic Math. It was Economics 101. It was a turquoise fingernail tapping a tip jar.

Rank told him how much.

Ivor said, "Let me talk to Rich."

Press pause. This is a little break to remind you that Rank was barely twenty years old. It's all very well to assume he would know better than to invest seriously in those five words: *Let me talk to Rich.* Words spoken by a criminal about a criminal. Spoken by a man who has a gun about the man who gave him the gun. Bad news all around, yes? Red flags abounding. Well, my friend, you give our hero too much credit. Earlier your humble narrator was riding poor Kyle pretty hard about his naiveté around the subject of Goldfinger's. About the fact that, as many rumours as Kyle might have heard about drugs and guns and various shady dealings, he couldn't quite believe it. The implication of course is that Kyle didn't have the kind of background to believe it — to believe that Richard and Goldfinger's could exist as anything but a joke. Well, let's face it. Rank didn't have that background either. Rank had years ago encountered a less clownish version of Ivor, a fatso of menace called Jeeves, from whom badness seemed to broadcast itself in radio waves. But that was pretty much as close as Rank had ever got to the kind of nasty that lay beyond Goldfinger's scummy surface, should you happen to scratch it with a turquoise fingernail.

Rank, even for his time in the Youth Centre, remained basically what social worker Owen Findlay had dubbed him in his earnest letter to the Provincial Judge's Office circa 1986: a decent kid. So let's not quibble with Owen on this one. Owen knew whereof he spoke. Let's give Rank, at least, that much.

But let's not forgive him. No, we can't. Sorry. Because his good-kid naiveté was only half of his mistake. Part two of this mistake is what's significant. Part two is what's outright unforgivable.

Part two being that, like any guy his age, Rank believed he was immortal. And no, just because this belief was typical of any guy his age doesn't make it okay for a guy like Rank. Rank, if anyone, should've known better. The gods had grabbed Rank by the neck a couple of times now and rubbed the barbed fact of mortality directly into his idiot face. And still the big lug ambled on his way, wiping the blood from his eyes, assuming it didn't apply to him specifically.

But what's even worse?

Rank had forgotten to remember the essential thing about himself. To wit: where there was a powder keg, Rankin Jr. was as fire. He was King Midas in reverse, our hero: fingertips Black Plague.

25 |

08/12/09, 10:52 p.m.

I DIDN'T THINK I would ever do this after I took up correspond-
ence with you, but I've started reading your book again. It has
to be my fourth or so time through it. I know I told you when
we started this up months ago — decades ago, it seems like —
that'd I'd read it quite a few times, but here's a confession: this
was and wasn't true. I read it the first time the way I would any
book, taking my time to get into it, wondering when in God's
name the action would pick up. And then the slow, cold recognition started to take over and I couldn't really concentrate
after that. I started reading specifically for the recognition — I
remember sitting rigid at the kitchen table holding the book
up in front of my face, the most unrelaxed book-reading posture you can imagine. I started blasting through paragraphs
and pages until I got to something I recognized and I would
feel my heart thumping in my face as my outrage reignited. It
was addictive, in a way. There he was, the character I knew to

be myself, lumbering in and out of scenes, and I'd be outraged when he was like me — because that was stealing — and outraged when he wasn't — because that was lying. I started folding down pages so I could go back and read these parts again. If there was a scenario I recognized, I'd go apeshit, marvelling at your gall, at how wrong you got it, or else how mercilessly dead-on the whole thing was. Either way, it was a violation. Lies and theft; theft and lies.

So when I said I read it three more times after that, what I meant is I read it in that same state, in that same way — blasting through the pages I'd folded down in a state of high piss-off, ignoring everything that didn't feel relevant to me personally.

Which maybe wasn't fair.

I want to say again that I am sorry if I scared you when I first got in touch. I was aggressive and creepy about it, and I apologize. All I really wanted to tell you was what I have just said — that I took your book personally. It felt as if you had reached across the decades just to poke me hard in the gut a few times, and I didn't understand why. What had I done to deserve this double assault? First: the angry guy, the football thug, the "innate criminal" with the eyebrow rash. Then, just as I'm recovering from him: the incident. The awful Incident. The awful, unspeakable, *inevitable* (as you paint it — and you have no idea how sick that made me feel) incident. Right alongside those occasional, sadistic, close-ups of yours: my rash, Wade's zit. Even worse: those throw-away lines — the most annihilating moments of my life dispensed with in just a handful of words: *His mother had died.* Jesus, Adam! Why this attack after twenty years? That's what it felt like — an attack, vicious, out of the blue, out of nowhere. I wanted to make sure you understood that. And the only way to do that was hit back.

Mostly I wanted to confirm whether or not you had done it on purpose, deliberately, hoping I'd see. Because you were trying to tell me something — or else tell the world something about me.

You have to admit, I've been trying very hard to see things from your point of view, Adam. The least you could do is acknowledge mine. I have been learning about you — and how and why you've done what you done — through every part of this experience. I figured out the thing about the noble purpose, and I figured out about getting caught up, and how the Noble Purpose is gradually shunted aside by something else, something deeper and more selfish, and I figured out about the lying, and how easy and natural and seductive it can be — to the extent that it starts to feel like a separate truth unto itself.

So what I'm saying is, I've come pretty far without any help or participation from you whatsoever.

I have been generous, if anything. I've been trying to understand you.

And you have given me precisely nothing back.

Anyway, I'll tell you why I started reading your book again.

Lately, I can't keep Gord out of my room, whether I'm in it or not. When I'm in here, typing, he tries to come in and dictate what I should say to "them" in my grand, cosmic appeal. That I can bench four hundred pounds, or used to be able to anyway, that I am a beloved soccer coach, that I graduated with honours from Teaching College, that I was a scholarship student (fact of it being a hockey scholarship, to a school I dropped out of, tactfully omitted), that I served for two years as an altar boy, that I was chosen to narrate the Christmas pageant in Grade 3 because I was the best and clearest speaker in the class, that my father started his own business from nothing, that my great-grand-uncle had a hand in starting the Co-operative movement.

And, it turns out, when I'm not here Gord's obsession with what I'm doing doesn't wane.

"Gord," I called to him yesterday afternoon after getting home from a run and ducking into my room for some clean clothes. "If you are going to go through my drawers, can you at least not leave all my stuff in a pile on the floor?"

"I'm sorry," Gord called back. "But I heard you coming in and thought you'd probably wanna get right back atcher book, so figured I better clear out. Did you tell them about that birdhouse you made for your mother in Grade 9?"

I ambled down the hall as he was speaking and found my father in the kitchen holding down the tab on the toaster. He'd broken it the day before — as I'd shouted at him he was about to do — by slamming it down repeatedly. (He said it never kept the toast down long enough to properly blacken it the way he liked.) We immediately started fighting about whether to buy a new one (me) or take a screwdriver to the old which was still "perfectly good" and had cost "an arseload of money" when purchased in 1982.

"Were you looking for something in particular?" I inquired as threads of smoke drifted up from the toaster and formed a stratus above our heads. "Needed to borrow some underwear?"

Gord released the tab and leaned over to check if the bread had been charred to his satisfaction. A second later, he pushed it down again.

He wasn't meeting my eye. This was about as abashed as I'd ever seen my father.

"Well I'm pretty anxious to read that book a yours," he confessed.

"Gord, the toast is done, okay?"

He leaned over to check, waving smoke from his view.

"Not quite yet," he said.

"I'm going downtown and buying another toaster tomorrow."

"Go right ahead and I'll just chuck er right on out the window because we do not waste money in this house, Gordie."

"There's no book, Dad. Just so you know."

Gord looked up, scowling, from his bread-blackening vigil.

"Well I'd like to know what you're in there tapping away on all day if there's no goddamn book."

"I mean I'm not printing out pages. There's no manuscript. So you can stop digging around in my shit."

He released the toaster and crossed his arms at me. "What do you mean no pages? What's the good a that? You just tap-tapping away into the air?"

"No, I mean it's on the computer."

"Well nobody's gonna read it on a goddamn computer!"

"Okay, one, lots of people read on computers —"

"Bullshit!" barked Gord.

I took a breath. "Two, someone is reading it. Right now. Friend of mine. I've been emailing it to him in chunks, okay?"

"Well why the hell does he get to read it and I don't?"

"Because it's not *for* you, Gord."

"Who the hell is it for if not your own goddamn family?"

I rubbed my face. There were no answers to these questions.

"I'm taking a shower," I said.

"It's all about me," Gord said as I turned to go down the hall.

I stopped. "It's not, Gord. You think everything's about you."

"That whole goddamn book is about me and what an asshole I am and I defy you — I *defy* you Gordie — to tell me any different."

I came back into the kitchen, feeling my major muscle groups bunch.

"Wow," I said. "I've been *defied*. Jesus. I think I just pissed my pants."

"You try and tell me different!"

"Gord it's *not* about you, don't be so narcissistic."

Gord picked up his crutch from where it was leaning against the counter and I thought, Oh great. He's going to do to the entire kitchen what he did to Sylvie's elephant. I've got to get that crutch away from him. But he just pointed at me with it.

"*You're* the one who's narcissistic," he shouted. "About *me!* All you do is sit around tap-tapping all day trying to come up with ways to blame your old man for every goddamn thing that's ever gone wrong in your life."

I was about to blow up, as per usual in these circumstances. I was about to yell at him to get over himself, and to buy a dictionary, and to mind his own fucking business, and to stay out of my room, and, oh, by the way a lot of the shit that went wrong in my life *was* his fault, measured against any objective standard. I was about to spew all this at him in one volcanic cascade when Gord added in a minor shriek:

"You're writing it all down for *posterity*! And sending it off over the internet where it could end up God knows *where*! Well maybe I'll just sit on down and write my own book, how do you like that Gordie? Maybe I've got one or two opinions of my own to contribute!"

I was about to laugh at the idea. Gord sitting down at the kitchen table with a big pot of tea, gearing up to write his own goddamn story of my life — answering my version chapter for chapter, page for page, with his own. I was about to laugh at the idea, except I could see that Gord was kind of terrified.

Long story short, I've started reading your book again. With a little more attention this time and maybe a little less adrenalin.

———

Kirsten said, Cyber-stalking? Sounds very high-tech.

And I said, It's not really, it's basically what I'm doing now, with you, the only difference being you write me back.

And Kirsten said, So if I stop writing you back will you officially be stalking me?

And I said, No, if you stop writing me back I'll stop too.

And after a while Kirsten wrote, I don't think I could be a cyber-stalker. I don't have the self-confidence for it.

And I said, You would be amazed how little self-confidence it takes.

And she said, So what does it take to be a really superlative cyber-stalker?

To start, I said, you need anger. Like a really good jolt, high-dosage adrenalin like someone's just kicked you in the ass for no good reason. And then you just need a bit of contact, a bit of back and forth to grease the wheels, to feel like you've really established yourselves in each other's vision. And then abrupt withdrawal — the contact has to be taken away just as you're getting comfortable; the moment you feel your fingers taking hold of something vulnerable — yank, it's gone. And you are in the dark. And you're alone, but it feels like something has been done to you and is continuing to be done, as if you have been tricked. As if you are a big stupid animal who's been led into a trap. So the only way you can think to get out of the trap is to chase down the guy who led you there in the first place.

And Kirsten wrote, Rank in all seriousness wtf?

And I said OMG you just wrote WTF. What are you, fourteen?

And she said IMHO, OMG is worse than WTF.

And I said, Do you mean because G is worse than F?

And she said G, as you know, is great.

And I said, F is pretty great too.

Ha ha, said Kirsten. I mean LOL.

RAOTFL, I said.

E2&ITCYP9, she wrote back. I just made that one up. My kids say you can't do that. It's a very lockstep sort of place, the internet.

Like religion, is what I wanted to reply. But stopped myself. We hadn't broached this yet — where exactly Kirsten stood on the whole Lord Jesus thing lately. There was that offhand *G is great* remark, but I had no idea how to take it. It could be anything from a fervent avowal to a smirking reference to our holy-roller past. This led me to remember that the problem with Kirsten and I back in the day is that we were basically incapable of having a serious conversation. We could talk about God, because that was sort of required — and, looking back on it, just another way of avoiding what was really going on — but the minute we tried to talk about each other, or our lives, or how we felt, we'd start joking around and never could quite get down to it. We entertained each other too much — it was always more fun to exchange quips than to dig into what was going on. She asked me once how I met Beth, for example, and I gave her the sitcom version. There I am in the bar when this fat, excessively bangled lady twice my age, who I can only assume is looking for some hot young meat, heaves herself into my booth and I decide in all my drunken beneficence to go for it and even try to buy her a drink. (*Beth!* Kirsten had screamed, dying. *You tried to buy BETH a DRINK?*) But I told her nothing about how the booth shook, how I gulped and sweated, how Beth's eyes were like a scalpel down my chest. Kirsten knew this was my conversion experience, and therefore the most important thing to ever happen to me, but she never insisted on hearing any version other than the joke. Anything else made us both uncomfortable.

And I'm noticing that pattern emerging again already, and it's great, don't get me wrong, it's as fun as it ever was but I also don't want to lose sight of the way it eventually sunk us. So before I replied to her *lockstep* note I sat and thought for quite a while.

And I wrote, So. I have told you about my irrational obsession. What about you? What kind of pointless bullshit is needlessly consuming all your time and emotional energy these days?

And she wrote back five seconds later, practically: I have kids, Rank. I'm not permitted pointless bullshit anymore.

Which was when I thought: For Christ's sake next year I'll be a forty-year-old man.

And I wrote, I would like to call you, Kirsten.

26

HEREWITH BEGINS OUR hero's life of crime, which is not really much of a crime-life at all since it consists basically of driving around with Ivor in a mud-coloured Dodge Aries making "drop-offs" and "pick-ups." Ivor, on Richard's instructions, doesn't even let Rank drive. Richard is perhaps the most cautious son of a bitch Rank has ever encountered. Rank is asked to do nothing but accompany Ivor — to climb into Ivor's barn-smelling K-car on departure, and out of it on arrival, at which point Rank follows Ivor into the abysmal apartment block or dilapidated household where business is being done. Glamour! Intrigue! Once inside, Rank stands there so that everyone present can get a good look at him before Ivor suggests to the host or hostess that they adjourn to another room to do business. Rank is not invited to come along at this point. Rank is instructed to stand by the door and wait. As he stands there — smelling stale cigarette smoke, or stale toast, or stale sweat, or stale macaroni and cheese — he wonders if this is yet another stage in the process of being brought up through the ranks of Goldfinger's — another tier on the hierarchical ladder.

During their time together on the highway, Ivor regales Rank with stories of his life (mostly to do with avoiding the rabidly obsessive efforts of the U.S. government to infect him with HIV) and attempts to impart to his younger cohort the occasional snippet of wisdom courtesy of Hard-Knocks High.

And, yes, more often than not the wisdom amounts to: Don't trust the U.S. government because it wants to give everyone AIDS. But every once in a while, when they've been driving a bit longer than usual and the road has become a hyp-notically undulating grey ribbon, Ivor's one-track mind slows down a little and even wanders far enough afield to allow him to talk about his life. A time before the Nixon administra-tion's diabolical plan to eradicate the black, gay and scummy had begun to take hold; a more innocent time.

Ivor grew up only a few miles down the river and even though his entire family are alive and live nearby, the only one he sometimes talks to on the phone is his sister Dini. He isn't able to go visit Dini because Dini's husband is an asshole who has never forgiven Ivor for breaking into their basement eight years ago to sleep off a binge and not paying to replace the window. Ivor argued that he had no memory of doing it, so the husband couldn't even prove he had. And the hus-band said he'd walked into the basement and Ivor had been sprawled beside the furnace in his long-johns and what more evidence did anybody need?

"But my point, Rank," explains Ivor, "the point I tried to make at the time was this. I am a man with a substance abuse problem. I will always have that hanging over me. There's nothing I can do about it — it's my cross to bear is what I'm saying. What I need is the compassion and understanding of my family. And I have never had that, Rank."

"That sucks, man," commiserates Rank.

"I never got that from anyone in my family except Dini."

"She sounds nice," says Rank. "I don't have any brothers or sisters myself."

"Well they can be a blessing," says Ivor. "My family isn't scummy like me, you know. I'm what you call the black sheep. My dad did a pretty good business selling Kawasaki bikes and ATVs and whathaveyou and he had this idea all his kids would go to college — first crop a scholars in his family history. But I kept fucking up at school. I had my own bike, so, you know, I was the king. I was Captain Motorcycle. Just wanted to fuck off and get high. Figured I was untouchable. Didn't graduate."

Rank tries to glance over and take account of Ivor without being too obvious about it. He has no idea how old the guy is. Ivor is balding, and greying, with a ponytail, but his face is as smooth as a baby's.

"You could always go back," suggests Rank.

"No, I can't go back to school Rank. I'm not a school guy."

"Hey, I never thought I was a school guy," says Rank. "And look at me."

"Yeah, but you are, Rank, whether you think it or not. Whereas I got a few years on you and I know. I know what I'm not. I know what you are. You keep doing what you're doing — I've known a lotta good kids like you who have done the same. Make your money offa Rich. Rich won't screw you over and he won't get all pissy when you tell him it's time for you to go find a real job. He's used to it. Meanwhile, you and he got a mutually beneficial relationship going. Pay for school and then get the fuck out of here."

Rank bounces along the highway beside Ivor feeling surprised. *Let me talk to Rich.* It never occurred to Rank before that Ivor might be concerned with anybody's well-being other than Richard's.

It is almost sweet.

"Hey," says Rank after a couple of minutes. "I just wanna say thanks for setting this up for me and everything, man."

"Pay for school," repeats Ivor, "and get out of here."

Before dropping Rank off back at the dorm, Ivor hands him a ten and two twenties.

"For the pleasure of your company," he says.

Fifty dollars was about what Rank got paid after a five-hour shift bouncing at Goldfinger's. Sometimes the rides in the Dodge with Ivor take no longer than fifteen minutes.

It is a good deal, no matter how you slice it. In the first week of his new position, he has already worked three such shifts with Ivor on top of the Thursday and Friday evening shifts he'll put in at the bar. All of a sudden, he's not making bad money.

All of a sudden, Rank begins to wonder if he shouldn't study for exams after all. What he should do is, he should call Adam, with whom he takes two courses, and set up an all-night grilling session. Do what he can to yank at least those two grades up by the bootstraps and then spend next semester doing his best Adam-imitation, pulling down A's across the board to make up for the shitshow that is sure to be his mid-term results.

All of a sudden, he's thinking about next semester.

The problem is he doesn't really call Adam anymore. They just sort of bump into each other, and not even very often. But Kyle has booked their boys' night out for the coming Saturday, the Saturday Rank has off, so he and Adam will see each other then. He plans to apologize for being such an asshole all semester. Maybe not outright apologize, as that would be kind of gay and over-earnest, but do or say something to sort of imply contrition. Mutter about how stressed out he's been lately. Buy his buddy an entire tray of shooters, tell him he likes his cardigan, slap him — ever-so-lightly — on the back.

And just before they get too shitfaced, ask his friend for help.

—

Wade has a girlfriend and it is ridiculous and sad. He won't shut up about her, goes around shamelessly burbling, *I am so freaking in love, man!* and is busy writing a series of guitar ballads to elucidate this point. It pains and embarrasses them. Wade and his girlfriend spend entire moony afternoons nuzzling each other on the grimy couch, so when Rank arrives to hang, he finds he can only sit so long watching them gaze and fondle before needing to be elsewhere. Worse, Wade insists that everyone must get to know and love his girl as he does. Kyle had to place him in an arm-lock to keep him from inviting her along on their Saturday blowout.

"I don't go anywhere without Emily now," Wade insisted. "It just can't happen, man. She's a part of me." So Kyle pinned him to the couch and wrenched his arm behind his back.

"Yoko Ono!" said Kyle, astride Wade who was busy suffocating among the cushions. "Say it. Say Yoko Ono."

"I will never say that about her," Wade protested from the
depths of the couch. "She isn't even Asian."

Emily was one of those awful neo-hippie girls who never
wore anything tight. It was all enormous, cable-knit sweaters
pulled down over ankle-length skirts, chunky boots and hair
going everywhere. *Little House on the Prairie* meets Janis Joplin.
And she smiled at you whether she liked you or not, no matter what you said — one of those secretive I-exist-on-a-higher-
plane kind of smiles — just to prove how laid-back she was.

"Just kill him," pleaded Rank. "Suffocate him now and get
it over with."

"Yoko. Ono."

Wade's reply was lost inside the couch, but his tone was all
defiance. Kyle rolled off him onto the floor and Wade sat up,
red-faced, victorious.

"Okay but she's not coming Saturday," panted Kyle.

"We'll see," said Wade.

The plan was to lock up the Temple for the night, because
if they hung out there for any length of time on a Saturday,
people inevitably would start dropping in, looking for a party.
Kyle, needless to say, had dictated the agenda for the night.
First stop was the Italian restaurant to treat themselves to
dinner. Rank, who was just getting used to having cash in his
pocket, thought this was a lame and needless expense — they
could easily pad their stomachs at a sub shop for a quarter
of the price then hit the bars — but since none of the other
guys balked, neither did he. Gordon Sr. sounded in his head

throughout the meal however, saying things meant to accompany a flitting hand gesture like: *My, my!* And, *La di da!* Also the occasional slur against Italians, whose traditions apparently involved pouring a greenish puddle of olive oil onto your side plate, meant to be soaked up by bread.

Rank watched as Kyle dumped some kind of brown syrup onto the plate to mingle with his olive oil. The two formed a greasy yin-yang.

"That's disgusting," said Rank.

Kyle glanced up, smiling at him indulgently like a kindergarten teacher. "It's balsamic, man. Try some."

I'd rather try my own toe jam, Gordon Sr. opined in Rank's head. So Rank made himself lean over and wipe his bread on Kyle's plate.

"It's good, right?" said Kyle.

"You know what else is good on bread?" grunted Rank. "Like, butter."

Kyle was about to crack a joke at Rank's ill-bred expense, when Adam, who had been silently hoovering his minestrone this whole time, remarked, "Why don't you just fucking order some?"

Kyle and Rank both turned to stare at him, but Adam hadn't bothered looking up from his soup. A couple of moments of silence went by, not at all in keeping with a celebratory evening among four raucous pals. Kyle dabbed a chunk of bread into his yin-yang, frowning, as Wade sat gazing obliviously out the window as if hoping for a glimpse of his neo-hippie beloved. Adam finished off his soup, not bringing it up to his face and slurping the dregs as Rank would have done, but tilting the bowl this way and that and

fiddling with the spoon forever to catch every drop and morsel. Rank watched Adam until finally Adam noticed he was
being watched.

"What?" said Adam.

"What," repeated Rank. "You know what."

Adam stared at him through his glasses. "What?" he said
again, scarcely moving his lips.

"You've got a bug up your ass is what," said Kyle.

There was something about Kyle's rejoinder that broke
the spell of hostility bouncing between Adam and Rank. It
had taken shape abruptly, for no fathomable reason, and Rank
was relieved to feel it dissipate. It was the opposite of what he
wanted to happen that night, but he'd felt helpless against its
weird surge.

Adam turned to Kyle. "I do not."

"Yeah, you do," said Rank, settling comfortably into the
familiar ganging-up-on-Adam group dynamic. "It's up there
so high you probably can't even feel it anymore."

"It's way up there," agreed Kyle. "Impacted-colon up there.
Way, way up."

"Like the Friendly Giant," exclaimed Wade, as if waking
out of sleep. This was so left field, they all cracked up.

"I have been locked in my room studying for the last three
days," admitted Adam. "I'm ready to kill someone."

"You wanna punch me?" said Rank. "I'll let you punch me
in the face."

"Maybe later," said Adam, smiling at his empty bowl.

Press pause. Zoom out. Look at the four of them giggling, pouring wine for one another, sitting around the table
in their jeans-and-sweater nice guy uniforms, the occasional,

innocuous swipe of hair gel and heavy whiff of Drakkar cologne. Fresh-shaved faces and napkins in their laps.

They're just kids — let's remember this, okay? That's the thing to keep in mind as this particular evening spreads itself against the sky.

Two bottles of wine at the Italian restaurant and Rank's lasagne ended up being basically a trough of mozzarella and therefore one of the most wonderful things he'd ever consumed — so the mood has improved by the time they hit the student pub. It's early and there are not a lot of people there but that's okay because the boys don't want to be tempted to stay for more than a couple of hours anyway. They have promised one another to conduct a pub crawl this night, as half-decent a crawl as is achievable in a town of only three pubs. They will start at the U, then hit the Leeside across from the strip mall to try out the karaoke machine, and finally polish the evening off at Goldfinger's nice and late when the action tends to be at its plastered, orgiastic apex. This, of course, another Kyle directive. Rank, personally, has experienced the aforementioned apex night after night — could frankly do without the apex. The apex often involves middle-aged women in various stages of undress laid out completely insensible on the dance floor, if not perilously animated, trying to climb up onto the bar and lead the crowd in a confused singalong/striptease. Or else some guy trying to break into one of the VLTs using the cranium of anyone he happens not to like the look of. Or vomiting. The apex often entails a great deal of human throwup.

But that's not how Kyle sees it, because Kyle hasn't seen it

enough. But whatever; it's Kyle's show, Kyle's pre-holiday hur-
rah. And what's a night on the town, in this town, without
Goldfinger's? Rank can only hope he won't be dragooned into
service as a bouncer upon the brothers' arrival at the bar — at
the same time, though, he can't see how he won't be. The
Goldfinger's clientele can keep a bouncer pretty busy come
one in the morning; Ivor is sure to need help at some point,
and Rank won't have much choice but to pitch in if he wants
to keep his lucrative new gig riding shotgun in the Dodge.

So, shit. Only thing for it is to get as drunk as he can
before then.

This happens to be the train of Rank's thoughts when
Adam, reading his mind like Kreskin, confides out of the blue,
"Seriously, I could do without Goldfinger's tonight."

And Rank says, "Oh God I was just thinking the same
thing. It's where I work now, you know? The novelty kind of
wears off after a while."

"You should say that to Kyle."

"Yeah. I just can't stand to disappoint the little guy."

They are huddled together at a table at the Leeside. Kyle
has gone off somewhere to schmooze the other tables, as he
is always helpless to do, even on an evening that is ostensibly
all about "the boys." Wade, meanwhile, is onstage doing
an actually pretty brilliant David Byrne. He makes his face
vacant and flails robotically and you can practically see the
oversized suit flopping against his limbs. Every once and a
while Adam and Rank stop talking to admire him.

"No, really, you should," says Adam. "People don't say no
to Kyle nearly enough."

"You could say something too you know," says Rank.

"He ignores me. He doesn't ignore you."

"Yeah," says Rank, watching Wade.

Better than this, sings Wade.

"You don't need to tiptoe around Kyle, by the way," says Adam.

"I don't fucking tiptoe around Kyle."

"Okay. Well if you thought you did."

Rank realizes what Adam is talking about: how Rank shoved Kyle that time. And he wants to say, It's not Kyle I feel like I'm on fucking eggshells around these days. And maybe he will say something like that after a few more drinks.

Somebody calls you, sings Wade, *but you cannot hear.*

"You know, he's really good," says Rank. "We ride him all the time about the rock star stuff, but he could do it."

"He's too lazy," replies Adam. Rank looks over at him.

"You said that with, like, no hesitation whatsoever."

"It's true," says Adam. "He doesn't want to work at it. He just fucks around."

"So he should be like you?"

"What's like me?"

Rank is still sober enough to know he should back off a little. "I mean like what you said at the restaurant — locking yourself in your room and studying 'til you wanna kill somebody. I don't know how productive that is either in the long run."

Adam grimaces up at Wade spinning around onstage in his imaginary big suit and says, "I'm trying to *get* somewhere. I'm trying to *achieve* something." And Rank is looking at him very closely because Adam says this in exactly the same way he once confessed to being afraid of fat people, of getting fat.

That is, with real fear behind it and also shame. And Rank feels the same instinct he felt then — a kind of fatherly need to reassure.

"Grix, you're a born brain. You're gonna kill on exams, don't worry."

"I'm not a born brain," says Adam. "Everything is actually really hard for me if you want to know the truth."

"Fuck off," says Rank kindly.

Adam puts down his drink and his hand, startlingly white, flies out at Wade like a dove. "Guy can sing, play guitar — easy. He doesn't even have to try. Just get stoned and follow Kyle around for the rest of his life. I don't have any talents. I have to work and I have to think. I have to force myself to spend a lot of time just thinking, Rank. I'm twenty already. I have to *get good*."

Rank doesn't have any idea what his friend Adam is talking about.

That knowledge won't come round for almost another twenty years.

All that it takes, sings Wade. *All that it takes.*

Kyle returns to their table then, arms spread wide.

27 |

I HOPE YOU don't mind if I take a break here. I'm not sure if you noticed but we're well into August already and Gord is basically healed up and I only have a couple of weeks to finish this thing and it's stressing me out. Really, I should be home by now, getting ready for classes. I've had to email the school and bow out of a couple of meetings already — an ailing father is pretty handy for that kind of thing, and as long as I'm back by the 23rd it's no big deal.

But, Christ, I just want to be finished this. And I know I'm coming up to the most important part, but then I think: Jesus, Adam, we were both there. Do I really have to do this? Why am I even doing this?

You could just drop me a line, you know, and tell me to stop. Tell me you remember, and tell me that you understand what I am doing, and why. After which you might even consider telling me your reasons for doing what you did — and for the way you did it, the half-assed way you told my story. Your approach, I'm noticing as I go over your book for the fourth time, was practically not to tell it at all. That is, to tell it second-hand, in barely a couple of paragraphs. To just allude to it, really, as if it wasn't even central to the plot.

In fact, I'm realizing as I reread the thing, it wasn't.

I didn't really notice that before — or else, on some level I guess I did, and that's part of what pissed me off so much. I remembered Gord yelling panicked in the kitchen: *It's all about me!* And how I laughed at his narcissism. Because it isn't, obviously. But then again, of course, it is. I mean, you had taken the time to put me there — to preserve the twenty-year-old me in all my misery like a bug someone had closed the pages on, squashing it between the covers forever — and didn't even end up paying me nearly enough attention. Same with the thing about the character's — my character's — mother. His mother who had died — who never even got to be alive in your version. Offhand. Sideline action. Just another squashed bug.

So I'm reading your book again, after all these other reads, and all of a sudden I find myself thinking Fuck! It's not about me at all.

So what am I doing there?

What am I for?

Anyway, enough. Enough about you and your book that didn't even do all that well or get all that much attention or even particularly good reviews, from what I can find on the internet. I was in the mall the other day to buy Gord a new toaster and stopped in at the Coles to see if they even carry it at this end of the country. Turns out they do. I found it tossed in a bin marked 60 percent off. I don't know why but for months after I first read the thing it felt as if you were the most famous man on the planet — your face on buses and billboards, magazine covers; hitting the talk show circuit, yukking it up with Oprah; throwing the first pitch at Yankee Stadium. When, really, it was just a few reviews in handful of papers.

But it seemed to me like you had taken over the world.

08/15/09, 1:00 a.m.

OK. I know I have to start again, but I have been writing my ass off to get this thing finished and the closer I get to the end the more the process seems to slow itself down — and this is exactly the opposite of what I want to happen. Today I actually got up from the desk, wandered into the living room and tried to strike up a conversation with Gord — that's how desperate I am. I just want it to be over now. I want to stop.

Gord, by the way, has been behaving himself beyond all expectation. Now that he doesn't need as much help getting around and can brew his own tea and blacken his own toast I've heard nary a crutch-bash out of the guy. That was part of the reason I ambled from my room to see how he was doing — the silence had been deafening. It was afternoon talk show time of day and I imagined him gearing up to yell at me to come see the guy with tattoos all over his head, or the brother and sister who got married and defiantly produced a special-needs rainbow of offspring, or the men who paid hookers to put them in diapers and offer them the breast. And then I imagined a jolt of pain in Gord's arm as he raised the crutch to bash me to attention, a feeling like a caber to the chest, his mouth working to produce one final, soundless *Piss on a plate!* before collapsing in his chair as the freaks on *Jerry Springer* shook their rattles.

"You okay out here Gord?"

"Jesus! Yes! You pretty near scared the dick off me, son."

I flung myself down onto the couch. "Anything good on?"

"I thought you were supposed to be hard at work in there."

"I was but you're so quiet out *here*."

"Well I know you're trying to work," said Gord, reaching primly for the box of Kleenex he kept stationed by his chair and giving his nose an elaborate honk.

"You getting sick, Gord?"

He eyed me over the wad of tissue.

"Listen, you don't have to worry about me. You get back in there and finish your book."

I sat up on the couch and stared at him. All of a sudden I was twelve and there was homework to be done.

"I'm taking a break all right? You don't even — look, it's not even a real book."

"Don't give me that bullshit. All week you've been growling around here like a bear how you gotta finish that goddamn thing before you head on back to school. Well get in there and finish it. I won't disturb you."

"Well what about lunch?"

"I've had my lunch. Had some Chef Boyardee. Oh and thank you very much for the new toaster, by the way, I put it in the trash."

"Oh for Christ's sake," I said, jumping to my feet, intending to head outside and upend the garbage cans.

"Leave it," barked Gord, picking up his crutch and brandishing it at me. "I told you, we don't waste money in this house. Now quit procrastinating and get back to work."

I stood there speechless, my arms spread out, appealing silently to the universe to for the love of God get off its ass and *do* something about Gord, until I felt a hard poke in my thigh. I looked over and saw him leaning forward, crutch extended.

"Git!" my father ordered, raising it above his head.

So back I went. And here I am.

Kirsten told me that she returned to Alberta to see her father, the town engineer, a few years ago. It was just after she got divorced, and just before she left the church. Her marriage, she said — second marriage, that is — had been the penultimate nail in the coffin of her evangelical faith. Hubby number two had been a fresh-faced, hard-working, upstanding Christian male, active in the church, an inspired speaker who had his oratorical skills honed by many years of AA meetings, and often brought his religious community to tears with stories of his parents' alcoholism and his own impious, dissolute youth. Also, he'd been "having an affair," as he delicately described it (once he'd been found out), with a teenage goth-girl from the homeless youth group he volunteered with. They'd been engaged in this affair-having while Kirsten was in the hospital giving birth to her twins, she learned, hence him showing up well after the fact toting two huge bouquets. Oh and also a woman — not even someone who was saved — who taught the cardio pole-dancing class at his gym.

"One cliché after another," Kirsten told me. "And I remember thinking, No more Christian guys."

"But how was that gonna work as long as you were in the church?"

"Well exactly," said Kirsten. "I tried not to think about that."

But it got harder and harder not to think about that after a while because the husband was tearfully repentant, even fled to the fleshy arms of Beth for support in his contrition — when he wasn't flying into rages at Kirsten over the telephone, that is, declaiming against her godless audacity in having initiated divorce proceedings against him.

Beth tried to act as intermediary.

Baby, she said to Kirsten (she referred to all female members of our community as "baby," I recalled as Kirsten told the story). Baby, she said. Carl is sorry. He's suffering.

But he's not sorry. He's actually furious at me. He can't believe I won't forgive him. The whole time it was happening, I'm convinced he told himself that if he ever got caught, I'd just forgive him and life would go on as it always has.

Men tell themselves a lot of things, baby, when they open themselves to Satan.

He believed, said Kirsten, realizing it as she spoke it, he was *entitled*.

Beth assured her it had been the devil talking, not Carl.

Yeah, okay, but in that case the devil's still doing the talking. Because you don't hear him when he talks to me, Beth, he isn't repentant. I mean, he tells me he is, but when I say, Well that's not good enough, he goes crazy. He curses at me, Beth. He threatens to take the kids. Not sue for custody but just *take* them. And disappear.

I can see Beth's face as Kirsten says this. Sorrowful; jowls fluttering as if windblown. Beth told her that she loved them both, so much, and this was killing her — which Kirsten believed, and I believe it too, hearing it in retrospect. She told Kirsten they had to try to work it out for the sake of the children and for, of course, Lord Jesus.

"So, my heart kind of broke then," Kirsten told me. "Because I knew I was going to have to let Beth down. And if I let Beth down — if I didn't do what Beth asked — because ultimately, you know, I believed Beth was wrong and I was right — then that would mean —"

"I know," I told Kirsten. "I know what that would mean."

(When I, your humble narrator, left our church, I didn't go see Beth first, even though I'd always promised her I would if I were ever entertaining "doubts." But it wasn't an issue of doubts at that point — I was too far gone, no doubt about it. And there was no way I could show my doubtless, godless face to Beth, the woman who'd found me when I was lost and wanted so much to see me saved. So I left without saying goodbye, or even thanks. Fortunately I had practice at this sort of thing. I stole away like the criminal I had long been, carried off on a mighty gust of grief and guilt, exactly the same way I disappeared when you knew me, Adam. It was kind of my forte by that time.)

The kidnapping threats were pretty much the breaking point for Kirsten. Once Beth, despite all her love and sorrow, had proved herself of zero use as mediator, Kirsten decided to pack up the twins and book herself a trip to Alberta to visit the town engineer, whom she hadn't seen since she was eleven. Practically the day she turned eighteen, however, letters had begun to arrive for her. He had sent them care of the church. Which made her think either her mother had been intercepting them up to that point, or else he had been politely waiting for Kirsten's adulthood to occur before reintroducing himself.

For a long time, she didn't answer him. Her mother had told her that this was a man who luxuriated in sin, who had gleefully opened himself to Satan and refused to shut the gates unto the evil one, even if it meant losing his own family.

"It's hard," Kirsten told me. "To overcome that fear when you've had it cultivated in you your whole life. And have cultivated it in yourself. Even when you start to know better. It's like those fizzy candies."

"Pardon?" I said after a moment of trying and failing to put her last sentence into some kind of context.

"When we were kids," she said. "And there were those candies that fizzed in your mouth. And people said if you drank pop with one of those candies in your mouth, it would explode in your head and you'd die."

I'd been lying on my side in bed with my cell phone squashed against my ear as we had this conversation. But at that point I rolled onto my back and bellowed laughter.

"Wow," I said, "you are such an apostate now! You're comparing the tenets of our faith to, like, urban myths about Pop Rocks!"

"What I'm saying is, if you gave me even one Pop Rock and a can of Coke to this day I probably wouldn't put the Pop Rock in my mouth and take a swig. I just wouldn't. Because I just spent so many years being afraid of it as a kid."

"So it was the same with your dad."

"It was the same with my dad. There was a part of me that was convinced we'd get off the airplane in Edmonton and he'd be standing there with horns growing out of his head."

"It's brave of you," I told her. "That you did that. That you just said, Damn the theological torpedoes, I'm going to Alberta."

"The day after I got there," she told me. "I woke up and my lips were cracked. And I looked at myself in the bathroom mirror in our hotel room and it was as if I'd aged overnight. I had all these little spider-wrinkles I'd never seen before. And I realized, It's because it's so dry here. It's the prairies and it's *dry*. And the minute I figured that out, Rank, this weird wave of nostalgia I didn't even know I had washed over me. And I realized I liked it, I've always liked dry climates. When I went to Arizona on my honeymoon to see the Grand Canyon, I remember standing there in the desert and heat and every cell in my body was going: Yes, yes, yes. This is what I like. This is home to me. And it didn't even occur to me that I came by that liking honestly — because of where I had grown up. I forgot I was a prairie girl."

I didn't say anything. I was picturing her happy in the desert.

"So that was like my dad too," she said. "I forgot how I felt about my dad. I forgot my dad was sweet. The girls and I spent a week with him and he drove us all over town. He brought me down to his old office, where he used to show me off to the secretaries. I remembered they kept toys for me in a box in the closet. He took us to Drumheller on the weekend so the kids could see the dinosaurs. I tried to talk to him about what happened and he kept saying, I won't say a bad word about your mother. And I was like, No, come on. I'd love you to; I'm dying for you to. Jeepers, if you won't I will. And he's like, No, honey, no. Let's just leave all that in the past where it belongs."

"So that was Satan."

"That was Satan. Or, Satan's backscratcher, as Mom used to call him."

"Satan's *backscratcher*?"

But that hadn't been the final nail in the crucifix. That wasn't what ultimately sent Kirsten packing from the faith. The final nail occurred not long after they got back from Alberta and one of her daughters staggered up to her after Sunday school as if punch drunk and announced to her mother that she was really, really sure she didn't want to go to hell and then burst into tears.

And Kirsten had said, like any mother would, Honey, that's not going to happen.

And the daughter, whose name was Gabrielle but who mysteriously had at some point managed to nickname herself Giddy, replied in that breathless, hysterical way of sobbing children, How is it not going to happen? I don't see how it can't. I hit Tyler with a block. I wanted to hit him. He smashed my tower and I wanted to hit him.

But even that hadn't been the final nail exactly. The final nail was when she spoke with Beth about it, and Beth told her: Baby, this is good. We want her to be afraid of hell. We want her to be *terrified*.

It was like dominoes, Kirsten told me. Something happened in her head that was like dominoes.

She thought: No.

Then she thought: But, yes. Of course. Of course I want her to be afraid to go to Hell.

(No.)

But, *yes*. That's how I was raised. To love Jesus. To fear Satan.

She remembered how she sobbed and rolled around on the floor of the dining hall at summer camp, while other kids performed variations of the same activity, howled and babbled on all sides. Ten-, eleven- and twelve-year-old disgusting sinners all. Hapless, helpless carriers of original sin, as rats once toted plague across Europe. Each of them panicking, Please Lord. Please Jesus. Oh my God. I can't do this. The flames practically blistering their heels. Save me! What can I do? Name it, Jesus!

(Not my daughter.)

But, *yes*.

Yes, agreed Beth. You know how Satan works, baby, as well as I do. He lies in wait.

(Like my father. Patient. Abandoned.)

No, thought Kirsten.

But, yes, thought Kirsten.

The way she tells it, it went like that for a couple of months. But each No constituted another domino. The Yeses weren't managing to set any of the dominoes upright again — the Yeses just stalled the dominoes' inevitable toppling — and never for very long.

Meanwhile, Giddy started having nightmares. Giddy dreamed, one night, that she'd been crucified as Kirsten watched from the centre of the jeering crowd and waved a blasé bye-bye.

"And that was it," Kirsten told me. "That was just freaking it."

We sat together on the phone in silence for a while. I thought about my cell phone minutes ticking away. The call was costing me a fortune, but I didn't want to use Gord's landline in the kitchen. I was hiding in my room like a teenager so he wouldn't know I was procrastinating again, talking on the phone to a girl.

"So," I said after a moment or two. "That must've been pretty hard. I mean, it was hard for me, and I hadn't even been raised with it. Truth be told, I kind of knew it was bullshit the whole time."

"Yes," said Kirsten. "I remember."

This was the first thing she or I had said that was even close to an allusion to our breakup. I said nothing. She said nothing.

Then: "I think now it's an addiction like any other," Kirsten told me. "Carl taught me a lot about addiction when we were together. I think you can get addicted to stories the way you can to booze or drugs."

"Stories," I repeated.

"It all serves basically the same purpose, right? It gives you some kind of comfort, even when it doesn't. Even when it's tearing you apart, it still has the comfort of familiarity, at least. Carl used to tell us when he preached: Yes, my liver hurt and yes I threw up every morning and yes people wouldn't come near me because I perspired pure vodka. But that first drink of the day — the ice cubes clinking into my favourite glass, that warm/cold swallow. Feeling my brain and my bones go loose with every sip. I just couldn't give that up, he said. It made him feel secure the whole time it was wrecking him."

"But I don't understand what you mean about stories," I said.

"It's the same with our stories. Jesus loves us, Satan hates us. One is in heaven and one is in Hell, and throughout our entire lives we just kind of balance on a clothesline strung between the two and the slightest breeze could send us tumbling where we don't want to go. Forever. It's terrifying and it's cruel and awful. But that's the story that we grew up hearing and that's the story that we know best and that's the story that makes us feel secure."

"That's your story," I said, "and you're sticking to it."

"It's really hard to give that up, Rank. To go cold turkey."

"I know," I said.

"Yes," she said. "Of course you know. Because you've done it."

"No," I said. "Because I haven't."

28

08/16/09, 10:04 p.m.

AND SO, what a coincidence. There sits Wade's beloved with two of her friends, huddled together around a pitcher of Long Island ice tea at the closest table to the door, all the more easily to greet the Brothers of the Temple when they at last present their half-cocked selves at Goldfinger's. Kyle is so disgusted with Wade, with this screamingly obvious set-up, he refuses to even look at him and simply heads to the bar with his hands in the air. Wade follows, laughing and protesting his innocence, but actually — you can tell — a little worried.

Emily sits there smiling like a sixties-era Mona Lisa. "Sit with us!" she calls to Rank and Adam. Rank casts an eye over Emily's friends and thinks okay. Adam also doesn't hesitate, maybe because he figures the university girls' table will provide a nice little bulwark of decency against the bar's progressively squalid atmosphere. Saturday night at Goldfinger's is hitting its stride.

It had been crazy even in the line-up. They'd tried to greet Ivor upon their arrival, but he'd been too distracted by the necessity of repeatedly shoving a couple of guys — two nearly identical brothers, a shitfaced, belligerent Tweedledee and Tweedledum — from out of the doorway, which they kept trying to rush.

"I said get out of here before I murder you," Ivor kept screaming.

"I know where you live! I am a human with human-being rights! And I know where you live!" Tweedledee was screaming in counterpoint. Tweedledum, meanwhile, was holding his gut and threatening to "blow chunks all over this shithole."

Rank stepped out of line and helpfully grabbed Tweedle-dum by the back of the collar, propelling him into the back alley where he could blow chunks in relative peace. Tweedle-dee, meanwhile, had taken issue with Ivor's gold chain. He had decided it was the stupidest, gayest, piece-of-shit gold chain he had ever seen and, furthermore, he wanted it.

"Gimme that fuckin thing," he said, blearily swiping a flac-cid hand toward Ivor's lack of neck.

Rank was about to lay a hand on his shoulder when Ivor grabbed the tweedle by his jacket and wrenched him forward, about a centimetre from his own glaring nose.

"Buh," remarked Tweedledee, twisting away, likely being baked by the heat pouring from Ivor's boiling face.

"You do not put your hands on me." Ivor spoke these words directly into Tweedledee's mouth. He was sweating and pant-ing to an extent that made his usual, workaday sweating and panting seem almost temperate — more typical of a senior's

cardio class. *"You do not put your hands on me because you will lose those hands, and you will lose the arms attached to those hands and that is when I fucking kill you, do you understand."*

This was something of a new side to Ivor. Ivor had never been much of an orator when it came to bouncing drunks. He did not typically veer off into rhetorical flights of fancy beyond: "I said get the hell out," punctuated with an inarguable shove.

"Ivor," said Rank. "Need help?"

Ivor responded by shoving the tweedle hard into Rank's chest.

"Whoa," said Rank, stumbling.

"You can help *this* scumbag by getting him the shit away from me."

But Tweedledee had already writhed away from Rank and was staggering off to find his bilious brother. Likely it was the nearness of Ivor's breath that had finally wrung the fight out of him.

"Jesus *Christ*," said Ivor, wiping his face on the sleeve of his T-shirt. "Just a onslaught of dicks tonight, Rank. You shoulda seen them going after each other on the dance floor. Broke a whole tray of glasses."

"They were fighting *each other*?" said Rank.

"Well until I stepped in they were. Then I had the two little dirtbags all over me."

Rank sighed. "You want me on the floor?" he asked at last. And didn't bother to look over at the groan this offer provoked from Kyle.

Ivor did look over, however — then looked around himself as if in surprise, like Kyle's groan had had the effect of an alarm clock. Then he wiped his face on his sleeve some more and smiled a slick, twitchy smile up at Rank. "No, no, no," he hollered. He reached inside the coat check booth and took a long haul from a beer he'd been keeping on the counter. "No, no, no, it's your night off. You have fun, Rank. It's Christmas. You go on inside and have some fun." Ivor was speaking so loud it made Rank flinch.

"Well — just . . . give a shout if you need me, okay?"

"I will," Ivor yelled, bouncing his head around by way of agreement. His nose had begun to run a bit dramatically, so he put his T-shirt sleeve to use again. "I will, son," he hollered as Rank was moving toward his friends.

"We thought you guys would never get here," Emily tells them with unmistakable relief. Rank can only imagine the calibre of sexual invitation the girls have been fending off for however long they've been sitting here. At the same time, he is thinking what a complete and total pussy Wade is. Wade has obviously made it clear to his beloved in advance that she and her friends would be both welcome and expected. Kyle will never forgive him.

Neither Rank nor Adam, however, particularly gives a shit. On the other side of the table, Adam is busy shaking the hands of the other two girls, so Rank turns his attention to Emily.

"Hey you've got some kind of sparkly crap in your hair," he observes by way of opening gambit.

"Yes," says Emily. "It's on my face too." She gives him a three quarter profile and her face shimmers like fish scales.

"Nice!" enthuses Rank.

"Thank you," says Emily, smiling her this-is-the-smile-I-give-everyone-whether-I-like-them-or-not smile.

Rank sets himself a task then. Rank decides to see if he can make her smile for real.

He asks Emily what she is studying, and Emily says art history.

"Really?" says Rank. "That's awesome. I love art."

"You do?" says Emily.

"Yep. The Impressionists. I like the Impressionists best." Rank has recently rented a movie that had to do with the Impressionists. Adam recommended it to him kind of as a joke because it was an actual film about Paris in the twenties. Consider it a primer, said Adam.

"Like who?" says Emily, testing him.

"Monet," says Rank, bullshitting happily. "Cézanne. You know, all the French guys."

"I wouldn't have pegged you for an art lover," says Emily.

Rank allows himself to sulk slightly. "Yeah," he says. "I'm not surprised. A lot of people pre-judge me that way."

He is gratified by the startled look this provokes in Emily. Of all the things she thinks about herself, he's betting she never for the world would have believed herself closed-minded, a pre-judger of her fellow beings.

"No, no, no!" she exclaims. "It's just that, you know, I thought you were a hockey player."

"Sports and art aren't mutually exclusive," Rank hears himself saying. Oh, Rank is on fire. Rank is at that ideal point of inebriation, a kind of golden mean where the percentage of alcohol in the bloodstream produces just the right balance of confidence and eloquence. No doubt after one more swig the whole thing will go pear-shaped and Rank will default into slurring and grunting obscenities. Meanwhile, however, he cups Emily in his very palm.

"Hemingway, after all," he adds, "was a boxer."

He glances over and notices Adam is watching him with a wide, incredulous smile. Rank hasn't seen Adam wear a smile like that for at least a couple of months, it seems. It makes him happy. Maybe all is forgiven — whatever it was that needed to be forgiven between them. He shoots his friend a grave, professorial nod, which causes Adam to cover his face abruptly, as if in a sneeze.

In a matter of seconds, Emily is leaning toward him, the drawn-on smile gone completely. Now, her pale lips are nicely parted and Rank understands that with her wild hair and shimmery face she is actually pretty hot. Conversation continues and Long Island ice tea is shared until a waitress comes to offer them a pitcher. Who knows how long they've been there at this point. The crowd roils on all sides, sometimes crushing against the backs of their chairs begrudgingly. Rank feels himself growing hoarse as the conversation wears on and he realizes he's had to shout progressively louder with practically every sentence in order to penetrate the crowd-sound and music. Emily is cupping one ear to catch his pearls of wisdom as they drop. Adam meanwhile seems to be holding his end of the table up quite nicely, a girl on either side, bending toward him. Way to go, Grix, Rank tries to transmit psychically. We should thank Wade later on.

It's at about this point when Kyle appears wearing a face like one of those Easter Island statues.

"Hi Kyle!" burbles Emily, who is deep into the Long Island

ice tea at this point and has been magically endowed with personality and charisma as a result.

"Let's go, you two," says Kyle, ignoring her. "I got us a table."

"We already have a table," says Adam, and he gestures to the two empty chairs that he and Rank have dutifully slung their coats over to reserve them for Kyle and Wade.

Wade, Rank sees, stands behind Kyle with arms crossed: a full-bodied pout.

"I got us four chairs up at the bar," says Kyle. "Lorna's watching them for us."

"Who wants to sit at the fucking bar?" says Rank. "It's a zoo up there."

"Come on," says Kyle.

Rank has seen Kyle like this only a couple times before — all his politician's polish and cultivated courtesy thrown completely to the wayside as a result of not getting his way. It's always an amazing transformation when it happens — all the animation leaves his face, his eyes go so dull it's as if they have filmed over like a zombie's, and you find yourself seized by the conviction that at any moment he might fling himself to the ground and start squalling like a 155-pound two-year-old.

"Kyle," says Adam. "We've got a great table right here."

"I've got us four seats up at the bar," repeats Kyle. "Come on. We're going."

"*We're going,*" Rank mimics, fake-sullen, causing Kyle's Easter Island expression to contort into an actual scowl. "Wow," remarks Rank at the sight of it. He glances over at Adam, who sits there looking as astonished as Rank feels. Their eyes meet. Psychic transmission: *Holy shit.* Kyle is beyond even being razzed.

But, press pause. They are drunk. They are peevish. They have been having fun with the ladies and have no desire to leave. They usually tolerate being pushed around by Kyle because that's just Kyle, and most of time it's friendly and well-meaning, if completely self-interested. But that kind of shit can pile up after a while. Both Rank and Adam are known to get quietly fed up from time to time, and avoid the Temple out of irritation with Kyle Jarvis's magisterial approach to friendship. When by themselves, Rank and Adam's running gag is to refer to Kyle euphemistically as "The Lord and Master." It's a joke, but one with a defensive edge.

Okay? We clear? And so to continue.

Wade is yelling over the crowd: "That's what I told him, I told him like fuck, we're lucky the girls saved us such an awesome table, let's just get some drinks and sit down."

Kyle starts shaking his head rapidly, like a furious dog, as if to shake off Wade's insubordination.

"I can't believe you guys. I just cannot believe you guys."

"Dude," says Rank, getting to his feet. The weary realization has set in that Kyle is going to require some big-time mollycoddling if the evening's fun is to be salvaged.

"I go to all this trouble to set this up," complains Kyle, "and you guys are like: *Yeah, whatever.*"

On the other side of the table, Adam says exactly the wrong thing.

"Oh come on, man, who gives a shit? It's a drunk. We've been getting drunk together all year and we'll get drunk together next semester. It's not like we're going off to war."

Kyle looks over and his eyes seem to take on an extra layer

of zombie-film. Rank intuitively steps in front of him to block his view of Adam.

"All he means," says Rank, "is that this is not worth getting pissed about. We're supposed to be out having fun together, right? That's all. Let's not make a big deal out of it."

"No, it's not a big deal," says Kyle. "Nothing's a big deal. Why don't you just go tend bar or bounce drunks or something, Rank? You'd obviously rather be working. We're not here five seconds and you're asking Ivor for a shift. Okay, fine. If that's all it means to you, whatever."

Rank cannot believe the soap opera this is turning into. "Kyle," he says, starting to laugh in his frustration. "We're having some drinks. Relax."

It's funny to think that with the crowd and the music, they are all actually screaming at each other. If the bar was empty they'd sound like lunatics.

Kyle turns his blank eyes to Adam. "Are you guys coming or not?"

"*Kyle*," says Rank, wilting with frustration. In the background, Wade throws up his hands.

"What's the matter?" calls Emily, who has been watching them open-mouthed and hearing only every other word.

"Fuck it," says Kyle, turning away. "I'm out of here."

"Man, come *on*," says Rank, reaching for him.

"No, fuck it man," says Kyle again, assuming a final, tragic pose — the Deposed King. He pushes Rank's hand away before it can land on his shoulder.

It's all so stupid. It's such a joke. Kyle's pride is wounded. He'll go home, stew all night, and the next day the guys will show up, apologize en masse, tease him a little until he allows himself just a hint of the old Jarvis twinkle, until finally they are laughing together and saying "fuck you" in the spirit in which it should be said among friends and Kyle is chasing them all around the room demanding hugs.

Rank follows him a couple of paces and reaches again to stop him from going. Kyle whirls around and bats Rank away using both hands.

"I'm warning you, Rank," says Kyle.

"Kyle," says Rank again, spreading his arms wide, thinking maybe he can just employ a little humour and fast-forward to the inevitable hugs-and-apologies segment of the evening. *Brother.* Hey. Come on, bro. Where's the love?"

"Screw off, Rank, I'm serious."

Rank advances on Kyle, neglecting to screw off. "Love me, my brother," he says.

Kyle's mouth is shut tight but Rank can tell he is clenching his teeth.

"Don't touch me, Rank."

"Let me love you," Rank insists, moving in. "Come, my brother. Let us love together."

Press pause. Is Rank aware of what he's doing? Does he know what's coming? Have he and Kyle locked eyes and — even from the depths of their mutual alcoholic fog — arrived at an understanding? Yes. Yes, yes.

Does Rank keep moving anyway, toward Kyle, with arms outstretched? Vulnerable? Heedless? In full knowledge?

He does. Let it be said. Let it be known.

Press play.

Kyle shoves Rank. It's not a particularly violent shove. It's half-hearted, if anything. But seeing as how the act is a surprise to neither of them, and even as he feels himself propelled backward, Rank has already decided to let it go. He's going to take the shove, turn around, sit back down at the table with the girls, drink more, and wait for his friend to cool down.

Before any of this can happen, Kyle goes flying into the abruptly shrieking crowd. And Ivor is standing in his place, one massive bulge of a human being — eyes, veins, belly, muscles — hoarse voice sounding trumpet-clear above the shouts and music, shouting at Kyle as he skids across the floor: DO YOU HAVE A PROBLEM? YOU GOT A FUCKING PROBLEM YOU FUCKING FUCKWAD YEAH?

Rank is in front of him going Ivor! Ivor! Ivor! And Ivor can't even focus on him, his baby's face entirely red and slicked as if with oil. Suddenly they are standing in an empty circle, as if the crowd has moved aside for them to breakdance. At the edges of the circle, Kyle wobbles to his feet, dripping in other people's beer, and Rank moves to block him from Ivor's view — the same way he'd positioned himself to block Adam from Kyle's only moments before.

Rank hears faintly a "Jesus!" from Wade. A "holy shit," from someone else. An "Oh my god," from Emily.

I WILL FUCKING TEAR YOU APART, says Ivor, somehow managing to look directly through Rank to Kyle. No matter how deep Rank sticks his face into Ivor's, Ivor seems incapable of focusing on him. Ivor's eyes are enormous and both stupefied and hyper-aware like a stunned animal's, a dying moose. Rank puts his hands out then and makes the mistake of glancing over to see if Kyle has done the wise thing and skedaddled for an exit. But apparently this is just what

Kyle is in the process of doing when Ivor shoves Rank aside and launches himself across the circle.

The crowd makes a tidal sort of noise as Kyle tears his way through, women's shrieks sounding above it like the cries of gulls. Rank plunges into the scattering human mass behind Ivor.

"Rank," says Adam from somewhere. "Rank. His gun."

Oh that's right, thinks Rank from some distant place in his mind. It's familiar, this distant place. He hasn't been there for quite some time, not since looking over at his mother in the driver's seat and thinking: Oh that's not good. I don't think that can be good.

Ivor does carry a gun, doesn't he, thinks Rank from his distant place. Yes that's right isn't it; that's what Wade told us.

There's no time, then, to develop strategy or think about what he's doing or try to holler some kind of sanity into Ivor. Rank simply pursues Ivor's black expanse of Motörhead T-shirt into the fluttering crowd and throws himself upon it. Ivor is a creature of flab but only the same way a bear is. That is, bears are fat, as Ivor is fat. But underneath, still bears.

What Rank must do is kneel on him; pin his arms.

The crowd is in his ears. Ivor's body is heaving and boiling against him.

Ivor has a fever, thinks Rank in his distant place — he is maybe a little insane in his distant place. He remembers looking at what happened to Sylvie's head and thinking: Oh — you know what? That's not too bad, actually. The doctors will be able to fix that.

Poor Ivor, thinks Rank. Flu season. Not enough vitamin C.

"Rank get off of me, you're heavy, guy," moans Ivor beneath him. And suddenly he bucks.

"Ivor, stay down."

"LET THE FUCK GO OF MY ARMS YOU PIECE OF SHIT I AM LOOKING OUT FOR YOU."

Rank braces his legs and rides him thinking *gun*. Gun. Gun.

"WE DO NOT TOLERATE SHIT IN THIS ESTABLISH-MENT. RICHARD WILL HAVE NO SHIT IN HIS PLACE. RICHARD IS FUCKING SICK OF YOU FUCKING UNIVER-SITY KIDS — OH RANK," Ivor interrupts himself abruptly and starts to shudder.

"Calm down Ivor, please," Rank says into the gulf of Ivor's sweltering shoulder blades.

"Ow," says Ivor. "Ow, ow."

Then Kyle is with him in the circle. "Rank you need help man?"

But Rank needs no help at all anymore. He climbs off Ivor, the front of Rank's body going cool where the two of them have sweat through each other's clothes. He stands for a minute beside Kyle, then kneels down again and even though he is very much in his distant place now, he is very much where he was the day his mother drove him out to serve his time at the Youth Centre, having insisted Gord stay home, so she could talk to him mother to son, so she could cry herself hoarse at the wheel and keep reaching up to blouse-sleeve the water from her eyes, even though he is very much in that dis-tant, delicate realm where his inner voice speaks with strange formality, prefacing all directives with polite preambles like: *Maybe you should; Perhaps it would be best.* As in *Maybe you should unbuckle her seatbelt for when the paramedics come. Perhaps it would be best not to move her.* Even though he is in that place now, or perhaps because he is, he manages to — without giving it too much thought — roll Ivor onto his back. Because if he were to give it any thought, he would be thinking it's probably not okay that Ivor needs Rank to roll him onto his back at this point. It's probably not okay that Ivor isn't doing it himself.

Rank can feel the sweat on Ivor, too, already cooling. He flops him over with a grunt and glances up at Kyle, Kyle already moving backward.

Kyle who helps by saying: "Whoa. Whoa, Rank. Jesus, man."

There's no music anymore. Somebody — it might be Adam again — says the word "doctor." Then "ambulance." Then "cops." Ranks look up, and he does see Adam, but Adam is turned away from him, submerged deep in the surrounding crowd, and all Rank gets is a blank, eyeless profile of jawline and the wire-glint of glasses. Rank feels a pair of legs close by, looks up, discovers Richard. Richard seems confused and pit-faced and a little sad, thinks Rank from his distant place. His distant place is a place, it seems, of a kind of unconcerned compassion for all men. Richard clears his throat.

"What the fuck," he wants to know, "is this?"

Ambulance, says somebody. Cop.

"Rank," says Richard. "Would you please help me get him to my office?"

Perhaps it would be best, thinks Rank, to go.

In thinking this, he has managed miraculously to transport himself into the parking lot — it's science fiction all of a sudden, beam me up, Scotty, beam us out of here, the planet's about to blow. And now he moves at warp speed, now the Millennium Falcon makes its escape as stars smear up against its windshield like gnats, Christmas lights on houses blazing streaks in his periphery.

29

08/17/09, 12:44 a.m.

GORD CRIED AND CRIED and cried and cried and cried. I can honestly say I've never seen a man cry like that, before or since. It's not something a lot of men do, and when you see it happen, you understand why. When men cry, particularly men who are your father, there is something huge and elemental about it — something that feels entirely wrong and yet entirely natural all at the same time, like volcanoes; like the planet regurgitating. And it continued for days, the crying, intermittently. In between, he would knot his face up and scowl at the hospital administrators and the funeral directors — anybody who had a whiff of "the man" about them, anyone who could potentially be considered managerial timber by the powers that be at SeaFare packers. He'd bark insults at them, urge them to kiss his scrawny Celtic ass, then the moment we were alone in the rental car or the house or the funeral home or cemetery the crying would start up all over again.

And he would cling to me at these times. I think his intention, through his grief, was to be fatherly and sort of take me in his arms and offer comfort, but it didn't work because I was so big and he was so small. He'd end up just sort of wrapping his arms around my waist and burying his face in my sweater like a child. It's okay Gordie, it's okay Gordie he'd say into my chest as if trying to speak through it and converse directly with my heart, and as I stood there feeling, even through my own grief, how ridiculous we were.

When I was in the hospital, being treated for absolutely nothing except the shock of seeing my mother caved in (and that shock more or less manifested itself in sleepiness — I was in the hospital for being *sleepy* as they pieced Sylvie together), I'd open my eyes every once in a while and a small, dark-haired man with John Lennon glasses and a sort of science-teacher look about him would be standing there. And he'd smile and glance over at me as my eyes were opening as if he just happened to be standing in my room this whole time enjoying the play of sunlight across my bed sheets or something, and wasn't it fortuitous that I was now awake so we could chat. And because my town is small, he was familiar to me, so I politely said hello.

"Your lawyer Trisha introduced us a while back," said Owen Findlay. "Do you remember?"

I didn't. Didn't matter. Owen was from that point on a daily fixture in the lives of Gord and me. He had apparently been appointed to welcome my mother and me to the Youth Centre that day, had been waiting for us, all set to guide us through some paperwork, offer a bit of a tour and — his particular area of expertise — be reassuring. The more I got to know Owen, later, the more I wished Sylvie could have lived just long enough to meet him, to see what a sweet guy he was, to hear his reassurances about the way my life would unfold in the following months. I think she'd had no idea what was in store for me — how could she? Juvenile detention was a phenomenon beyond her realm of being. I think she must have been imagining prison tattoos, forced gay sex, eventual heroin addiction — that's the only thing that can account for the way she lost it in the car. If only she could have been greeted at the door by Owen's open, well-shaved face, sniffed the humble waft of Ivory soap that hung about him, seen the calming way he had of rocking on his heels, hands-in-pockets, in his science-teacher loafers and cords.

But in the car it had been a frenzy. She managed to hold on to the wheel but her demeanour was that of a bee that had flown in through the car window just as it was being rolled up and now was trapped and slamming its body against the glass in ever-increasing alarm. The conversation became pure adrenalin — neither of us quite knew what we were saying, or what the other one was talking about. My mother and I, we had never spoken like this before. It was always Gord I shouted and railed at, and he who did the shouting and railing in return. Sylvie and I usually turned to each other for relief — for a little peace and quiet once Hurricane Gord had finished raging.

She had pretty much liquefied the moment we pulled out of the driveway, when only moments before she'd been entirely in control. She had explained to Gord he would not be coming along on the drive to deliver me to my punishment for having brained Mick Croft, and Gord, surprisingly, hadn't kicked up too much of a fuss. Sylvie made her case in theological terms. Like any good Catholic, Gord could only bow before the inviolable bond of the Madonna and child, so when Sylvie explained things on that level — *we need to talk mother to son* — he had little choice but to nod and flick on the TV. Gord had exhausted himself in the courtroom anyway, and now that the verdict had come down and Trish had refused to hand over the judge's home phone number and/or address, he didn't quite know what to do next. My father's wrath, and the immense, inexhaustible supply of energy he always drew from it, was, for the first time I'd ever witnessed, spent.

She even kissed him on the top of his prickly head before we left, which troubled me because my parents usually took such care to not go near each other, at least when I was around.

She was being, I think now, very careful.

But at the first stop sign we came to, she let go, braking the car and collapsing across the steering wheel as if gone boneless.

I remember her telling me, "You don't have to *be* this. You could be anything."

"Be what, be what?" I was saying, freaked out because of the way she was crying — great whooping sobs that convulsed her entire body. And I had done that to her. It was because of me.

"Don't have to be what? I don't know what I am, let alone what I'm supposed to be."

"What they're going to try to make you be now. What your father tries to make you be."

"I never wanted to be that anyway," I shouted.

"*I know* what you are," Sylvie shouted back.

"No *you don't*," I continued to shout (and, warning: it gets very teenage here). "Everybody thinks they know *all about me* but they don't! Nobody knows *anything* about me!"

I was thinking about Constable Hamm — *I see exactly where you're headed, son.* I was thinking of Gord thwacking me in the sternum. *This son of a bitch right here.*

We went back and forth like this in our mutual incoherence. That is, I was incoherent and panicky, whereas Sylvie, I think, was in the process of elucidating something, however heartsick she may have been while attempting to do it. We were on the highway now. I just wanted her to stop crying that way. It would be okay if she were trickling a little, but the sobs wracked her body like she was being flogged. I even thought she might pull over and ralph out the driver's-side door at some point, like one of my high school buddies on the way to a dance.

"We can't continue like this," she gasped after a few heaving moments of speechlessness. "We don't have to."

"I have to go to jail, Mom," I said, watching her because there was a weird momentousness to the way she was speaking all of a sudden. "We can't, like, go on the lam."

"After this, Gordie," she said, shaking her head and reaching up to swipe an entire forearm across her eyes. "After this, everything changes."

Needless to say she was right. Of course, that wasn't what she meant. She didn't mean that in about eight minutes she would take a blind turn while driving slightly on the wrong side of the yellow line as she finished blouse-sleeving another gush of tears from her eyes and a car would be coming just

a titch over the speed limit in the opposite direction and the
vehicles would brush against each other like two illicit lovers
at a party, spin in opposite directions, they into a ditch, we
into yet another oncoming vehicle before discovering a ditch
of our own. That's not what Sylvie meant by *everything changes*. At the time, however, I didn't understand exactly she
what she meant.

She meant, it took me years to understand, that she was
leaving Gord. She and I, that is. The thing I always wanted;
my ultimate, never-spoken wish.

Which of course is what ended up happening anyway.

08/17/09, 3:25 a.m.

I just realized I've got one more story to tell you.

I started playing hockey again a few years ago, can you
believe it? Twelve years after stumping out of the locker room
back in university and making my buddy Adam so proud of
my principled stand against the cracking of human skulls. It
happened not long after I bought my house. One of the first
things I noticed about the neighbourhood, standing with the
realtor at the upstairs window, was an outdoor community
rink a couple of backyards beyond mine.

I watched it fill up with kids from the first snowfall in November and not empty out again until March. On especially
cold days, rink sounds — the *pock* of pucks hitting the boards
and the slash of skates gouging ice — flew across the frozen
air into my yard. It sounded like all the games were taking
place directly beneath my bedroom, and if I jumped out my

window I'd land smack at centre ice like a dropped puck.

I'd stand there some evenings watching the kids going around and around, making their touching Hail Mary passes from one end of the ice to the other, and eventually I noticed that during a certain block of time on Thursday evenings, the kids got bigger. I took in the occasional pot belly here, a face-ful of beard there. I saw how different guys seemed to come and go from week to week, some of them even showing up in the middle of a game, brandishing their sticks and being immediately accepted onto the ice. Next thing I know I'm at Canadian Tire buying extension cords but standing, for some reason, in the sporting goods section, feeling annoyed at the crappy selection of skates.

Flash forward two years later and at the age of thirty-four I'm finally doing my father proud — heading downtown to the arena every week to play in a league. And let me tell you, old-timer's hockey is the best hockey going. There are no psychotic parents in the stands, no purple-faced coaches, none of that sweaty, draft-pick desperation. Guys can be old, guys can be pudgy; guys are slow. Guys are sometimes even — as in the case of our goalie for a couple of years until pregnancy interrupted our winning streak — women.

There's only one downside, which is this: when guys go into cardiac arrest.

The first time it happened, I didn't understand what I was seeing. On the opposite side of the ice from us, Hamish Powell from the Stoney Creek Choppers bounced off the bench where he'd been sitting, mouth agape, exactly like someone from my former church might have done in a moment of holy ecstasy. The spirit could hit you like that if you happened to have the right preacher — say, a preacher like Beth — in front of you, egging it on. One minute you're letting the words wash over you, weaving back and forth in relative peace, hands in the air, and the next it's like a holy bolt has entered through your anus.

But that wasn't what had happened to Hamish, even if that's what it looked like to me. Wow, I thought. Here of all places. Hamish has seen the light. Hamish has been *saved*.

I remarked to a guy on the bench beside me: "Hamish —" but didn't have time to say anything else, because my teammate, an internist at Saint Joseph's named Wally who had helpfully identified my broken tibia the year before as I lay writhing and gasping on the ice, was now flying across the rink.

As I watched Wally arrive at the other side I still didn't grasp what was going on. Meanwhile another guy had positioned himself on top of Hamish. *They're fighting*, I thought. *Hamish has gone nuts!* But that was when I realized the other guy was a colleague of Wally's — an EMT, to be precise. And that's when I heard Wally yell for a defibrillator.

Did you know sports arenas are legally obliged to keep heart defibrillators on the premises, precisely for occasions such as this? It happens, I was soon to discover, all the time. Old guys like us who spend our weekdays in desk chairs and our weekends on couches and our mealtimes dumping gravy all over everything decide we can just lace up a pair of skates one fine winter's day and hit the ice like we were seventeen again. It's a bit sobering, Adam. It's sobering to be sitting in what you realize is a kind of temple devoted to the worship of youthful, masculine vigour and watch a guy get taken down so decisively, as if in reproach. Like a too-big kid getting his hand slapped reaching for cookies. *You've had enough,* decrees the fucker-in-the-sky.

Hamish was okay, but I would never meet him on the ice again. I found this out from Wally a few weeks later after a game. Usually I liked talking to Wally, because he often shared gross details from his medical career. He once told me he'd learned to do stitches in med school by practising on the flesh of dead pigs. I couldn't get the image out of my head — a bunch of guys sitting in a room sewing pigs.

Still. I wasn't all that keen to learn the details of what happened to Hamish. Wally was keen to give them, however. Wally loved talking about his work, and he was, he said now, perpetually fascinated by the workings of the human heart. We men, he told me, we walk around with no idea how fragile our hearts might be.

We were standing in my kitchen, Wally watching me slather sauce onto spare ribs in preparation for a post-game barbecue, one of my all-time favourite rituals of defiance against the winter months. I have been known to barbecue while wearing ski-goggles, to protect my eyes against ice pellets ripping at my face in gale-force winds.

I replied something like *Yeah yeah yeah* as I slathered, just letting Wally ramble about ventricles for a while. I was happy Hamish was still with us, but the image of him popping up from the bench like a jack-in-the-box with his mouth in an agonized gape hadn't left me.

Then, from out of nowhere (or at least that's how it seemed to me, considering I'd been working so hard at not paying attention), Wally started talking about the tasering deaths in the news. Do you remember that scandal, Adam? The cops got a bit zap-happy with their new, supposedly non-lethal toy and a handful of people getting zapped promptly disproved the whole non-lethal thing. Whoa, remarked the cops as multiple zap-ees dropped like stones. That wasn't supposed to happen. Cue public outrage.

So Wally got very exercised on this subject. Wally appeared to be among the outraged, and because I'd been following the details on the news pretty carefully — you can imagine how stories of accidental deaths tend to claim my sympathy — I shoved the platter of ribs aside and gave him my full attention.

"I mean, Christ," Wally was saying as he struggled to open a non-screwtop beer with his hands. "You send up to fifty thousand volts of electricity through a guy's body — and maybe the guy is freaked out as it is, maybe the guy has a heart condition; he's angry, he's terrified. You are pretty much begging for the worst possible outcome."

"That's not a screwtop, Wally."

"I've almost got it," said Wally. He didn't, but it was a matter of face-saving now.

"Dude," I said, holding out a bottle opener. "You're a doctor. Save your hands."

"So anyway," continued Wally, accepting it quickly. "They say it's perfectly safe, right, all this electricity coursing through your body, but for who? An eighteen-year-old maybe. A guy who runs ten K every day and watches his cholesterol. But they have no idea who they might be jazzing, what a guy's heart might be doing, what kind of shape it might be in. They're dealing with crackheads? Drug addicts? The guy's in a state of excited delirium — just holding him down could stop his heart."

At Wally's last remark, I responded, as you can imagine, "What?"

"It's a controversial term, but generally it just means if a guy's all cranked up his heart could blow. The last thing you want to do is zap him."

"But what about holding him down?" I said. "You said you can't even hold him down."

"It's not a good idea," allowed Wally, "with someone in that state."

I had picked up my own beer once I shoved the ribs aside, but now I placed it on the counter again without taking a swig. "But how do you know? How are you supposed to know if someone's in that state or not?"

"Well I suppose the dilemma for the cops," said Wally, "is probably every other guy they wanna taser is in that state."

"Excited what-did-you-call-it?"

"Excited delirium."

"And what happens?"

"When?"

"When a guy's in excited delirium."

Wally rolled his sleep-deprived eyes to an upper corner of my kitchen and seemed to recite from a memorized textbook. "He's agitated, violent. Sweats profusely, seems unusually strong — doesn't really feel pain. I mean, definitely the kind of guy the cops are going to want to tase. But definitely the last guy that you should."

This painted something of a familiar portrait, would you agree?

"But you said you don't even need to taser him."

Wally's eyes rolled back to me and he leaned on the

counter, smiling, making himself comfortable. He seemed to almost wallow now that he had my full attention.

"Just by restraining him, yeah. Because he's in a heightened state, right? The heart is just flailing, it's going flat-out, it can't go any harder, and then you grab him from behind, throw him to the ground. What's it gonna do next?"

I was in a bit of a heightened state myself at this point. My beer, I noticed, had overflowed after I placed it — gently, I'd thought — on the counter, so I moved on autopilot to get a rag and wipe it up, still firing questions at Wally so he wouldn't get the idea the conversation was winding down. I kept him there in the kitchen for a while, making him go over a few details of particular interest to me. Pretty soon he stopped wallowing and took on the demeanour of what he actually was, i.e., a guy under interrogation. He'd finished his beer and just stood there and fidgeted, wondering why I wasn't offering him another, why I wasn't putting on the ribs and letting him get back to the party. A few of our teammates wandered in from the living room, wanting to know the same thing. I dumped a bunch of chips into a bowl and shoved it at them and told them to go sit down.

"Not you," I said to Wally, who'd made a move to sort of unobtrusively attach himself to the other two and wander unnoticed from the kitchen.

I didn't offer him another beer until I was sure I had all the facts straight. Not that the facts of the initial revelation really changed much under my questioning. I just needed them affirmed, and then re-affirmed.

So here's what I learned.

You can stop a guy's heart, Adam — an over-excited guy,

say, a guy who has abused drugs his entire life, a guy who means well, who is only looking out for you, a guy who has to live with the fact that the most powerful forces in the universe have marshalled themselves against the scummy likes of him — and what difference does it make if that fact is a fantasy, and how can it be a fantasy anyway, when the loneliness gouges his face like scars? So a hunted, haunted guy. A guy who just happens to be coked out of his head at that very ill-starred moment. The very moment the powers eternally gunning for him finally muster themselves to gather overhead and funnel their way into a convenient, waiting vessel. A vessel who happens to be a bit of a hard-luck Charlie himself, let's face it. Therefore, what better vessel? The point is: such a vessel can stop a guy's heart simply by, it would seem, restraining him. As the obliging vessel does. Just by holding the guy down; applying force. Just by kneeling on the dude.

"Does he die?" I said to Wally. "Does he die? Every time? Does the guy die?"

Wally was looking at me vaguely — he was leaning against the refrigerator now and his big eyes had glazed over and were watering as if I'd been shining a flashlight into them this whole time.

"Well . . ." he began. "Hamish didn't die."

"But all the tasering guys. All the excited delirium guys. They croaked from it, right? That's why it's such a huge scandal, they die every time."

"Rank," said Wally, raising his hands and scratching either side of his head with them. "You only hear about the ones who die."

"What's that supposed to mean?"

"I mean the guys who live — it doesn't get reported. Why would it?"

"Why wouldn't it?"

"There's no story there."

This was when Wally actually yawned. Like the absence of a good story was getting to him.

30 |

08/17/09, 6:46 a.m.

HATE IS NOT the opposite of love, Kirsten told me once: indifference is. Adam, I accept you didn't write your book out of hate or love for me, your former friend and sort-of brother. I accept what really pissed me off was your indifference. What I mean is I'm accepting your indifference.

I accept you know the answers to pretty much every fucking question I have put to you this summer. And I accept that you are never going to give them to me, are you. You know, ultimately, what happened to Ivor and you know why the police never came after me and you could have put that stuff into your book, you could have couched the answers in there somewhere, secretly, as a little nod and wink to Rank, in a book I once thought consisted of nothing but such nods and winks, however malicious. And I accept that I was wrong in this regard. I still don't quite get what you were doing. But I accept, at least, you weren't doing that.

I accept that you will never respond to my emails. I accept that you have maybe not been reading them since May.

I accept that you exist, or else you don't, and everything that happened from the point at which we became acquainted with each other to the point where we stopped being acquainted with each other, either did or did not take place the way I said.

Or maybe it's what happened in your book that actually happened. And maybe the guy in your book, the alcool-guzzling football player, maybe he only exists around the edges, just the way you made him — big and bad, huge and crazy, marginally tragic, marginally interesting, somewhat related to the story itself.

I don't expect to hear from you. I told you what I had to tell you, and you told me something back, and that's our story, isn't it Adam?

I told you how my mother died, is what I told you — exactly how. And the dominating way the blood announced itself that day, exploding everywhere, uncleanupabble: it was like I'd stuffed it in some kind of pressurized container the night I made it flow from Croft, tucked the thing beneath the driver's side seat and breathed a nice, forgetful sigh of relief as the pressure built up, day after day. How else to explain my guilt, my immediate thought the blood belonged to me; that *I* had made this sudden mess and, what's more, I should have known, I should have seen it coming and prepared.

So I told you all that, you'll recall I sort of crucified myself in front of you, and as the morning light fingered its way through Kyle's shit-green velvet curtains, I asked you the question, and you gave me the answer. You *gave* it to me already, is the thing. And somewhere along the way I just forgot.

That's what this has been about, I guess — trying to wrench from you an answer you've already given. This whole summer I've just been haranguing you to repeat yourself. So I am sorry for that too. All right? I should have listened, Adam, but I was beyond listening then, I was beyond belief or doubt.

Was that God? Adam? Yes? I think it was God. It was a God-joke, right, my mother? Because it had to be. Because it's like that story, "The Monkey's Paw," where you wish for your ultimate, never-spoken wish and getting what you want becomes your punishment. Joke's on you — someone has to die. Giveth; taketh. But wait, you have more wishes, so you wish for that person back, you're stupid, you just never learn, and, sure, you get her back but you get her back dead and now she's always with you, and she's dead. Death is the only reply, no matter where you look, no matter how you phrase the question — it's your cosmic smack upside the head. This is what you make happen.

Maybe I didn't say it that way exactly, I can't remember what I said exactly anymore, but I remember saying something along those lines to you, I remember basically blubbering a ranting stream of nonsense punctuated by the ultimate nonsense: *God. God? God!*

And you telling me, intermittently — frozen hand against my boiling forehead — you must've told me in a hundred different ways that morning: *No.*

And I seem to remember saying to you that night, after going into so much more explicit detail than I have here — and it just occurred to me that I should say I'm sorry for that too, by the way, Adam. All that explicit detail. I realize it was a lot of gore and grief to lay upon some twenty-year-old kid whose life experience has come entirely out of books, who's never left the east coast of Canada and has a perfectly nice, perfectly intact mom and dad of his own living merely a three-hour drive away and looking forward to his return at Christmas. Let me just stop right here and tell you I am sorry for it all — for offering it up to you, of all people, all that gore and grief. I am heartily sorry for having offended you, as we say in the confessional — the good old Catholic penalty box. Whatever it was I did to you that night, that morning (we both know it was something; I struck a match, I flicked a switch), I'm sorry.

And thank you for not putting it in your book.

And fuck you for not putting it in your book.

Your friend,
Gordon Rankin

Acknowledgements

My heartfelt thanks go out to the following for their witting and unwitting support:

Melanie Little, Sarah MacLachlan and Christy Fletcher

The Department of English and Film Studies at the University of Alberta

The Banff Centre, Literary Arts Program

The Alberta Foundation for the Arts

The Canada Council for the Arts

Karen MacFarlane and Judge Richard J. MacKinnon

Kurt Stenburg, EMT

Marguerite Pigeon, francophone blasphemer

Karen Engle, prairie apostate

my parents, whose hunting trip I stole

Peter Sinemma, Peter Ormshaw, Curtis Gillespie — consultants/hockey thugs

Rob Appleford, Paris in the twenties.

To those I haven't even asked:

Thank you;

I'm sorry.

About the Author

LYNN COADY is the author of the acclaimed short story collection *Hellgoing* and the novel *The Antagonist*. *Hellgoing* won the Scotiabank Giller Prize, was a finalist for the Rogers Writers' Trust Fiction Prize, and was a national bestseller. *The Antagonist* was a finalist for the Scotiabank Giller Prize, and a national bestseller. Her other works include *Mean Boy, Saints of Big Harbour, Strange Heaven*, and *Play the Monster Blind*. She has been a finalist for the Governor General's Literary Award and the Stephen Leacock Medal for Humour, and has four times made the *Globe and Mail*'s annual list of Top 100 Books. Originally from Cape Breton, she now lives in Edmonton, Alberta, where she is a founding and senior editor of the award-winning magazine *Eighteen Bridges*.

www.lynncoady.com
www.twitter.com/lynn_coady